D0490483

A Strange Man Named Will

SLEEPER CHRONICLES

Ray Zdan

"As a man's desire is, so is his destiny. For as his desire is, so is his will; and as his will is, so is his deed; and as his deed is, so is his reward, whether good or bad."

Brihadaranyaka Upanishad

～☆ ❀ ☆～

Will spent his usual Friday evening in the gym pumping iron. He used earphones to shield him from the outer world allowing him to focus on the smooth movements of the barbell – up to the highest point, spending a few seconds there just enough to breathe out, then slowly back, along with an airstream down his nostrils to the lowest point barely touching the chest. Blood rushed to his temples in unison with the loud beat from the earphones as Will repeated the presses until warm numbness filled his chest and arms. He finished the set and got up, sipped a few mouthfuls of water from his bottle, then wiped the sweat from his forehead, catching a few envious glances at his chest from skinny guys fooling with the chest machine. Will always only used free weights to build his core, not relying on any fancy equipment. Barbells and dumbbells were his friends, and while guys called him old-fashioned, they envied the way he looked at the same time.

Will was used to furtive attention and gossip around the gym and sometimes teased guys by taking his T-shirt off and playing with his pecs or biceps or carefully touching his eight-pack in front of the mirror. He was proud of his body, and he knew he was the best. No one dared to challenge him.

Will permitted himself a few minutes of rest. Girls sweated on the treadmills on the other side of the gym, and he gave them a wink before rolling up the cuffs of his shorts to expose bulging quadriceps while flexing his calves in front of the mirror. His face remained serious, and he couldn't hear their sighs over the crazy music still beating through his earphones.

Will stopped fooling in front of the mirror and returned to the barbell. He adjusted the bench for incline press and carefully lowered his torso. The numbness in his pecs was more intense when he had finished. Will wiped off the sweat and took two more gulps of water. His short ginger hair was wet, and several drops of sweat glistened on his neatly trimmed three-day beard.

Only a set of dips remained to complete his workout. He felt drops of sweat rolling down his back and took off the T-shirt to the delight of the girls and envious looks from the guys. He was the centre of the secret attention of everyone and enjoyed every glorious moment of it before attacking the barbell again.

Will finished the workout and struck a few poses for his phone camera before hitting the showers. He smiled and hummed his favourite tune as streams of lukewarm water splashed over his skin, soothing huge numb muscles that were fully pumped with blood.

Will wrapped a towel around his waist and returned to the locker room, checking the mirror on his way. The light in the locker room was cold white, and his skin looked pale pink, like whipped cream with just a hint of strawberry. Will frowned disdainfully, quickly dressed, packed the sweaty T-shirt into his rucksack and headed out. There was one more thing he must do.

Back on the street he turned left and slipped into the nearby tanning shop. The receptionist was flirty with a painted smile, fluttering her long fake eyelashes.

"Seven minutes," he said, giving her a fiver and not waiting for the change.

"Do you need goggles for eye protection?" she asked, knowing that he never used them.

"No, thank you," Will shook his head and went down the corridor.

He knew the way. Inside the cubicle, Will carefully closed the door and put his rucksack down. He stripped naked and spent several minutes looking at himself in the large mirror on the wall inspecting his sculptured body from different angles. Everything seemed perfect. He was almost willing to kiss the mirror when his gaze wandered down to his pubic hair – the fire-red lumberjack desperately needed trimming. It wasn't precisely a jungle yet, but he did use to have much less vegetation down there. Frowning, he turned around and nearly cursed aloud. His butt was too flat compared with his sculptured back! It was the direct consequence of taking shortcuts on the leg days, and that must change. Will slapped his butt with frustration and made a mental promise to be more careful with his leg routines.

Upset, he slipped onto the tanning bed and closed the lid. Seven minutes passed like a breeze.

Once out, Will looked at himself in the mirror again. His butt still seemed disproportionately flat and not worthy of his magnificent back. But it was that horrible reddish glow of his skin after a good workout and a few minutes of ultraviolet that he hated the most. Will mouthed a silent curse. The colour was dull pink with ugly freckles on his shoulders. He must do something about that too.

Slowly, he dressed and went outside without even noticing the hopeful gaze of the receptionist.

The traffic moved down the street as Will headed uphill upset by his flaw finding as he absentmindedly chewed his favourite protein bar. His body wasn't as perfect as he thought it was, and he had to address that urgently. The butt problems weren't overly of concern. He decided to add a few more routines to his workout, and things would improve in no time. That wasn't a big issue. But he had to address that pale pink skin somehow. He needed something capable of drawing the attention of any secretly glancing admirer and keeping it away from that awful pink paleness and freckles.

The day was dying, and darkness slowly crawled from every corner, but Will wasn't scared. He was a tall, well-built guy in his late twenties – nobody would dare to threaten him. He plugged in his earphones and scrolled through the playlist, searching for some inspiration. Nothing caught his eye, so Will pressed on a random track filling his ears with the beat. His discomfiture, however, didn't go away. He has always been envious of the darker skin tones of his gym mates and hated his ugly freckled pink covering. That mirror in the tanning shop had splashed the bitter truth at his face. He could have a better butt – that was just a matter of a few weeks' work, but he couldn't change the colour of his skin. Even tanning was virtually useless – his ugly pink coating only grew redder and was too resistant to acquire any darker shade.

Several hundred yards further on, his worries took over, and the music began to irritate his ears. Will took the earphones off when something creepy caught his gaze. He stopped to have a better look at the large dimly lit shop window where a three-foot-tall skull made from *papier mache* with eerie-looking red and blue illuminations stared out. "Custom Tattoo & Piercings" was written in Gothic-style letters. Will looked through the window, shading his eyes from the incoming traffic lights. A skinny man was sitting at a table facing the window and shuffling through some papers with his long bony fingers. His thin arms and shallow chest, barely visible through the loose T-shirt, were covered with countless illustrations, climbing up to his chin. Both his earlobes were pierced with enormous tubular ivory earrings. A much smaller shiny metal ring was at the left side of his nose. The man was much older than Will, perhaps in his late forties already – it was impossible to guess with such a strange appearance and the poor illumination. His mouth was disproportionately large with tightly pressed thin lips. His chin was long and narrow, and the man sometimes rubbed it with his fingers.

A wailing ambulance passed down the street, and the man lifted gaze from his papers attracted by its noise and blue flashing lights. His black eyes spotted Will, and the man smiled, inviting him with a gesture of his bony fingers.

Strangely, Will thought that it might be a good idea. He smiled back and opened the door.

"What can I do for you?" asked the man.

His voice crackled, and he nervously picked a pack of cigarettes, opened it, and then tossed it into the bin, frowning.

"Do you want a Superman sign on your chest? Or a rose on your neck? Or a fish named Wanda preparing to dive into your asshole?" he asked with a foxy smile.

Will grinned too. That sounded funny but wasn't what he would like. He needed something extraordinary, something that could outshine his pale skin, making his bulging muscles more defined.

"I haven't made my mind up yet," Will shrugged. "Do you have any samples?"

"Oh, yes," the man nodded, standing up. "I have plenty of samples. Make yourself comfortable."

He was wearing torn skinny jeans, and Will could see illustrations on his legs and calves through the gaps in the torn fabric. The man pointed to a leather sofa in the corner and disappeared through the side room door. Will lowered himself onto the couch, placed rucksack on the floor at his feet and patiently waited.

Something heavy dropped down in the side room, and a few shy curses sneaked through the opened door.

"Are you all right?" Will asked, still sitting on the couch.

"Yes," the scraggy man said, emerging with several folders in his arms without offering any further explanation.

"There *are* plenty, indeed," Will indicated the folders.

"Take your time," the man smiled and placed the folders in front of Will. "Here we go – Chinese, Native American, Celtic, Comics and Various…"

Will put the Chinese folder aside without even opening it.

"You don't like Chinese?" the man observed, raising his eyebrows.

"I don't understand Chinese," Will said and opened the Celtic folder. "You could scribble whatever you wanted in Chinese, and I don't like the idea of walking around like the label from a packet of instant noodles."

The man chuckled, but Will failed to see the funny side. He was busy shuffling through the Celtic crosses and ornaments, tree shapes and leaves – nothing caught his attention. Will hadn't yet decided if he needed an embellishment on his back, or his arm, or his chest. He hadn't even decided if he needed any at all.

The man returned to his papers.

"Feel free to ask if you have any questions," he muttered, but Will merely nodded, entirely immersed in the illustrations catalogue.

One more ambulance passed down the street as Will put the Celtic folder aside and opened Comics. He only took a quick glance through the pictures; most of them were dull and silly. He set the folder aside and began to look at the Native American. He spent several minutes wondering how the wings of an eagle would look on his back. They could nicely cover those freckles on his shoulders, but the shape of the wings would obscure his perfectly carved trapezius muscles. He didn't dismiss the idea entirely, just put it aside for now.

Will briefly thought about getting a drawing of a roaring mountain lion on his right deltoid which was usually facing the row of treadmills when he was doing his workout but then discarded the idea. The open mouth of a lion with that red tongue would look like a wound with its eyes hiding on top of the deltoid, and the image would be entirely invisible when he was lifting weights. The pictures of bears and wolves in the catalogue were just not worth considering.

"Have you had anything inked already?" asked the man lifting his black eyes from the papers.

Will only shook his head and carried on looking at the illustrations. The inking didn't seem a bad idea anymore. He just needed to find the right image. His perfect body required something truly unique, not some second-hand mainstream artwork that he was looking at in those folders.

"It's always tricky with the first one," the man smiled.

"I know," Will sighed. "Is the inking painful?"

"It depends on the body part," the man shrugged. "Least painful are the shoulders, I think, but the private areas may be tricky."

"I have no intention of having anything in my private

areas," Will told him and picked up the last folder named Various.

He found several captivating illustrations with a 3D effect there. Will carefully inspected the pec tattoo, giving an illusion of the skin having been torn apart with bare muscle fibres exposed, but then decided against turning his life into an eternal Halloween. Snakes, spiders and skulls looked creepy and repulsive. He closed the folder and stood up, picking up his rucksack.

"Not found anything suitable?" the man looked surprised.

"I need something special," Will said firmly. "These are too trivial. No offence."

"I have a few more sketches," the man stopped him, standing up too. "If you could wait a minute, I'll fetch them for you. Nobody has ever inked them."

"Let's have a look," Will agreed.

The man disappeared into the side room again and several minutes later squeezed out, holding a bunch of loose sheets. He brushed the folders away and carefully placed the sheets on the table in front of Will. These did indeed look different.

The first few depicted strange idyllic landscapes with hills, rivers and forests, looking vibrant and alive. Birds floated in the sky, barely moving their wings. There was a lonely tree on a hilltop, painted red by an epic sunset.

Will spread the sheets all over the table and grinned – these images looked fabulous. He glanced at the lonely castle with a shadow of a dragon passing across its proud walls, at the enormous expanse of water with a few sails tossed by a high wind – you could almost hear a seagull crying!

Then he picked up a creased sheet depicting a beautiful blonde woman dressed in black standing in front of the dramatic background of an erupting volcano. The image was vibrant with red and black, but the most unusual thing was the deep blue eyes of the woman and a certain hint of sadness and desperation in her pretty face.

"Who is she?" Will asked, holding the sheet.

"I've no idea," the man shook his head. "One crazy artist drew these sketches. I know nothing about them. But honestly, I've never tried to ink them."

"Why not? They're beautiful. Do you think you're not skilled enough to ink them?" Will challenged the blackness of the eyes in front of him, but the man remained unperturbed.

"The technique isn't very complicated," he said casually. "I can do this easily, that's not a problem."

Will was still holding the picture of that beautiful blonde.

"You see," the man continued his explanation pointing at the sketch. "Some inks are pretty usual – that red and black. But I need special ink for her eyes, and that's what's holding me back with this drawing."

"What's so special about that ink?"

"The colour is unique and very expensive. This pigment goes deep into the skin and might be very painful to ink. It will stay for life – no laser removals if you have second thoughts," the scraggy man said, rubbing his chin. "It's not for the decision of a moment."

"I see..." Will looked at the beautiful face again. "I need to think then... Can I take a picture of it on my phone?"

"Well... You can. But don't even bother to have it done somewhere else – I'm the only one who has the right pigment for the eyes," the man warned.

"I understand," Will said and placed the sheet on the table. He fished out his phone. "I'll delete it if I decide against having it. Promise. I only need the image to help me make a decision."

Will took a photo of the sheet and returned it to the skinny man.

"Am I to understand you haven't made your mind up yet?" he asked, accepting the sketch.

"As you said – it's not the decision of a moment," Will grinned.

He went back into the night, continuing his way uphill along with the traffic. A light rain started to sprinkle from the dark sky, and Will pulled his hood up without slowing down. His bulging muscles beneath that hideous pale pink skin hovered before his eyes, tormenting him with stubborn persistence. A beautiful tattoo might be a solution. He just needed the right image in exactly the right place.

For the remainder of his journey, Will was deeply immersed in doubt – he wasn't sure if he needed any tattoos, but the image of the blonde woman had already hooked his imagination.

"You're late," his mother observed, opening the front

door.

Will just shrugged and dropped his rucksack in the corner of the hallway next to his shoes. He then quickly stuffed his stomach with some tasteless chicken breasts and poured down a protein milkshake. But his troubled mind wouldn't release him.

He locked himself in the bathroom and took off his T-shirt. The light was dim here, and his torso looked impressive. He messed about in front of the mirror for a while before his little sister forced him out.

Back in his room, Will undressed and slipped into bed. He took out his phone and looked at those sad eyes of the blonde lady again. Something weird and magnificent was in this picture hiding behind the vibrant colours and dramatic background. He just couldn't decide what it was.

The next morning Will got up early and made himself a sizeable but tasteless omelette from egg whites. He gulped it down and rushed to the gym.

The morning was bright, but Will caught a bus to travel downhill. He was hoping to find the gym empty and perform those embarrassing butt related sit-ups without any awkward glances. The traffic was light, so it was a very smooth ride without too many stops.

Will's assumptions were right – the gym was empty and still pristine clean with a sleepy receptionist drinking his morning coffee. Will quickly changed, grabbed his bottle of water and rushed to the barbell corner. His butt desperately needed some training.

He quickly went through the warm-up routines and then put a decent weight on his barbell and rushed to do squats like mad. Soon, Will was sweating profusely, but he finished the set without slowing down and only then did he permit himself a few mouthfuls of water. It was getting hot. Will took off his already wet T-shirt and hung it on a nearby chest machine then he plugged his earphones in and scrolled through the playlist, selecting the most insane beat. The first set of walking lunges went like a breeze. Will wiped his forehead and took a few minutes' rest. The music beating his eardrums was in unison with his heartbeat. He smiled and grabbed the barbell again, struggling through the second set. It felt more difficult.

Two sets of hips thrust with a barbell followed. Will drank several more gulps of water and then gave himself a full three minutes of rest.

The gym was slowly filling with people – girls were already sweating in the treadmill corner. He secretly grinned looking at the lean guy who was fitting his skinny butt into the leg press machine and casting several envious glances at the gorgeous quads of Will. The guy still had a very long way to go to grow some meat on his sticks.

Will casually changed the weight of his barbell again and started a long and strenuous set of deadlifts watching his bulging pecs in the mirror. The skin looked less pale than yesterday but was still awfully pink although the freckles were nearly invisible. After a few more repetitions, the music in his earphones ended with a longer than expected pause before the next track. Will froze with the barbell in his arms when a loud bout of insane laughter broke the silence in the gym.

It was so unexpected and humiliating that Will dropped the barbell on the floor with a thud. He ripped out his earphones – the laughter in the treadmill corner was almost hysterical. Will's face blushed deep crimson as he carefully glanced over his left shoulder.

One of the girls was looking at her phone, nearly rolling on the floor but paying no attention to him. *What had just happened?*

Will sighed quietly, slowly regaining his colour, but his reaction puzzled him. What had happened to all the pride and confidence in his body? Were those flaws in his perfection now so obvious?

He picked up his wet T-shirt, put it on and silently resumed his deadlifting routine until he was utterly exhausted. He kept the volume of his music down and his ears sharp, but the gym remained silent with everybody minding their own business.

He then ran a quick maintenance routine for his legs and quietly hurried to the locker room. That girl who had laughed was running on a treadmill and didn't raise her eyes as he passed by — *false alarm!*

Will took a quick shower, dressed and paid one more visit to the tanning shop.

He spent a good ten minutes in front of the mirror looking at his naked body before climbing onto the sunbed. His muscles were still bulging, perfect in their shape and proportion if you didn't count that slightly flat butt. *Was it that too noticeable?* Was his butt spoiling his ideal frame and crushing his confidence?

Will was torn in doubt and impatiently waited for those seven minutes to pass. Then he dressed and took a bus ride home. The weather outside was beautiful, but he saw only darkness.

The growing paranoia haunted him for several next days. Will spent less and less time in the gym doing only the essential basic routines to maintain his core. The rest of the day passed slowly either in front of the mirror in the bathroom or looking at that picture of the beautiful unknown woman on his phone. He even cut out a piece of dark paper in the shape of that sketch and tried to stick it onto his naked torso, searching for the best spot.

His efforts were in vain. Will couldn't make his mind up. Sometimes it seemed that his body *was* perfect and needed no improvement, but the next moment those beautiful, slightly sad eyes floated into his consciousness out of nowhere like a distant mirage.

He rushed to the gym then and trained like insane, trying to suppress the feeling. Sometimes he succeeded, but not for long.

The tanning shop mirror continued to reflect his disproportionate figure and ugly skin. He felt like an impure diamond, but, unlike the imperfections of diamonds, his flaws didn't make him feel unique. They drove him insane.

A few weeks passed like a single day. Will ran like a hamster in a wheel between his home and the gym while real life outside of his routine was ablaze with flamboyant colours but went unnoticed.

By the end of the third week, Will decided to visit that "Custom Tattoo & Piercings" shop with the massive *papier-mache* skull again. The man appeared to be waiting for him.

"I need to have a look again," Will said after a short greeting.

"Which folder do you need? Chinese? Celtic?" the man asked, getting up.

"No," Will stopped him. "I need one of those special sketches."

The man shrugged and disappeared into the side room. A few minutes later, he returned with the sheets in his hands.

"Keep in mind, these are expensive," he warned giving them to Will.

"How much?" Will asked, shuffling through the images.

"Which one do you have in mind?" the man demanded.

Will quickly found the sketch with the lady and lava flow and silently showed it to the skinny man.

"That would be around twelve hundred," said the man, scratching his chin.

"What?! It's just a small tattoo, not a whole-body inking…" Will almost dropped the sketch.

"The design is distinctive and complex, and as I mentioned last time, it uses a unique dye for the colouring of these eyes," explained the man taking the sketch from Will's hands. "No other pigment can do the job, and the amount I have is sufficient for one job only. There'll be no duplicates."

Will felt a wave of heat in his temples. Twelve hundred was a ridiculous amount of money, even for an intricate and unique job like this.

"The price is non-negotiable. You can choose something less sophisticated if you haven't got the money," suggested the skinny man carefully studying the portrait of the blonde woman. "Do you want me to bring the other folders?"

"No need. I don't like anything else," Will said firmly. "I need to think. It's a lot of money."

The skinny man frowned, displaying the sketch across his chest.

"Better be quick with those thoughts," he grinned. "You're not the only one who is thinking. First come, first served. There is no dye for a second one."

Will's heart skipped several beats.

"I understand. I will," he mumbled, leaving.

The chill outside cooled him down. Will found the nearest ATM and looked at his meagre savings – five hundred and thirty-six, which was far from enough. Very far.

Back home, Will locked himself in his room and spent the rest of the day, staring blankly at the ceiling. In his imagination, the lovely blue eyes of the blonde woman were staring back. He skipped dinner, which was unusual for his training regime.

"Are you ill?" his mother asked from behind the closed door.

"No," Will said. "I've got no appetite. Leave me alone, please."

That night he had a weird dream. The blonde lady was smiling at him from in front of the erupting volcano. They were standing amidst the flames but didn't feel the heat. The hissing flow of molten rock parted just in front of her and then united again in its flow down the slope. *Who are you?* Will asked, but the lady only smiled. She slowly waved her hand – a gesture as gracious as an arabesque – inviting him to swim in that river of flames. How could he refuse? Her clothes perished as soon as they were touched by the heat. His clothes were gone too, but the lava felt warm and comfortable. They swam laughing, fooling about and teasing before they had fiery sex on the black beach.

Her image haunted the next few sleepless nights and long days. Will skipped a few sessions at the gym (which was unthinkable!). His inflamed brain just refused to allow him to leave the room. His mother prowled outside the door several times, worried by Will's behaviour. He tried to reassure her that everything was okay but wasn't very successful in convincing her.

Will was sure that he badly wanted that tattoo. He was firm on that decision but couldn't think of any way to raise that ridiculous amount of money. He couldn't ask his mother. She would never understand his need. His younger sister wasn't that rich either. And time was ticking.

He mostly ignored his mother's mumbling, but when he did choose to listen, he caught the word *hospital* a few times. Will knew he must do something about her worries, or he might end up there. Being in a hospital could complicate matters beyond repair, so Will decided to pay a visit to the gym after spending a few days in bed. He got up early and sneaked outside, leaving a note on the fridge. He hoped she would be relieved, but he would hate to have to go into any explanation.

The gym was nearly empty. Will quickly changed and went straight to the free weight corner as his gaze fell on a black guy with huge bulging muscles, who was already sweating there.

Will hated to share his weights, but it looked like he had no other choice. The guy was murmuring a cheerful tune under his breath as he juggled dumbbells with enormous speed. Will noted the thick gold choker around his neck and the corresponding golden bracelet, accompanied by several large rings with clear sparkling stones on both hands. His posh golden phone lay on the ground with a wireless connection to the black earphones sitting on his ears.

Will quickly did some warm-up, trying to ignore the guy. He turned to the barbell and started to fit the weight when a gentle tap on his right shoulder stopped him. He turned around and met a wide sparkling smile in front of him.

"Ricky's the name," the black guy extended his right palm in a friendly gesture.

"Will."

"Could you safeguard me with that barbell?" Ricky asked, still smiling. "I promise to return the favour."

"Sure…" Will stepped aside watching how the black guy lowered himself on the bench and got a grip of the barbell. "How many repetitions do you do?" he asked.

"Twelve," Ricky answered.

With growing envy, Will watched the bulging muscles

move under Ricky's shiny dark skin. He secretly compared his own physique to the Ricky's – the size of the muscles and proportions were almost the same, but Will's gorgeous torso was wrapped in that pitiful piggy skin. He couldn't even get a decent tan!

"Twelve," whispered Ricky exhaling and waking Will up from his dreamlike state. "You didn't count."

"Sorry," Will said and grabbed the barbell.

"Your turn," Ricky got up with a broad smile, flexed his muscles and took a stance at the head of the bench.

Will wasn't used to being pushed in his workouts, but the weight was challenging, and the barbell was guarded.

"How many?" Ricky asked while Will was making himself comfortable on the bench.

"Fifteen."

Blood rushed into his pecs as he lowered and lifted the barbell, swelling and numbing his chest.

"… three, four, five, six…" Ricky counted loudly. "Fifteen! You are good, man! You are really good."

Will smiled and got up. He gulped a few mouthfuls of water secretly admiring the ebony colour of Ricky's sculptured legs. The man was flawless.

They repeated the press several times at different tilts of the bench, and it was an excellent workout. Will's black mood faded into nothingness. He knew it hadn't gone far away. It was just hiding around the corner, waiting for the right moment to sneak back.

Then they fooled with dumbbells. Ricky showed Will a few new tricks which he was eager to learn. They laughed loudly, ignoring everybody else in the gym. Will felt great and just tried to avoid glancing directly in the mirror where his bright pink skin was shining like the morning sun. Ricky didn't seem to mind.

They hit the showers together joking and chuckling like two kids. Cool streams of water brought Will back to reality and his problems. The joy was over.

"That was a decent workout," Ricky observed, spitting the water from his mouth and rubbing shower gel on his torso.

"Yeah…" Will sighed. "I've never seen you in the gym before. Are you going to train here regularly?"

"No," Ricky winked and answered chuckling. "I was only here for a day on business. My train is the afternoon. I had to kill some time."

"Oh…"

The streams of water washed the soap away, and they returned to the locker room, rubbing their bodies with towels.

"You still look very tense," Ricky observed, slipping into his trendy underwear. "Problems?"

Will only sighed.

"Shoot," Ricky encouraged him. "It's always easier to tell a stranger everything."

Will was reluctant, but his tongue took on a life of its own.

"Well…" he said, rubbing his ginger hair with a towel. "The main problem is to do with money."

"That was easy to guess," Ricky chuckled. "We all need

money. How big is your problem?"

"I need something desperately," Will said fiercely, surprising himself. "I need less than a grand to make it happen. How can I raise it without selling my kidneys?"

"I'm not giving you money. It doesn't work that way," Ricky sighed. "But the advice is free."

"I'm listening," Will stopped rubbing his body, the towel still in his hands.

"It depends on how desperate you are," Ricky gave a wink. "No need to sell your kidneys. You have a very nice sample of meat on your bones and a very decent tool down there – rent it out. You could make that grand you need in a night."

An awkward silence followed. Will only blinked, unable to say a word.

"As I said," Ricky smiled and whispered. "It depends how desperate you are."

Will put the towel away and sat down.

"And what if she's ugly?" he asked, still shocked by the thought.

Ricky winked.

"You just need to close your eyes, and the hormones will do the rest," he smiled. "But I can see you're too innocent for that. Forget it."

They finished dressing in silence. Then Ricky left with a short goodbye, while Will still was busy sorting his things.

He paid a visit to the tanning shop on his way home.

"To be honest," the receptionist said, flashing her fake eyelashes. "I don't think you can get a decent tan from those sunbeds. They're not suitable for your type of skin. Maybe you should think about a spray tan instead?"

Will simply gave her a fiver, silently shook his head and sneaked into the first available cubicle. His face was bright red. He sat down and waited for a few minutes until he managed to calm down.

Then he stripped and looked at the mirror with the professional approach of a butcher. He flexed his muscles. His meat moved attractively in lovely shapes, if not to mention that ugly skin tone. His gaze wandered down to his tool below the glistening red pubic jungle – it looked normal but not exceptional as Ricky had implied – only a little larger than a toothpick. Still, the idea was repulsive, and he dismissed it entirely.

Will slipped onto the sunbed and spent those few measured minutes sweating in the ultraviolet rays. He came out and glanced in the mirror again – he looked as red as a grilled lobster. *Shit!* Will angrily turned away from his image and quickly dressed. He absentmindedly chewed a protein bar back in the street on his way home, placing one foot in front of the other. Then he stopped at the window where the *papier-mache* skull sat. The man was inside, reading a newspaper.

"Is she still with you?" Will asked, sticking his head through the door.

The man raised his skinny smile from the paper.

"Yes," he nodded. "She's still here for a while, I suppose. Five people are making their minds up, including you. Or are you dropping out of the race?"

"Not yet," Will shook his head vigorously.

He thanked the man and closed the door.

Back in the street, Will cursed aloud, which was unusual for him, and stormed back home and locked himself in his room.

He would lose her. He was almost certain – *he would lose her.*

Will slumped on his bed like a bunch of rags with his eyes suddenly full of tears. He fished out his phone and looked again at the features of that mysterious woman. Could he dare to lose her? That thought was unbearable. Will shook it away, but it kept returning and banging at his temples.

The day had been wasted. His mother knocked on his door several times, but he had lost his appetite altogether. All day long Will lay on his bed staring at the lady in his phone. Suddenly he realised that four other people somewhere in the city were doing the same.

This thought brought a cascade of sweat and a stomach-churning sensation of failure. Will hastily looked around the room searching for something suitable to sell. Nothing was worth even trying. Who could be interested in his few smelly trainers or used T-shirts? Even his humble old laptop collecting dust in the corner was hardly worth more than a hundred. It was still very far from enough.

Will moaned, feeling the ground slipping under his feet. He had never wanted anything so badly.

He slipped into the bathroom, locked the door and stripped off. Ricky's slip of the tongue kept bouncing in his brain, every time meeting repulsive resistance. Had it been bad advice? Will wasn't that sure anymore. "How desperate you are?" – Ricky's question still rang in his ears. Will sat down on the loo and carefully inspected his manhood. The idea was monstrous, and he closed his eyes, frightened, trying to imagine the process. His manhood twitched in approval. Will cursed.

He stood up and looked at his bare chest in the mirror. He *must* get that blonde girl inked on his chest. *Left pec*, he decided.

A loud knock on the door brought him back down to earth. His younger sister was persistent, and Will had no other choice but to dress and go back to his room.

"Will you have something to eat, Willy?" his mother asked on his way. "I'm fed up of wasting food."

"I will," he nodded reluctantly.

"Then come down in fifteen minutes!"

Will only sighed. His head had spun into action mode already as a firm decision to get that tattoo cut some circuits short and forced his body into motion.

Back in his room, he shuffled through the photos on his phone. He had plenty of images of himself in different poses and environments and at various stages of undress.

He quickly uploaded an advert online and tossed his phone on the bed as if it was a poisonous spider.

"Willy!" it was his mother. "Get downstairs!"

Will was about to shout back "not hungry", but remembered his promise. His mother would be furious. Silently he got up and went to the kitchen where she looked at him with concern in her eyes.

"Are you okay?" she asked, placing his usual chicken breast and vegetables on the table in front of him.

"I'm fine," Will said, picking up a fork and sitting down.

"Don't lie to your mother," she was persistent. "Are you using drugs?"

"No, that's ridiculous," Will frowned. "What makes you think that?"

"You've never skipped meals before," she complained.

"I'm fine," Will started to stuff his stomach in his usual manner without offering any further explanations.

Mother sighed. Will felt that she hadn't been convinced by that banal statement and made a mental note not to skip any more meals. He felt guilty for making her worried, but he had a right in his late twenties to keep a few secrets for himself.

Will finished eating in silence, then dutifully washed his plate and left the kitchen. Back in his room, he grabbed his phone, hoping for some phenomenal sale of his meat that Ricky had promised, but the mailbox was empty – nobody was interested.

The rest of the day he spent in bed, toggling between the photo of *that* sketch and his mail inbox. Things hadn't improved even after the usual protein shake later in the evening. Will nearly wept in desperation. He kept looking at those blue eyes on the sketch and fell asleep at some point when it was already late into the night.

The next morning Will woke up with a headache but decided not to worry his mother even more, and rushed to the gym after a quick breakfast. He popped into the tattoo shop on his way.

"Is she still available?" he asked the man.

"Yes, sir," the scraggy man nodded with a military salute, smiling.

The workout was dull. Will kept checking his inbox every few minutes with diminishing hope and absentmindedly messed with the dumbbells which were too small for his regular weights. The phone remained silent.

Will hit the shower in the blackest of moods. He rubbed his body thoroughly for a long time, allowing the cold stream to chill his skin, shaking the nerves. When he came out of the shower, drying himself with a towel, a message was waiting for him.

"Nice pictures of yours," the message said. "I am interested. What is your name?"

"Will," he responded immediately. "Your name?"

"You can call me Jill," the response came a few minutes later. "How much do you charge for a night?"

"A thousand," Will felt breathless as he typed that into his phone. "That's non-negotiable."

For a painful fifteen minutes, the phone was silent.

"Okay," the answer finally flashed up. "Your job starts at 8 pm. My place. Don't be late."

And the address followed.

Will quickly dressed and sprinted into the street. The day seemed brighter than before, despite the low clouds and sprinkling moisture. He nearly ran uphill and stopped just in front of the tattoo shop with the skull. The skinny man was talking with someone on the phone, and Will waited patiently outside until he finished.

"I'll have the money tomorrow," Will said with a broad smile.

"It's still first to come – first served principle," said the man indifferently.

"Can't you reserve her for me?" Will was nearly begging. "I'll be here tomorrow, first thing in the morning."

"I'll be closed tomorrow morning," the man frowned. "I'll open at 2 pm. Be the first here then. If you're late, she's back on the market."

"Agreed," Will quickly nodded.

Back home, he ate his usual chicken breast while increasing waves of worries splashed him from every corner. He had no idea if Jill was attractive. He hoped she was. Otherwise, his task would become nearly impossible. A doubting voice continually whispered in his head – *what are you doing? Is that tattoo worth the effort? Anyway, it was only a tattoo… Wasn't it?*

Will skulked to his room and locked the door. For a few minutes, he just looked around helplessly, as if trying to find some salvation. Did he really need that image on his chest? Will fished out his phone and looked again at those bright blue eyes and lovely features. *Yes, he needed it.* Will was still adamant about that.

This last thought brought about some action, and he sat down on his bed, checking the map and finding the address where he was supposed to make an appearance this evening. It was quite a long way from home, in a suburban area on the other side of town, so Will decided he would leave early just to get there on time. His heart was fluttering. He felt like a rabbit preparing to pay a visit to a snake hole. He tried to ignore that dreadful feeling, encouraging himself with some empty hopes: *she will be young and pretty, they will just spend a romantic night reading poetry in the candlelight, she will only need a hug and a lullaby, she will just need some company…*

A swarm of thoughts buzzed in Will's mind as he prepared his perfect body for the task ahead. He ate his lunch, then took a quick shower and put on fresh underwear. Will spent a few minutes in front of the bathroom mirror. His short ginger hair didn't need combing, but his skin now looked even paler and less rosy as he battled the doubts and fears within.

Will quickly dressed and went outside. The street met him with a downpour of rain and unpleasant gusts of winds. He almost ran to the bus stop.

The bus arrived several minutes later, and Will took a seat next to the window. Angry thoughts kept attacking him – *stop, what are you doing?* But then the lava flow brought back those blue eyes into his troubled mind, and Will carried on sitting there helplessly and staring out of the window at the endless stream of cars passing in the opposite direction.

He had to change buses several times on his way. The skies grew darker as he travelled, but the rain had stopped.

Will found himself standing in front of a dark red brick house at the far end of a street. Tall shrubs guarded the house on both sides, partially obscuring the dimly lit windows. He checked the email on his phone – this was the address she had given him.

Will's heart pounded as he approached the door, ready to jump and run away at any moment. *It must be the wrong address, it must be the wrong address* – the thought kept rolling around his head.

He rang the doorbell. A minute of silence followed, which poured more uncertainty in his growing tension. Then he heard slow and heavy footsteps on the other side.

The door opened.

"Yes?" a messy grey head with specs on peeked outside.

The head belonged to a large lady in her sixties. *This must be the wrong address* – the thought was now overwhelming.

"Is Jill home?" Will cleared his throat and asked, hoping for a negative answer.

"I'm Jill," said the lady. "And you must be Willy? Come in..."

She stepped aside, letting him in and closed the door.

Jill was enormous, much shorter than Will, but her body, twice as wide, resembled a shapeless blob on short legs with thick arms sticking out on both sides. Will instantly felt trapped. His naïve hopes for a romantic night with an attractive girl were crushed to dust under Jill's weight.

"The bedroom is to the right," she crooned, pushing his butt in the right direction.

Will suddenly felt a weakness in his legs, but the push was persistent, leaving no room for objections. It was clear that it wasn't poetry that was waiting for him in Jill's bed.

Heavy footsteps followed him as he entered the boudoir and stopped. The room was dimly lit by several scented candles, making the air thick with a sickening bitter-sweet smell. Jill rolled in after him.

"Here's the money," she indicated a wad of banknotes on the table in front of the draped window. "You can count it if you like. The money is yours in the morning but no sooner."

Will was about to turn around and run as fast as he could, but that bunch of banknotes glued his feet to the floor. Instead, he went closer to the table and touched the money. It looked like a grand's worth. He closed his eyes, clearly imagining that tattoo on his chest. That dream was now only moments away. But he had to survive the night somehow.

"I'll count it in the morning," he uttered, licking his dry lips. "What do you want me to do?"

"Undress," Jill told him and sat down on the bed. "First, I want to have a good look at what I'm buying."

Her request shook Will back out of his daydream. Despite all the surrealism of the situation, the reality was crude. He dutifully took off his hoodie. Jill offered no place to hang it, so Will dropped it on the floor. His T-shirt, jeans and socks followed.

"Those must go too," Jill pointed to his underwear with a finger crooked by arthritis.

Will flushed but obeyed and stood up stark naked in front of her.

"Come closer," she ordered, adjusting her specs.

Will shuddered, feeling like a mouse in front of an adder. He had no other choice but to step forward.

"It's so small," Jill complained, pointing at his manhood. "I thought it would be much bigger."

"It was cold outside," Will was unsure how to react.

Jill dismissed his explanation with an impatient gesture.

"Now I want you to undress me," she told him and placed her specs on the bedside table. "And I want to get some pleasure out of that. Put a smile on your face, please."

Will acted dutifully like a robot with a freaky smile on his face, releasing the blob from the restrictions of its apparel.

"I guess you won't object if I will take my dentures out? They're a bit lose, and I don't want to choke on them," Jill said as he finished messing about with her clothing.

She didn't wait for his approval. Her face imploded slightly without their support as her teeth found their way to the bedside table next to the specs.

"Kiss me," she ordered, closing her eyes.

Will closed his eyes too. That helped a little.

Will didn't remember much of how he spent the rest of that night. All he could see each time he opened his eyes was a lolling sea of fat. Then he closed his eyes again, letting the hormones do the job. The candles burned out at about midnight, and they spent the rest of the witching hours in darkness. Finally, the morning sun broke through the window.

"That's enough," Jill told him in a firm and commanding voice and put her false teeth back into her mouth. "You may go now."

She didn't offer him take a shower, though he felt dirty and smelled awful. Will hastily jumped out of bed and dressed before she could change her mind.

"Don't forget to count the money," Jill reminded him and adjusted her spectacles. "I keep my promises."

Will counted the banknotes before carefully placing the wad in his pocket. It *was* a grand.

He felt nauseous and rushed outside without her offering a farewell kiss. Back in the street, he turned right and ran as fast as he could until he reached the bus stop. The morning chill cooled him a little, but his head was still dizzied from that thick sickening smell of Jill's bedroom.

Fifteen minutes later, the bus arrived. It was full, but Will somehow managed to squeeze inside. He couldn't even bear to think about spending another half an hour in that neighbourhood.

The journey home seemed endless. Again he had to change buses several times until he finally reached his street.

"Where have you been all night?" his mother demanded.

"I was with my friend," Will lied. "We talked about training, and I didn't notice the time until it was too late to come back, so I just slept there."

"You could have called," his mother shook her head, worry still in her eyes. "I've spent the whole night waiting for you."

"It won't happen again," he promised firmly. "Sorry…"

Back in his room, he took out the banknotes and counted again. It was a grand! That desirable tattoo now was within reach!

Will was deadly tired but couldn't bear the thought of

the remnants of Jill's sticky touch on his skin. He locked himself in the bathroom and spent a full hour in the shower scrubbing and scrubbing his skin until it felt shiny again.

"Will you have some breakfast, Willy?" his mother banged on the closed door.

"Yes, mum," he answered.

Life was about to get back to normal. Will decided to skip training and took a short nap instead. It was well past noon when the alarm woke him up from the dreamless oblivion. Will got up and dressed. It was time.

He carefully placed his hard-earned money in the breast pocket and headed out. On his way, he paid a short visit to the ATM to get the two hundred pounds he still needed. At half-past one, he was standing in front of the *papier mache* skull. The "Custom Tattoo & Piercings" still was closed.

Will nervously paced in front of the locked door, checking the time on his phone every few minutes. Fifteen minutes past two – there was still no sign of life behind the closed door. Will grew increasingly impatient. He almost jumped when his phone vibrated in his pocket, notifying him of a new email.

"Thank you for a fantastic night. Could we meet next week – same place and same price?" it was Jill.

He cursed and slipped the phone back into his pocket, choosing to ignore the message. The scraggy man was unhurriedly strolling down the street and smoking a cigar. He stopped in front of the "Custom Tattoo & Piercings" and greeted Will.

"Am I still in business?" Will asked with a sinking heart.

"It depends if you've got the money," the skinny man shrugged as he unlocked the door. "Another candidate is due to come at five."

"I have money!" Will followed him into the shop.

"Well, then she's yours," the man shaped a foxy smile. "Are you sure about it? I've warned you about the consequences and the pain."

"I'm sure," Will nodded.

"Okay…" the man sighed, locking the door. "Where do you want it?"

"On my left pec," Will pointed firmly.

"Oh…" the man winked. "Closer to your heart? Very well. Let's do it."

"How long will it take?"

"A few hours, at least," said the man leading him to the side room. "It'll be a neat job."

The side room was smaller than the reception area without any windows. Several large luminescent lamps hung from the ceiling and along all three walls except for the one with the door. The leather-covered table was in the centre of the room with several shelves on two walls, stuffed with phials, papers and strange ink-stained tools.

"You better take your T-shirt off if you don't want it to get stained," the man said, shuffling through his papers. "And you'll need to sign these."

"What's this?" asked Will.

"This is my safeguard, in case you ever think of suing me," the man wasn't smiling. "I've explained everything to you, and you're giving informed consent. Just sign it and assume the responsibility for your own decision."

Will hesitated for only a second. *What could go wrong with a tattoo?*

"Very well," the skinny man smiled. "Can I have the money now before we get started?"

Will took out the banknotes and put it on the table. The man carefully counted, then tossed the wad into one of his drawers.

"All is good," he said and put on black latex gloves. "Let's get the job done."

Will took his T-shirt off and put it on a chair in the corner. His skin looked terribly pale in the bright light, and he suddenly felt even more embarrassed than he was in front of Jill, his face blushing red. The skinny man grinned but refrained from making any comment.

He spent the next hour carefully transferring the image onto Will's chest.

"Almost ready to start," he said, finally standing up.

"Do you have any mirrors here?" Will asked, curious about how his new look was progressing.

"There's not too much to look at right now," the man told him. "And I warn you. I'll charge you another hundred if you suddenly decide to change the location. But you may have a look. The mirror's in the reception. I'll get ready to ink."

Will impatiently sneaked into the reception and spent a few minutes in front of the mirror. The man was right – the contours of the image on his left pec now looked like a shapeless web without any colour, but it already detracted the eye from his freckles. Will grinned and returned to the table where the skinny man was waiting for him with the inking machine in his hands.

"All okay?"

Will just nodded and lay back down again on the table.

"Here comes the pain," announced the man, looming over him with the inking machine.

The machine began to buzz, and Will felt a light pricking on his chest.

"It's not so bad," he observed.

"I'll just do the conventional red and black inks first," said the man working on the pattern. "The main attraction will come later."

Another hour passed as the machine followed the intricate curves of the picture, leaving first red tracks then later – black. The needle that pricked the skin was just surface deep which was unpleasant, but far from painful. Will relaxed and only frowned a couple of times when the needle hit more sensitive areas.

He looked at the man's face – he was locked in complete concentration with his black eyes closely following the pattern. His lips were tightly pressed together, letting out no sounds.

Suddenly he stood up and stretched his spine.

"What?" Will asked.

"Don't worry," the man said. "We've reached the fun part."

He went back to the shelf, shuffling a few things around and picked up a few phials. The sharp odour of antiseptic followed.

"Here," he returned and handed Will a piece of wood. "Bite down on this, or you might damage your teeth. And you can scream as much as you like, but just don't move."

Will's heart sank to his ankles as he bit on the wood. Anyway, there was no way back. The picture would be incomplete without those beautiful eyes.

The machine began to buzz again, but this time it felt like liquid metal was being poured onto his chest. Luckily, Will only blinked and fainted.

The sharp odour of ammonia brought him back to his senses. Will blinked at the bright lights until he was able to focus on the skinny smile.

"How did you do that?" the man asked. "It was a neat trick."

"It wasn't a trick. I've no idea what happened," Will shrugged with his gaze still wandering without a proper focus. "Are we done?"

"Yes," the man chuckled. "You can get up when you're feeling strong enough."

"I need a mirror," Will requested.

The man helped him to his feet.

"I've covered it with a film," the skinny man explained. "Don't remove it for a few days, and don't wash it. Let it heal. It might be a bit sore to start with."

"I need a mirror," Will repeated firmly.

The man helped him to the reception area. Will carefully inspected his chest. A magnificent river of liquid stone was visible even through the film. The shape of the lady was slightly blurred, but Will smiled, touching her bright blue eyes shining through the film.

"Everything okay?" asked the scraggy man.

Will quickly nodded.

He spent a few more minutes in front of the mirror. Then the man helped him to put his T-shirt on keeping the protective film in place.

"Good luck," the man unlocked the door and let him through. "It's been a pleasure to do business with you."

A few gusts of chilly wind outside finally blew away all remnants of dizziness. He felt his chest. The deep throbbing pain was still there, and his left pec felt numb and swollen. Will frowned – it was too painful to touch. He only hoped that this would pass in a few days as the skinny man had promised.

He went uphill slightly hunched because straightening his shoulders caused a sharp pain in his chest. But that pain brought a broad smile of victory on his face. The other four contenders could eat dust!

Back at home, he silently stuffed the usual portion of chicken breast into his stomach and washed it down with the usual protein shake. Will then locked himself in the bathroom and carefully inspected the image on his chest. He was tempted to remove the coating but remembered the warnings.

The lady behind the film smiled at him, and Will smiled back.

Back in his room, Will carefully lowered his body onto the bed. He tried to imagine the envious looks at the gym where he would have the chance to display this beauty – he just needed a few days to let it heal.

He had a restless night and was unable to sleep. The throbbing pain in his chest was not too intense, but it kept him awake. He alternated between lying flat on his back and his right side but still couldn't get any sleep.

Deep in the night, Will decided to answer the call of nature. He sneaked out of his room, keeping the lights off – he could easily find the way in the dark with his eyes closed. He went down the corridor and stopped abruptly in front of the bathroom door. The white paint on the wood had a barely perceptible bluish glow, and Will extended his hand out carefully to touch the painted surface. Only then did he realise – it wasn't the door that was glowing. The ghostly blue light was emitting from his left pec! The tattoo was even more incredible than he thought. Will rushed into the bathroom giggling like a kid. He kept the light off and spent nearly half an hour in front of the mirror, admiring the faint blue glow of the lady's eyes. This was wonderful, much better than he had expected. Pity that the light was so bright at the gym, nobody would be able to see this miracle.

The pain in his pec was slowly subsiding, but Will was still unable to fall asleep – now he was too excited. Three or four times he went to the bathroom again just to have another peek in the mirror. He couldn't wait to remove the film and have a closer look at those glowing eyes.

"Are you ill?" his mother asked in the morning as he was eating his breakfast. "You went to the bathroom a lot in the night."

"No, mum, I'm fine," Will answered, eating scrambled eggs.

"Don't lie to your mother," she was persistent.

"I'm not," Will said firmly. "I'm fine. I've had a tattoo done. It was a bit sore so that I couldn't get to sleep."

Mother placed her fork down on the table.

"*What?*"

"I badly wanted it, mum," Will muttered defensively. "It wasn't expensive."

"Willy…" she sighed. "I would be much happier if you at least pretended that you were looking for a job. That gym is not a job. It only plants crazy ideas like that in your head."

"I'll find one, don't worry," he nodded. "Promise."

She just shook her head, looking miserable. Will quickly finished his breakfast and sneaked outside without saying another word. He knew it was pointless to argue with her.

He wandered aimlessly around the town for several hours. The pain in his chest slowly subsided so that he could touch the pec without even frowning, but the soreness was now replaced by itchiness. It wasn't too bad, but he was constantly on alert, forcing his right hand to stay in his pocket to keep it away from the precious picture.

Will wasn't ready to go to the gym yet. He couldn't show his half-baked treasure to anyone with that protective film on.

He wandered around the park when his phone beeped to indicate receipt of an email. He fished it out of the pocket. It was Jill.

"I'll pay you a fifty per cent premium if you could make

it next week," said the message.

Will made a horrible face before replying "not interested". He then hummed a sickly tune, sat down on a bench in the park and watched the pigeons and squirrels. Twenty minutes later came a reply.

"Name your price," Jill wrote.

She definitively was desperate. Will grinned but was firm in his decision. He felt sorry for her loneliness, but he had no intention of slipping back into bed with her.

"I'm swamped with requests for the whole month," he typed, trying to soften the blow and hoping that the problem would just fade away given enough time.

"I'll wait," Jill replied within a few seconds. "Just remember me when you have a free slot."

Will put the phone back in his pocket, watching how the grey squirrel in front of him sank its teeth into a hazelnut. A pang of hunger suddenly hit his stomach. It was time to go home.

Will retraced his steps back to the street and unhurriedly made his way uphill. Several minutes later he stopped in front of "Custom Tattoo & Piercings". The skinny man was reading a newspaper, but spotted Will and waved his hand, smiling.

"Hello," Will poked his head through the door.

"How are you? How's the inking?" the man asked.

"It's not painful anymore, but itching like hell," Will complained.

"Let me have a look," the man took Will to the side room.

Will frowned as the man put his skinny fingers on his still tender chest and slowly ripped the film off, inspecting the picture with his sharp black eyes. The itching stopped.

"Looks fine to me," was the verdict.

"Could I look at it without that film?" Will asked. "Please…"

"You can," the man rubbed Will's chest with antiseptic. "I'm not going to put it back. Everything's healing perfectly, and you can look at it as much as you like. You can even take a shower, just don't rub it too vigorously – the skin is still a bit irritated."

"Great!" Will's smile was as broad as a full moon.

He stood up and got dressed.

"That tattoo is exceptional. You never mentioned that wonderful glowing in the dark that it does," Will was still grinning widely, shaking the man's hand.

The man's skinny smile froze.

"Glowing?"

Will nodded still exposing his teeth in a smile of cheerful happiness.

"I had no idea that the pigment glows," the man admitted hesitantly. "I knew it was special but had no idea of its features."

"I'm very happy about it," Will assured him. "It's really cool."

"Glad you like it," the man muttered.

Back in the street, Will's smile shone like a second sun. It was ready! Finally, it was ready!

His mother still looked unhappy, as she opened the door

for him, but Will's grin softened her attitude a little.

"Get your lunch, Willy," she put the chicken breast on the table without saying another word.

Will quickly gulped down the meat.

"Thanks, mum," he kissed her cheek, bringing a shy smile to her lips.

Will spent the next half hour in the bathroom, carefully washing his chest with the gentle shower gel until the eyes of the lady shone like two precious gems. He quickly dressed and rushed out to catch the bus. He was very impatient to see the envious expressions in the gym at the sight of his new look.

The journey was short. Will got off the bus just in front of the gym. He looked with concern through the windows for a few seconds then he smiled contently – the gym was full of people. It was the perfect time for a display.

Will quickly changed and marched to the free weight corner, ready to put on a show. He decided to go for a shoulder routine and postpone the chest workout for a few days just to let the pec heal completely.

Girls giggled as he proudly marched in front of the row of treadmills. Will could barely keep a straight face.

The free weight corner was empty since all the low-meat guys were sticking to the machines as usual. Will adjusted the bench into the sitting position. He was already being followed by envious looks and secret admiring glances.

Will deftly did a few sets of shoulder presses with the heaviest dumbbells he could find. Then he switched to the barbell and did a few sets of military presses sitting on the bench. The workout was great. Soon his skin began to sweat and acquired that pink colour he had always hated. Not this time. He put down the barbell, took a few gulps of water from his bottle and slowly took off his T-shirt.

Hushed envious gasps spread through the gym like wildfire. Will looked in the mirror. The liquid stone on his chest perfectly blended with the pink colour of his skin and the moving muscles gave an impression of an actual living flow. The lady smiled, staring back at him with her blue, slightly sad eyes. Will absentmindedly smiled back, then grabbed the dumbbells and performed three sets of lateral raises in front of the mirror, pausing just to drink some water.

The effect was ultimate. Skinny guys secretly added more weight to their machines and cast glances over to him. Will grabbed the barbell and performed several sets of the upright row, without slowing down with a wide grin still lighting his lips.

A full hour passed like the blink of an eye. For all of that time, he was the centre of attention. That felt great.

Will hummed a victorious melody as he hit the showers then he got dressed and paid a short trip to the tanning shop. Will requested five minutes but all he needed, in fact, was to use their big mirror. He spent almost ten minutes there, looking at his naked body from various angles. Each time the lady firmly grabbed complete attention and kept the eyes away from his skin, freckles and that still slightly flat butt. It was perfect. He needed to thank that skinny man – it was worth every penny he had paid him.

Will impatiently spent the next few minutes on the sunbed, then got out. The lady looked even better when his skin had acquired that awful pink colour. He quickly dressed and went out onto the street. The evening was chilly, and he decided to take a walk uphill. Traffic moved up the street in an endless flow, but Will paid no attention to the cars. He stopped only in front of "Custom Tattoo & Piercings" – it was closed, and the lights were out, maybe the skinny man had finished early today. Strangely, that terrifying *papier mache* skull and weird illumination of the window were missing too. Will shrugged and resumed his walk. *Maybe, tomorrow.*

Back at home, he decided not to trouble his mother and made a huge omelette from egg whites – not as tasty as mother used to make (Will knew nothing about salt and spices), but it was still edible.

He spent half an hour in the bathroom, brushing his teeth and messing about in front of the mirror. He couldn't feel happier.

That night, Will dreamed of a strange place. He found himself in a cave, dressed in strange garments and clutching a spear in his right hand. It was dark and dusty inside with the faint stench of rotten eggs. A peculiar low rumbling sound could be heard in the distance, and the earth shuddered under him in convulsions. That was frightening at first, but he soon got used to it.

Will stood up and went outside, still clutching the spear. The panorama was vast but grim, mainly black frozen lava fields. Sparse blades of grey-green grass circled the cave mouth and stopped about a hundred yards later, giving way to the bare black boulders. But it wasn't the grass or those black rocks that immediately caught Will's attention. It was the erupting volcano that looked similar to his tattoo, although the view was obscured in part by several massive cliffs on the left.

The river of molten rock slowly flowed down the slope almost a mile away, spitting out blue flames. There was a lifeless plain between him and the flowing lava, paved by bizarre black rocks which had been spat out from the depths of the mountain many years ago and then frozen into the black glacier. The clouds were low and dark, slowly floating to the right with their curvy bellies painted pink by the volcano.

The scenery was frightening but familiar – Will had memorised it in the slightest detail when he had looked at the lovely lady on his phone. He quickly checked his chest – the tattoo had gone! Will cursed aloud in frustration and then remembered that it was only a dream, and he would find his treasure still there in the morning. He clutched the spear, preparing to explore that dream in full and slowly went downhill towards the flaming river, carefully stepping on the jagged rocks.

"Where are you going?" the voice behind him sounded frightened.

Will stopped and turned around. A girl, dressed in strange rags, stood in the cave mouth. Her dark hair was a mess, and her black eyes were wide and set deep in their sockets, giving her a frightened expression. She was leaning on the stone wall as if afraid to step any further.

"I want to have a closer look at those flames," Will told her, indicating the flowing lava.

"You can't go that near to Death," the girl whispered.

"I'm not going to take a dip, don't worry," Will shrugged. "It's my dream, and I'm going to get a closer look. You can't stop me."

"Your dream is wrong," she told him firmly. "We should stay away."

"I'm not asking you to follow me," Will was persistent. "You can go back if you want."

"You're so stubborn," the girl complained.

Will dismissed her with an impatient gesture and turned to face the lava. He resumed his slow stroll forward, carefully choosing his way.

"No!" the girl sounded desperate. "Don't step off the grass! She'll kill you!"

"She?" it was like a strike of the lightning, adding even more determination – the possibility of meeting the lady from his tattoo felt dizzying.

Anyway, it was his dream, and he could do as he pleased.

"No, no!" the girl was crying.

"Wait here or go back," Will told her harshly without even glancing behind him.

The way was tricky. Some stones were loose, and he had to watch his step carefully before putting his feet on the ground. Several times he tripped and almost fell, but his spear came in very handy, steadying him like a walking stick.

Will slowly approached the edge of the grass and then stopped. A hushed wailing reached him from the cave.

"I'll be back," he said, trying to calm her down, then stepped forward grinning. "Don't worry."

Nothing happened.

"See?" he grinned again.

The silvery blades of grass were still wafting in the gentle breeze. The earth was still trembling with each outburst of molten rock from the crater and lava still flowed – nothing had changed. Will waved to the frightened girl and resumed his journey. He was determined to reach the river and have a look at what was there.

Progress became even slower. The light wind brought waves of heat from the lava, but the views opening in front of Will's eyes kept pushing him forward. He carefully bent round the large crag that towered on the left and stopped. There was a massive cliff half a mile uphill on the slope of the volcano, facing the fiery river at its foot. But it wasn't the cliff that caught Will's attention – it was the black castle that sat on top of it.

It *was* a strange dream, Will decided. He hadn't met the lady, but he had found her castle! Or was it somebody else's castle?

Will was about to set his feet uphill, closer to that lonely cliff when the eerie reversed V-shaped formation of ghostly shadows appeared as if from nowhere. It was several dozens of knights in black armour floating like ghosts a few feet above the ground at the very shore of the flaming river. Their speed was incredible, making the view even eerier. Will stopped with his mouth gaping. Several hundred yards behind the line of dark knights, a shiny black stallion galloped uphill. When the animal came closer, Will got a view of the blonde rider in the saddle and gasped – she was his beautiful lady in the dark leather garments with her long hair flying in the wind.

The knights stopped at the foot of the volcano and parted to let her through. The stallion rushed up the narrow road and disappeared behind the high gates of the black castle.

Will leant on his spear. The dream had enormous complexity and looked almost real. It was like a computer game; only he couldn't understand its rules yet.

He was sure the knights were guarding the lady, but why?

Then another bout of eruption shuddered the volcano as it spat out an enormous fountain of lava knocking Will off his feet.

"No, no, no, no..." he whispered as the blazing stream took a new path down the slope, threatening to engulf the castle, the knights and Will on its way.

At the same moment, a cloud of black fumes appeared from the depths of the castle, circling into a slowly expanding whirlpool, and covering first the black walls then the knights. *Was the castle on fire? She might die there!* Will gasped, staring at the closing wall of dark fumes – it roared like thousand claps of thunder spitting flames and streams of sparks. And it approached him down the slope with the speed of a racing car. He had no time even to blink.

Will rushed back to the safety of the cave as fast as he could on the loose gravel. The earth trembled, knocking him to the ground several times. Only when he reached the edge of the grass did he dare to glance back. The insanely circling wall of flames and fumes was at the same spot where he had been standing just minutes ago. It stopped advancing, but the speed of its rotation increased.

Will straightened up and laughed out loud. The view

was frightening, one of those that cover your skin in goosebumps while still being breathtakingly spectacular.

"Hey!" he waved happily to the flaming tornado and watched it slowly dispersing.

"Why are you doing that?" came a question from the cave. "She might see you!"

He turned back to face the frightened girl, hiding in the cave mouth.

"I must go back," Will told her. "I need to check the castle. She might be injured."

"You can't walk on fire," the frightened girl shook her head frantically. "Look…"

Will looked – the whole field up to the lava river was scattered with blazing embers. Everything that had come out of the volcano on that outburst was now evenly spread as a new layer across the lava field, breathing waves of scalding heat.

"Let's go home," the girl said. "It'll take ages to cool down."

"You can go if you want to," Will mumbled. "I'll wait here."

"Bryn, please," she was almost crying. "Bryn…"

The name was strange, even in a dream.

"Why are you calling me Bryn?" Will demanded with a frown.

"Because it's your name," she pulled an angry face. "What's happened to you? You're out of your mind. Let's go back!"

Will sat down, leaning on the rocky wall at the cave

mouth. The girl was disturbing and was spoiling an otherwise exciting dream.

"You go back," he said firmly. "Stand up, turn around and go. And don't come back. And don't even look back."

"Why are you doing this?" she began sobbing. "I love you, Bryn…"

"I don't love you," Will growled. "Go!"

"Bryn…" she covered her mouth in a burst of lament. "Bryn…"

Will lost his patience with the stupid love story. He had no idea who that girl was and didn't care to find out. She was just making him nervous.

"Go!" Will repeated, dismissing her with an impatient gesture. "Don't make me force you!"

The wailing slowly retreated into depths of the cave, half an hour later it was gone. Will wasn't sure if she had left him or had just stopped crying. He looked at the fiery field, waiting for it to become cool enough to put his feet on. Still, the process was slow. The field was transforming from a bright blaze into dark ruby at the pace of a sleepy turtle. Several times he stood up and carefully approached the edge where the sparse grass gave way to the lifeless rocks. Each time he was forced to go back. It was still too hot to proceed.

Cliffs and boulders on the left obscured the view of the castle, and Will could only imagine what was going on there. Was the castle still standing? Had the lady survived the eruption? What had happened to her black knights who were left to face the rage of nature in the open field? Had they survived the flaming tornado?

Will returned to the cave mouth and sat on the ground staring at the field in front of him. The dream had become boring. Nothing was happening. Will made an attempt to find an alternative route to peek at the castle, but steep impenetrable cliffs barred the way, and he was forced to turn back. He cursed several times, but that didn't make the rocks cool any quicker.

Will sat down, leaning against the cold wall of the cave and waited, gazing at the ruby red field in front of him. The dark clouds grew even darker as the evening closed in, their bellies still painted in pink. And that was the last thing he remembered of that dream before he woke up.

❧❦❀☙❧

The morning was beautiful, with strong sunshine beaming through his window. Will spent a few lazy minutes in bed simply recalling the fancy visions he had seen overnight until his mother came banging on the door.

"Breakfast's ready," she said.

"What's for breakfast?" Will demanded. It was unusual for him to ask.

"Scrambled eggs" came the reply. "Be quick. It's getting cold."

"Okay."

Will sprang out of bed and rushed to the bathroom to brush his teeth. The blonde, blue-eyed lady on his chest smiled as he thoroughly washed away the remnants of toothpaste from his mouth.

The scrambled eggs were much tastier than the omelette he had made the day before. Will quickly stuffed his stomach, thanked mother, collected his stuff and went to the gym.

He rushed downhill with the dream still vivid in his

mind. The "Custom Tattoo & Piercings" was still closed, and he stopped only briefly but long enough for a glance through the window at the empty premises. Maybe the man had decided to do a makeover in the shop now he'd got that money? It wasn't essential to thank him, but his absence was a little unsettling.

The gym was almost empty as Will went quickly through his leg routines. Several "skinnies" were sweating uselessly with the pec machine and messing about with the cable fly, but Will barely paid them any attention. Each time he closed his eyes, the black castle on that lonely cliff facing the river of flames floated into his mind, and Will wondered if the blonde lady had survived the cataclysm. He wished he could get back to that dream and find out, but he had always had a tricky relationship with dreams – they never came to him on request. Only nightmares had a certain stubborn persistence, staying in his mind for much longer. Will sighed – that dream hadn't been a nightmare.

He headed to the lockers, absentmindedly ignoring the sighs from the row of treadmills – he even forgot to flash his eight-pack and remembered that teasing trick only when the cooling stream of the shower touched his skin. He skipped the tanning session and took a slow walk uphill, still trying to remember the smallest details of his dream. That lady had been in a hurry to reach her castle and hadn't even noticed him. Maybe next time if she still was there… If there would be the next time.

Will spent the rest of the day eating and messing about on his phone. He took several pictures of his new self, but none were satisfactory, and he deleted them all.

Will brushed his teeth in the evening glancing at the lady on his chest. Would he be able to see her again?

The sad face of the full moon gazed at him in his bed through the closed window. Will shut his eyes expectantly and let his mind slowly sink into darkness, almost praying for the continuation of that adventure.

"Bryn..." it was a barely audible whisper.

The dark eyes of that annoying girl were staring at him when his vision finally regained sharpness. She was still frightened and still crying.

"Why are you still here?" Will growled, with unconcealed disdain in his voice. "I told you to go away!"

She irritated him with her constant wailing and groundless fears, but how could he get rid of her? Maybe she was some essential but annoying part of his dream designed to make him nervous and place obstacles to his path to the flaming river. *Was that river still here?* Or was he having another version of that dream? Will raised his head but was unable to see anything outside from where he was lying.

"I love you, Bryn," the girl whispered. "Don't get angry."

Only then did Will notice that his wrists were tightly bound with rope. He cursed. Of course, his ankles were bound too.

"Why? Why have you done that?" he screamed at her

angrily.

The girl jumped back and raised her hands in fright.

"She's put a curse on you," the girl muttered. "It's the only way to keep you alive. I'll get some help, but you must promise me to wait here. Don't go anywhere."

"Go?" Will burst into laughter. "Untie me. Now!"

The girl retreated into the black depths of the cave, slowly shaking her head.

"Just wait, please," she said before disappearing into the shadows. "I'll get some help."

Will cried out in rage and cursed. His voice reverberated from the walls of the cave and died somewhere in the dark. Then the earth trembled.

Will became impatient. It *was* the same dream, he was sure, and he had a chance to meet the lady! He must get out of that cave somehow and crawl that half mile towards the flaming river.

He checked his bonds. The rope was tight, and Will cursed again but managed to sit up, leaning against the wall. It was a small victory, and he grinned again when he noticed his spear nearby. He crawled those few feet to the weapon, but his victorious smiled faded when he looked at the spearhead more carefully. It was made of stone and had no sharp edges, only a rounded tip.

Stupid girl – how dare she interfere with his dream?

Will screamed again in feckless anger, but only echoes reverberated from the rocky walls. The girl had gone.

The ground trembled as the night before, and he uttered an endless tirade of curses in frustration – his dream wasn't playing by his rules. He managed to stand up, clutching his spear despite his bound wrists. It was another small victory, but he was still far away from even a glimpse of the black castle.

He hopped outside like a drunken kangaroo hoping to find a sharp rock on his way. The scenery was unchanged, it looked just as he had remembered, and Will grinned – the molten splashes which yesterday were scattered across the field like countless embers, were now merely black rocks. The way was clear. He only had to cut the ropes somehow.

He jumped a few more steps and searched around. The damned rocks were smooth and curvy rather than sharp – just drops of frozen lava. He couldn't find any sharp edges to cut through those ropes.

Will cried out in desperation. All he could do was to jump forward, hoping not to land on any loose rock. Will was sure he risked being dragged back by that unnamed help the girl had gone to find if he stayed long enough by the cave mouth.

He kept jumping until he tripped and fell, painfully hitting his left shoulder. Cursing, Will sat up and looked back. The cave was still too close. He had to get up and keep jumping.

The task was difficult. Will jumped, trying to keep his balance with the spear. He tripped a few more times before reaching the invisible line where the sparse blades of grass gave way to the lifeless frozen lava fields. He grinned, looking back. Whoever emerged from that cave – they were too late! They wouldn't dare to cross the line.

He continued leaping among boulders of black basalt, keeping his eyes fixed on the flaming river. A few jumps later, he finally got a glimpse of the castle. Will grinned widely – it had survived. He had no idea how and what kind of magic rules operated in his dream, but the castle stood on the same cliff unharmed. That meant the lady had survived as well! He just had to find her.

Will carried on around a few more boulders and raised his eyes to the castle again. The dark knights were there as well, standing in the same formation as he remembered. How had they survived that flaming hell? And would he be able to pass them?

He took a few more jumps but landed on a slippery rock and fell flat on his face, losing his spear in the process. Silently cursing, he managed to sit up, keeping his watering eyes on the castle. *Why must everything be so complicated?*

"It seems you need some help?" a calm voice asked behind him.

Will turned around.

It was her!

The lovely features, long blonde hair, clear blue eyes and the sad smile on her lips – everything he dreamed of was now there in front of him.

"Where are you going?" she demanded.

"I just wanted to see you," Will admitted, clumsily trying to rise to his feet.

"I don't remember anybody trying to get to see me so desperately," she smiled, approaching and producing a small golden dagger.

Will forced a silly smile, struggling with his restraints. It took just a few light strokes with the dagger for her to cut his ties, and she stood back, still smiling. Will got up to his feet, ready to face her.

"What's your name?" she asked.

"Will," he said as speech almost failed him.

"A very strange name," she observed. "That's why you are so persistent."

Will grinned. The statement sounded like a compliment.

"What's your name?" he remembered to ask at last.

"That's an even stranger question," her smile faded. "People here usually know me quite well and never have to ask. You must be from a very distant land then… I am Hel. Why do you seek me?"

"I was worried," he shrugged. "That was a huge eruption yesterday."

"Everything's fine now," she picked up his spear and handed it back to him. "You're a strange man, Will. You don't know me, but you're worried."

"It's hard to explain," he said hesitantly. "I've seen your image, and I was keen to know you better. But the one who showed me your picture didn't even know your name."

He decided not to mention the tattoo.

"That's a very unusual story," although Hel didn't seem to be worried one bit by that oddity. "But he showed you where to find me without knowing my name? Let's take a walk."

They walked through the basalt field among the weirdly shaped boulders.

"Would you have a cup of tea with me?" Hel asked a few moments later.

"I'd love to," Will nodded, his eyes shining with enthusiasm.

"*Love*? That's a strange word for you to use," she said gesturing to the right, where an elaborately carved white metal table stood between the tall black pillars of a frozen flame.

Delicate china lay on the table with plates full of cakes, biscuits and pastries, complete with a vase of white and blue orchids. It was the most unusual and surreal scene in his strange dream yet – Will thought as he helped Hel to take a seat on a matching white metal chair. He picked up the teapot and poured her some tea. He filled his own cup with the light-brown liquid smelling of cinnamon then sat down in front of her on a similar chair.

Hel thanked him. Will grinned with the awe of a shy teenager sitting opposite the object of his wildest dreams and desires.

"Have some cake," Hel offered. "It's quite nice."

"You're so kind," Will nearly spilt his tea. "You're making me feel very special."

Hel chuckled, politely covering her mouth with her palm.

"I don't have too many guests here," she admitted.

"It seems like everybody is afraid of you," Will tasted the brew. "Why?"

"Are you afraid?" she parried the question, looking at him with her serene blue eyes. "Does it matter to you?"

"No," Will said. "But you haven't answered my question."

She chose to remain silent, then placed a piece of cake on her plate and took a tiny sip of her tea.

"People have very strange prejudices," she said at last with a hint of sadness clouding her smile. "I hate to discuss them."

"Sorry, for the asking," Will apologised. "I don't want you to feel uncomfortable."

Hel shrugged and took another sip of her tea. They spent nearly two hours talking that sweet little nonsense, interrupted only by a few more rounds of tea. Will beamed a happy smile. He had become used to paying no attention to the occasional shudders of the ground, the hisses of blue flames in the river of molten rock, the thick clouds mixed with black fumes from the volcano and her squad of black knights guarding the foot of the mountain. All he saw were the beautiful features, the shy smile and the slightly sad blue eyes of the lady in front of him.

"Bryn! Bryn! Where are you?"

Will frowned at the cry. It was the voice of that stupid girl calling, joined by a few male voices, but the table was shielded by basalt pillars and remained invisible to them.

"Are they looking for you?" Hel asked. "You said your name is Will. Why are they calling you Bryn?"

"Honestly, I don't know them," Will shrugged. "But that girl is just so annoying. She's mad. She thinks I'm her lover."

"Are you?" Hel's face remained calm.

"No, of course, not," Will shook his head vigorously.

"I've no idea who she is or why she's after me. I don't want to see her again."

Hel studied his face as she raised her hand to make a fleeting gesture. Will shrugged again with a guilty smile, looking back at her. He hadn't seen that several of the black knights had moved from their position and had silently hastened downhill to where the cave was. There were no sounds of a fight, but there were no more cries either.

They spent another hour talking.

"It's time for you to go, a strange man named Will," said Hel after their final words of that sweet nonsense finally fell into silence.

The thought was sad, but Will had a feeling that it was an imperative rather than a suggestion. He didn't like to question the goodwill of Hel, so he stood up.

"Thank you for the tea," he said. "It was a pleasure to spend time with you."

"The pleasure was mine," said Hel seriously, standing up.

"Will I see you again?" he asked, looking at her lovely features. Suddenly, it was unbearable to part, and his voice sounded almost beseeching.

She shrugged and picked up the blue blossom of an orchid from the vase.

"I've no plans for the next few days," she said carefully pinning the flower to his chest. "You can if you want, but you must go now."

Will mumbled a short goodbye and stepped onto the trembling ground finding his way to the cave between the splatter of frozen stone. Several times he looked back, trying to catch another glimpse of her, but the basalt pillars shielded the table from his sight.

Will sighed, reluctantly stepping back towards the cave. Maybe she had her reasons for sending him away, but he still wondered why. It was his dream, and he was willing to spend more time enjoying that lovely chat and banter they had had. Was she busy? *Or was she going to meet someone else?*

Will stopped and turned around to face the fiery river. Nobody walked in that black field, not a living soul. Dark clouds were hanging low, entirely covering the caldera, and only the blood-red glow was visible at the top of the erupting volcano. He waited patiently for almost an hour, but Hel didn't show up. Only her knights stood in the distance like ghostly statues in the light of a fading day.

Will suppressed rising disappointment. He must be patient. She had promised to meet him again, and that was the most important thing.

It was almost dark when he finally reached the cave. Will felt deadly tired and sat down on the rocky ground, leaning against the wall and looking at the ruby aurora outside. The volcano still rumbled in the distance, and the earth still trembled but tiredness finally gripped him and lulled him into sweet oblivion.

⊷ℬ❀ℭ꧂

There was a strange emptiness in his chest when Will woke up. He jumped out of bed and rushed to the bathroom, frightened. The portrait of Hel was still on his left pec, and her lips still smiled at him, but the feeling didn't go away. He touched his chest, but that strange numbness went deeper than the skin and maybe even deeper than the muscles tool. It wasn't particularly painful, and Will tried to ignore it as he vigorously brushed his teeth until his sister banged the door to get him out of the bathroom.

"Your breakfast is ready, Willy," his mother said from the kitchen.

"In a minute, mum," he said, returning to his room to dress.

Will slipped into his jeans and his favourite T-shirt, feeling like his usual self again. He ate the scrambled eggs smiling at his mother. But he was sure; the feeling lurked somewhere deep in his soul, waiting for an appropriate moment to surface again. *What was it?* Will had never experienced anything like it before. He put on his "no-

nonsense" face. *It must be a strain.* He just needed to stretch his muscles, and it would go away.

Will collected his gym stuff, wondering why Hel had ordered him to leave. Was there some other danger coming? Would he be able to protect her? It seemed that his dream had a life of its own, forcing him to be merely an observer, but he hoped to have that dream again.

The weather outside was lovely, with only a few fluffy clouds in a bright blue sky, but Will decided to catch the bus. Cars rushed by in both directions in the usual morning traffic. Will barely noticed them as he waited at the bus stop. The lovely features of Hel still hovered behind the blue and white orchids in his mind. His heart now beat faster, and another sudden wave of chill and emptiness engulfed his chest.

It was at that moment when his mother's generous portion of scrambled eggs decided to take a look at the sunshine and splashed onto the pavement in front of him in a foul looking fountain. Will suddenly felt weak at the knees and lowered his body down next to the mess he had made. The traffic indifferently moved by without stopping. Nobody cared. Will looked around, but his head felt dizzy. *What was going on with him?*

He closed his eyes, waiting for the sickness to fade. The tension and knots in his stomach eased a little, but that weird emptiness returned with renewed vigour.

He flinched at the sudden shriek of brakes in front of him, followed by the sound of a door opening.

"Are you ok?" asked a strangely familiar voice.

Will started to nod but froze, opening his eyes. The huge physique of Jill shaded the sun from him.

"Are you ok, Willy?" she repeated her question.

"I'm fine," he managed to say just before another fountain of the foul-smelling scrambled eggs escaped from his throat.

The next moment Jill was clutching his shoulder.

"Stand up," she gasped in his ear. "I'll take you to the hospital."

"I'm fine," mumbled Will, protesting weakly.

"No, Willy, you're not," Jill was persistent and lifted him with surprising force. "You look pale."

She stuffed him into the back seat of her car and closed the door. The next moment Will noticed her squeezing behind the wheel and the car jumped back into the continuous line of traffic again.

"Where are you taking me?" he asked, his unfocused gaze still wandering around.

"To the hospital. I told you already," Jill adjusted her specs, staring straight ahead with her both hands firmly gripping the wheel.

"Where is this hospital? I think you're driving in the opposite direction," observed Will glancing at the street signs.

"Don't worry. I know the way."

Will spent the next few moments coming back to his senses. This situation was weird.

"Stop the car, please," he asked Jill. "I'm fine. I don't need any hospital."

"Let the doctors decide that," she was busy looking at the road ahead. "You didn't look very well, sitting next to that pile of vomit."

"I'm feeling fine now. You don't need to worry," Will said firmly. "Let me out."

"Great," squeezed Jill through her gritted teeth, still looking at the road. "If you are fine, what about visiting me for another bundle of banknotes?"

"I'm not interested," Will had to suppress another wave of rising nausea when he recalled that formless blob of fat moving in the flickering candlelight.

"I won't take no for an answer," Jill responded. "Name your price."

"I'm not doing that type of thing anymore," Will said. "Stop the car!"

"I must be mad," Jill's lips crooked in a freaky smile. "But let's triple the price!"

"You are mad," Will admitted coldly. "Stop the car."

Jill simply giggled, pressed on the accelerator and moved along the traffic queue. Will looked helplessly at the people and houses flashing by with sickening speed. The situation was becoming dangerous, and he somehow had to escape.

"Don't rush," his voice trembled. "You'll kill us both."

"I don't care," she laughed, gripping the wheel.

They were rapidly approaching the High Street where the traffic was heavier in the morning rush hour, finally forcing Jill to slow down. They stopped at a red light, and Will didn't think twice – he grabbed his rucksack and jumped out of the car, leaving a surprised Jill only able to gasp out loud.

He ran across the street, narrowly avoiding being hit by oncoming vehicles. Angry shouts and gestures followed him until he was swallowed up by the crowd and disappeared into the nearby shopping mall.

Will ran along the large terrace before finally realising that Jill wasn't chasing after him. He stopped at the nearest bench and put his rucksack on the floor before sitting down. Still breathing heavily, he looked around – nobody paid attention. The place was safe just for long enough to calm his racing heart, but for no longer, Will was sure.

His phone beeped indicating receipt of a new email.

"I don't give up easily," it was Jill. "I'll find you."

Will closed his eyes and took three deep breaths before standing up and moving along, now at a slower pace. He took a different exit out of the mall and carefully peeked at the oncoming vehicles before crossing the street.

The imaginary menace of Jill hid behind every large female frame walking along the pavement, coming out of a shop or waiting for a green light to cross the street. This felt insane, and Will muttered a few silent curses as he waited for the bus.

The journey was short. He got off by the front of the gym and quickly slipped into the locker room. Changing took him longer than usual. Will put his earphones on to shield him from the outside world and quietly sneaked into the free weight corner, secretly glancing through the window on his way. Jill was nowhere in sight, and Will got into his leg routine, feeling some relief. The free weights were away from the window, and he could easily avoid any unwanted glances from the street.

He scrolled through his playlist searching for an appropriate beat, but couldn't make up his mind. Every track he tried seemed dull and inappropriate, and eventually, he put the phone away. A skinny guy was sweating in the chest press, and Will slyly smiled, secretly wishing him the best of luck.

Will adjusted the weights and took a grip of the barbell as he performed the long and strenuous set of back squats. He paused just long enough for a few gulps of water, then switched to the dumbbells wearing himself out with Romanian deadlifts. Will took a full three minutes of rest. Rivulets of sweat ran down his back, and he took off his T-shirt, sneakily admiring the lovely features of Hel on his chest.

The skinny guy raised his eyebrows in surprise and looked at him twice as Will adjusted the weight on the barbell and went into a long set of Zercher squats. Will's core was rock solid, and to an outsider, it looked like a breeze, but his muscle fibres gave their very best performance every time he was lifting his body into a standing position. His skin turned shiny pink with large drops of perspiration, but Will kept forcing his body into motion, squeezing out every ounce of power he possessed.

An hour passed as he alternated between squats, lunges and lifts, barbells and dumbells.

Will hit the showers with a happy smile. Jill seemed

light-years away, and he was impatiently waiting for the evening to have that strange dream and meet Hel again. He longed for that silly, sweet nonsense chat. He longed even more for her presence.

On the way out, he paid another visit to the tanning shop. Will gave a fiver to the bored receptionist with the painted smile and proceeded to the cubicle. He stripped and spent the next fifteen minutes in front of the mirror, looking at the beautiful eyes of Hel on his chest.

"Are you ok?" a soft tap on the door brought him back to reality. "Is there anything wrong with the machine?"

"No, it's fine," Will said told the receptionist. "Sorry for the delay."

He slipped onto the tanning bed and waited impatiently while artificial sun rays roasted his skin. He was back in front of the mirror as soon as the machine switched off. The flowing lava now blended with his bright pink skin, and large drops of sweat gave the eerie impression that Hel was crying.

"She must be missing me," the thought flashed in Will's brain as he dressed.

He left the cubicle, smiling. Back in the street, Will remembered the gross and fat menace in the form of Jill again – she would be wandering somewhere in the streets, creepily sniffing his footsteps. She had sworn she would find him! He hurried to catch an approaching bus and got there just in time to join the last of the passengers entering through the closing door.

The journey home was uneventful. Will spent the rest of

the day in bed aimlessly scrolling through the playlist on his phone and playing random tunes. None suited his mood. Several times his mother banged on the door trying to feed him. She succeeded once.

Will received a few more emails from Jill which he deleted without reading.

The day was dying, and he took a long shower, carefully brushed his teeth and combed his hair as if preparing to meet Hel in person. He could barely hold a straight face as he marched back to his room.

The last thing Will saw before slipping into the dream was the moonlight painting his room in silver through the window.

It was dark in the cave. Only the faint ruby aurora was framed by the black walls of the cave mouth. It was quiet. Too quiet. The earth wasn't trembling, and a wave of fear instantly sneaked into Will's heart – *it might be a different dream!*

Will cursed, finding his way out as quickly as he could in the darkness.

The field looked the same with the lava flow in the distance, and he sighed with relief. Then three scorched bodies which had been dumped on the rocks to the left of the cave spoiled the joy, and he cursed again. Will got closer and recognised that crazy girl. Her empty gaze was fixed on the sky, and her mouth was slightly agape. Both of the men next to her were unfamiliar. All three were dead.

He wasn't sure how they had been killed but wasn't interested in finding out either. A tiny voice in his head squeaked that those people had died because of him, but Will didn't feel any guilt and silenced the voice immediately – he had sent that girl away, and it was her stubborn stupidity that had made her come back bringing those men with her. It was entirely her own fault.

Then Will gasped – he must get rid of the bodies or Hel might see them. With the tea drinking going so well, he didn't want any disturbing sights to upset her.

Will shaded his eyes, scanning the surroundings but nothing of worth caught his eye – no holes or trenches, only rocks and boulders. *Shit!* He hated to stash the bodies into the cave as sometimes he slept there but saw no alternative. It was a dream (*wasn't it?*), and maybe the stench of decaying flesh wouldn't be that horrible here? Will frowned, unsure if he would like to put this to the test – there was no way the corpses could smell of roses, and that cave was the only roof he had.

Then Will's gaze stumbled upon the blazing river. He was sure the bodies would be quickly wiped out of existence in those flames. And the distance wasn't great, he was strong and could easily cover it carrying one corpse at a time.

The venture he was planning was risky – Hel could spot him from her castle, but it was early morning, and she was probably still sleeping. He must act quickly!

Will didn't think twice. He grabbed the bigger man by his ankles and heaped the corpse on his back. The weight was challenging, and Will quickly found out that his body wasn't as strong in his dream as it was in reality. He cursed, carefully picking his way among the large frozen splashes of black basalt, trying not to step on any loose stones and maintain his balance. That was tricky.

Will had to stop and rest twice on his way, but he was afraid to put his load down. In those brief moments, he could allow his gaze to wander up the slope of the volcano and search for Hel's whereabouts. The black castle on the high cliff was dark without light in any of its narrow windows, and Will grinned – she *was* still sleeping!

The heat grew with every step, and he soon realised that it would be impossible to get close enough to drop the body into the flow as he had planned. He needed a cliff that hung over the flames where he could dump the man down without any risk to his own precious skin.

Will spotted one suitable cliff slightly uphill, closer to the castle, and hurried there as fast as he could with that macabre load on his back. The ground began to tremble, and he was afraid that this might wake Hel up.

The cliff was easy to climb, and he lowered the body onto the rock. The heat was barely tolerable, and he didn't dare to stick his head over the edge. Even the black stone which formed the cliff was too hot to touch, and only the thick soles of his shoes kept his feet from frying. Will hastily rolled the body over and dumped it down into the moving lava. It didn't sink into the liquid rock, but the flames instantly shot around the corpse like hungry snakes and began consuming the robes first, then the flesh. Will backed away from the cliff and watched the pyre for a few minutes as it slowly floated downstream, then turned around and rushed back to the cave. He still had to deal with two more bodies.

The line of dark knights halfway to the castle stood still

and silent, but Will was sure – their eyes were on him. *Would they tell Hel about the bodies or how he had disposed of them?* The thought was disturbing, but Will wasn't prepared to leave the work unfinished.

The second man was skinny, and Will had to rest only once. When he got back to the cliff, the first floating pyre was already out of sight – either it had burned out or moved further downstream – Will had no time for guesses. He quickly dumped the skinny man into the flow and rushed back to the cave, this time without watching the body float away.

The girl was small and fragile. Will easily lifted her body in his arms. Her eyes were wide open, and he felt a strange and uneasy sense of guilt, carrying her like a child through the fields of frozen lava. Yes, she was annoying, and her death had been entirely her own fault. She should have listened to him when he told her to go away and never return. She would still be alive. Why didn't she listen? And she had brought those two men to die with her. It was her crazy idea to save him. He didn't need any saving. Will cursed, but the girl carried on staring at the cloudy sky, and the sense of guilt kept sneaking back each time he dashed it away. *Damn! It wasn't his fault!*

A few times, Will secretly glanced at the castle just to make sure that Hel wasn't watching, but the windows were still dark and empty.

He went on carrying his load to the cliff overhanging the fiery river.

The girl was mad. She kept repeating that she loved him.

Was this the explanation for her madness? Will had no idea. He didn't know that girl. He hadn't even bothered to ask her name – it seemed irrelevant when she was alive, but now it suddenly felt important.

Will decided to call her Girl and whispered a short farewell while laying his load on the rocks at the edge of the cliff above the flaming flow. The girl looked quiet and peaceful, and the unwanted sense of guilt for her death again sneaked back and filled Will's heart. He closed her sightless eyes, then took the blossom of a blue orchid, which still was pinned to his chest, and placed it in her palm before pushing the body over the edge.

A sudden scream made him quail, and Will carefully peeked over the edge at the lava flow. The girl was screaming among the splashes of liquid rock with her body arched in pain and her robes aflame. Will silently cursed – this dream had become such a weird nightmare! Was that girl still alive? Why hadn't she even gasped when he took her in his arms and carried her to the lava? *Why had she been silent then?*

The sense of guilt mixed with horror as he watched the bright stream of lava carrying the convulsing body, entirely engulfed in flames, away. A few more heart-piercing screams followed, and Will cursed loudly – that stupid girl was spoiling everything again. He cast a glance to the castle, hoping those screams hadn't disturbed Hel's sleep.

Then he followed the pyre with his gaze, as it moved along the fiery surface, then caught the rapid current and crashed down the slope. Moments later, the girl was gone.

Will stood at the top of the cliff, without realising that the soles of his shoes were already smoking. He looked down the slope at the blazing streams of molten rock. *Had he just killed that girl?* But she *was* dead when he took her to the top of the cliff. He cursed again remembering that it was only a weird dream. The thought brought ineffable relief. It had been her fault anyway…

Will got off the cliff to the cooler ground and stood for some time watching the castle. Had those screams attracted Hel's attention? Not a single flash of light escaped through the windows behind the grim line of her knights. Nobody and nothing moved there either. That was strange. It was late morning already, and Will hoped that Hel would be glad to see him.

He crawled a few steps closer, making his way through the piles of stones. *Was she okay?* The castle remained dark and still, but her knights stirred into motion. Will froze – all of them now faced him with their spears ready to be thrown.

It was a clear indication that he should not even think of getting any closer. Will felt disappointed. It was his dream, and they were threatening him! But he still wasn't ready to give up. He still hadn't seen her.

Will hastily backed several paces, and the spears moved up, pointing to the sky. It was his clear boundaries provided by the dream. He sat down on a flat rock and began waiting. The ground was slightly trembling, but the castle remained dark. Hel was nowhere in sight.

Several hours passed, waiting. The skies were grim with thick clouds almost touching the erupting peak. Finally, they broke with heavy showers pouring onto the hissing lava. Hot steam instantly filled the field, obscuring the view. Only the spikes of spears marked the line where her knights stood guarding the castle.

It was clear that she would not show up in such nasty weather. Waiting any longer was pointless.

Will crawled back to the cave, stepping on slippery stones and crying in desperation. The dream was ignoring his wishes and desires. It had its own rules.

He leant against the stone wall next to the cave mouth, waiting for the rain to stop. The field slowly filled with thick fog with occasional splashes of red where the volcano was. It was silly, but he kept staring at the milky wall, hoping that she would emerge at any moment.

He patiently waited, but nothing changed. The sky still leaked endless cold streams, and the lava behind the thick wall of fog flowed down the slope without interruption. Hel didn't show up, and Will couldn't see from the cave if there was a light in any window of the black castle.

It was getting dark, and Will closed his tired eyes just to give them some rest. At some moment of weakness, he slipped away.

❦❧ ✿ ☙❧

Will was back in his room again, and his mother was banging on the door.

"Get up, Willy!" she said impatiently. "Breakfast is ready."

Will cursed before getting up. The feeling of failure was still fresh. Unhappily, he slipped into his jeans and rushed to brush his teeth.

Hel on his chest looked sad, and he was worried if she was all right. Maybe he could try to find another way to the castle? The thought was comforting, and Will smiled as he put his T-shirt on.

He gulped down the scrambled eggs on the go, grabbed his stuff and kissed his mother goodbye. It was the day for chest exercise, his favourite, and he felt a rising inspiration to move his pecs.

The day was sunny, with only a few fluffy clouds dotting the clear blue sky. Will was tempted to run all way to the gym but remembered Jill. That woman was crazy. Will was sure about that. She could be stalking him. The thought was unpleasant, and he carefully peered at the oncoming cars before running across the street to the bus stop. He didn't like being an easy target and only hoped that she would give up trying if he kept ignoring her for long enough. The bus arrived a few minutes later. He took a seat next to the window and put his earphones on, selecting some crazy beat on his phone. A few stops later, his attention wandered to the red car positioned in the middle of the street next to the bus. Jill's specs peered out of the window with a broad prosthetic smile below them. She was waving happily at him.

Will looked away, feeling embarrassed, and pretended to read something on his phone. He hoped that she would drive away with the traffic, leaving him alone. It didn't happen.

Two stops later the tenacious blob of fat was still jammed into her red car and slowly driving next to the bus with a mile-long queue of traffic crawling behind her.

The problem was growing bigger with every minute and required an immediate solution. Now that she knew the stop where he usually boarded the bus, her stalking ground had narrowed to a minimum. Will had no desire to show her where his gym was. He would be held up to ridicule if that crazy woman spotted him there, and started peeking through the windows, waving and shouting at him. Will just couldn't let that happen.

He missed his bus stop on purpose. He kept staring at his phone and pretended to ignore the hysterics unfolding in the street entirely. Several miles later, Jill was stopped by the police, and Will sprinted off of the bus, hiding in the nearest convenience store.

He slowly circled the aisles twice while the police officers tried to bring that mad woman back to her senses. When the traffic jam had finally cleared, and Jill had driven away, Will caught the shopkeeper, giving him a few angry stares. He quickly bought a protein bar and left, slipping into the shadowy side streets, away from the main routes where Jill would be able to spot him again easily.

It was quite a long way back to the gym. Will sneaked down the streets, cautiously looking around. Every red car now seemed like a threat. He tried to move into the shadows each time one passed by. Jill didn't show up again, but he had become paranoid about the situation. He was already tired when he reached the gym through the backstreets feeling like a fugitive thief.

Will quickly changed, and then waited for several minutes behind the treadmills until he was sure that it was safe to pass alongside the window.

But the training session had already been utterly spoiled as his mood drained quicker than his sweat. Will only did a few basic routines and then hit the showers. His life was steadily rolling downhill with Jill poisoning and overshadowing everything, and the only remaining ray of light was the possibility of seeing Hel in his dream.

He dressed and went home, sticking to the side streets, back alleys and cul-de-sacs again and skipping his usual tanning session. He was afraid that Jill might begin pounding on the door of the tanning cubicle.

Back at home Will went straight to his room, locked the door and spread his aching muscles on the bed, angrily looking at his phone. Jill's emails were steadily incoming every fifteen minutes. He deleted them at the same pace without reading any of them.

Several attempts by his mother to feed him were unsuccessful.

"Not hungry" was the answer.

The day was slowly dying, and Will carefully prepared for the dream hoping that he would be more successful this night.

A full moon looked through his window again carrying his consciousness away.

The rain had stopped, but it was cold. Will's wet robes clung to his skin, and he shivered as the damp chill drenched his bones. The fog had cleared a little, and he braved to take a peek outside.

The dream was still the same, and Will smiled like an addict at the sight of another dose. He might succeed in meeting her! He stretched out his arms, trying to keep his trembling body balanced on the wet rocks, but his legs began to shake even more.

He had to dry his clothes somehow – the chill they were causing was unbearable. Will looked around searching for some wood, but who would need to build a fire when there was a volcano nearby? The bloody glow of the flaming river seemed too inviting.

The day still was dark and gloomy, and the grass outside the cave seemed black. Will crawled on the slippery stones, shivering and trying to keep his balance, failing several times. The fog was burning his skin, but Will kept on going where the flow of liquid stone spat blue flames at the gloomy sky. The waves of heat met him midway, pushing the fog back, and Will stopped a few paces later, waiting.

The warmth pleasantly wrapped his body, and streaks of vapour began to rise from the wet robes. Will stretched out his arms, embracing the heat. Only then did he dare to look at the castle.

The line of knights was in the same position as before, but every window in the castle was now brightly lit. *She was there!* He must be patient.

Will backed a few paces towards the wall of fog and sat down on the rock, waiting. Nothing changed in the scenery, but he kept staring at the castle in the hope of spotting her lovely silhouette.

"What are you doing here?" asked the voice behind him.

Will sprang to his feet and turned around. Hel was sitting on a huge shiny black stallion, looking at him and frowning without a smile.

"I just wanted to see you again," Will muttered.

"Why?"

"Simply to be sure that you're fine," Will smiled widely, but Hel maintained her face straight.

"I'm fine," she cut him. "You can go now."

"Couldn't we just talk?" Will nearly begged. "You're very important to me."

"Am I?" Hel chuckled with bare irony. "But you've lost the blossom I gave you. You just don't care enough."

Damned stupid girl! Will cursed the moment of weakness when he had placed the blue orchid on that dead body. *It was her fault! She had made him feel guilty for her death!*

"It was only a flower," he sighed. "And everything happened by accident. I didn't mean to lose it."

"Go away, a strange man named Will," Hel said and urged her stallion into motion. "It wasn't just a flower. And it wasn't an accident. You know that."

Stunned, Will looked at her slowly riding past him, then taking the almost invisible path uphill, winding between black rocks, before crossing the line of her knights and disappearing behind the castle gate. Will's heart nearly jumped out of his chest. He dropped to his knees, feeling crushed and loudly cursed that stupid girl and her stupid love, but nothing changed. Hel didn't show up.

Will spent the rest of the day on the rock looking at the castle windows and hoping to see her again. *Would she be able to forgive him?* Will hoped she would, but that hope faded with every passing minute.

It was close to the evening when the fog cleared. The skies were still dark, cloudy and gloomy, tinged red by the volcano.

Will stood up in frustration, watching the castle windows growing dark one by one. His waiting was in vain. He had not had one glimpse of her silhouette.

He slowly retreated to the cave, barely seeing the path – his eyes were watering, and a few hot drops rushed down his cheeks which he quickly wiped away, hoping that nobody could see them. He crawled deep into the darkness of the cave, away from the opening, sat down on the floor, leaning against a cold wall and let his feelings out.

❧ ❧ ✿ ❧ ❧

Will's pillow was wet when the morning sunshine touched his cheek through the window. He jumped out of bed, ashamed of his weakness, put his pants on and quietly sneaked into the bathroom.

He took a long shower, washing away the remnants of the night, but the feeling of emptiness remained deeply rooted in his chest, and his eyes still held traces of sadness. He looked at Hel's image on his chest and nearly broke into tears again. *How could she do this to him?*

Will rubbed his skin dry with a towel and peered at his face in the mirror. His eyes were red and slightly swollen, and his face looked irritated. *Damn!* He looked a mess, but, surprisingly, this time, he didn't care. That woman from his dream had captured his imagination entirely. All he wanted was to meet Hel again.

He bumped into his mother on the way back to his room.

"Why are you so red, Willy?" she grabbed his elbow and dragged him to the window. "Are you taking drugs?"

"No, mum," he tried to break free. "I'm fine."

"Don't lie to your mother, Willy," she looked at his face with obvious concern. "Get dressed. We're going to the hospital."

"I'm fine, mum," he hated the idea.

"It's not up to you to decide," she cut him short firmly. "Be ready in ten minutes!"

Her frowned eyebrows left no room for argument. Will returned to his room and put a fresh T-shirt on. She was full of determination waiting for him in the hallway with the car keys in her hand.

"Don't even think about running away," she warned him.

They were silent all the way to the hospital.

Will stood meekly next to the entrance while his mother booked him in. He looked at the waiting area and felt increasingly uncomfortable. Other people there had real problems, even broken limbs. His redness seemed so trivial. It was simply a waste of time, but his mother was adamant.

They took seats between a smiling elderly lady with bright yellow skin and a grim-looking man squeezing a bloodied towel onto his left palm.

The passing minutes slowly grew into hours. The place was busy, and people rushed about in every direction. Will gazed at all that topsy-turvyness with an apathetic alienation. He still saw Hel proudly riding her black stallion away from him every time he closed his eyes. He couldn't understand why she had turned him down. It was only a flower...

The injured grim man was called first. His seat was empty for only a few seconds when a huge bottom squeezed between Will's mother on one side and the bright yellow lady at the other side.

Will's heart skipped several beats. *Jill?*

He sank into his seat with his skin suddenly becoming bright red and began to sweat profusely.

"Are you okay?" his mother asked.

"I need the loo," Will whispered.

"Go," the mother told him firmly. "But be quick about it. We might be called soon."

Will sneaked into the corridor and spent a few minutes trying to get a better view of the large lady sitting next to his mum. She was grey-haired and wore specs like Jill, but she wasn't Jill. Immensely relieved, he paid a trip to the loo.

The nurse was already chasing him when he returned to the waiting area.

"I'm going with you," Will's mother stated, getting up.

"It's up to him," the nurse shrugged. "He's big enough to decide."

"Willy?" mother looked at him, furrowing her brow.

Will didn't dare to say no.

They walked along the narrow corridor with closed doors on both sides. Will felt trapped. He didn't feel ill and had no desire to meet any doctors, but a glance at his mother crushed all hope of sneaking away. The nurse stopped at the last door, opened it and led them through.

The lady at the table shuffled some papers, but stood up and greeted them as soon as they entered.

"What's the problem?" she asked Will after a short introduction.

"His problem is there on his face," Will's mother explained, instead of him. "Have a look – he's as red as a lobster, and his eyes are red too."

"Yes, it looks slightly irritated," the lady agreed, frowning. She came closer to have a better look. "Have you had any recent exposure to chemicals?"

"Are you taking drugs, Willy?" his mother demanded in an angry voice. "Don't lie to the doctor!"

"I'm not taking anything, mum," he addressed the mother, and the doctor quickly scribbled something in her notes.

"Any chemical exposure?" the doctor repeated her question, still scribbling. "Any fumes? Sprays? What kind of work do you do?"

"No," Will shrugged. "No chemicals. And I'm not working."

"When did it happen?" the doctor asked and lifted eyes from her papers.

"Overnight," his mother answered the question. "He was fine yesterday. I saw that for myself."

"Let me check your blood pressure," the lady doctor smiled, trying to fit the cuff on Will's huge biceps. "Have you had any fever?"

Will shrugged and shook his head – he felt fine. It was only that stupid redness. It would go away, he was sure, only his mother was too impatient.

The doctor finally succeeded in fitting the cuff around

his arm on her third attempt and with a sense of victory pressed the "Measure" button. All three patiently waited for the reading while the white box beeped as it pumped air.

"It is slightly elevated," the doctor frowned, looking at the readings. "Do you have any headaches? Nausea? Vomiting?"

She stuck a digital thermometer into his ear before he was able to shake the head again.

"Is it serious?" the mother gasped.

The lady doctor didn't answer. The handle beeped, and she took her fancy piece of equipment out of Will's ear. "The temperature's slightly elevated too," she frowned again.

No wonder – Will grinned inside – he had spent the whole night next to an erupting volcano!

"Is it serious?" the mother repeated her question.

"I don't know yet," the doctor said and turned back to Will. "Anything?"

"I did vomit yesterday," Will admitted at last.

"You didn't tell me that, Willy," the mother said reproachfully.

Will only shrugged. It didn't seem relevant. The lady doctor scribbled something in her notes again.

"Are you taking any steroids?" she asked casually.

"No," Will said firmly, interrupting the almost silent gasp from his mother. "I don't need them."

"Any stressful situations?" she continued the interrogation watching his reactions. "Are you sleeping well?"

That question sounded strange. Will wasn't prepared to

discuss his nightly visions, so he shrugged again, shaking his head.

"Have you had any recent interventions? Visits to a dentist? Have you recently had anything inked?" the doctor demanded, making yet more notes.

"Yes, yes, he has!" the mother gasped.

"Was it a certified tattoo shop?" the lady continued. "Were the instruments sterilised properly? Were certified inks used?"

How could she know all this? Will slowly shook his head. He was afraid to tell her about the special ink which had been used for Hel's eyes. Not in front of his mother!

"May I see it?" the doctor asked.

Will felt like slowly sinking. An image of the doctor taking out her lasers and destroying the image of Hel flashed through his brain. He couldn't let this happen. Then he recalled the assurances of the skinny man that the pigment used for her eyes was indestructible! Will sighed in brief relief, but remembered that the other inks were ordinary – that grinning doctor still could destroy the image leaving only Hel's eyes. *Shit!*

"Willy!" his mother sprang into action. "Show it to the doctor!"

He hesitantly took off his T-shirt. Hel was sadly smiling on his massive pec, but neither his muscles nor his tattoo made any impression on the doctor. She carefully inspected the skin, then took a magnifying glass from the shelf and looked again.

"Did it heal properly? Was it painful? Itching?"

"It was slightly itchy to start with," Will admitted. "But everything healed quickly."

The doctor looked at her notes.

"We'll have to do a few tests," she said, filling in some forms.

"Is he ill?" the mother whispered and gasped, covering her mouth.

"I don't know yet," the lady doctor said firmly. "The tests will show that. His blood pressure is elevated, you can see irritation of his skin and eyes – it could be an infection if the inking machine weren't properly sterilised, or it could be an allergy. Let's find out."

The doctor was wrong – Will was sure about that. He felt fine. His skin was slightly itchy, but he knew the *real* reason why that was. The burning had begun when he walked through the fog last night. He had felt itchy when he got back to the cave. That dream was dangerous, but he wasn't ready to give up his nightly visits to the volcano. He still had a tiny hope that Hel might forgive him.

"We'll check his blood," the lady doctor said. "It would be best if you could see your GP next week. We'll send all the test results there."

"Doesn't he need any treatment?" Will's mother was persistent.

"Not until we know what's wrong with him," the doctor smiled.

"I'm perfectly fine," Will decided to share his opinion but was instantly hushed by the mother.

"Here," doctor handed them the brown envelope

containing the forms and directed to them to the Phlebotomy room.

"I'm fine, mum," Will began protesting in the corridor, but his mother was determined to bring the matter to a satisfactory conclusion.

"It's not up to you to decide," she mumbled under her breath, pushing him through the door and handing the envelope to the nurse.

In no time Will was seated, and a thick needle was stuck into his arm. The nurse smiled at him as she filled five phials with his blood, then placed a piece of strapping on his vein and hurried them out, where more serious patients were lining up with brown envelopes in their hands.

Will felt immense relief when they finally left that busy factory of cripples and headed to the car park. All the way back home, they were silent.

"Where are you going?" the mother asked with suspicion when he began packing his rucksack.

"To the gym."

"That's out of the question, young man," she locked the door. "You're going to your room and will stay in bed until we know what's wrong with you!"

"I'm feeling fine, mum," Will said. "And I am a grown man. I can decide whether I'm ill or not."

"Don't argue with me, a grown man," her voice was as hard as steel. "I decide everything as long as you live under my roof and eat my bread! Go to bed. Now!"

It was pointless to argue. She would always stand her ground; Will knew that. He dropped his rucksack by the door and went upstairs. He spent almost fifteen minutes in front of the bathroom mirror looking at his face. The redness was still there, but it didn't feel that bad. It seemed silly to spend the whole day in bed, but he knew that he had no other choice.

His mother checked on him several times with a worried look on her face.

"Do you want something to eat, Willy?"

"No, mum, I'm not hungry," was always the answer.

All day he hugged his phone and listened to sad tunes while deleting occasional emails from Jill. Later in the afternoon, he managed to swallow only a milkshake. He took a long shower and brushed his teeth. A sad feeling of being abandoned traced his steps like a hungry stray dog. Will had no idea how to persuade Hel to have another look at him. Was it all over?

He had a burning desire to run to the gym and wear himself out in an insane training sequence, hoping that this would make the feeling go away. Then he looked in the mirror and carefully touched the lovely features on his chest. The image was there forever, and it wasn't just skin deep – he knew that it had also sneaked into his heart.

Will crawled back to bed with a sense of emptiness in his chest. His mood was grim, and he put his phone away, unable to stand the music any longer. His eyes watered when he looked at the clouds outside the window. He curled on his side, hugged his knees and closed his eyes. The entire world seemed to be acting against him, and he only wanted to shield from everything and run away.

Suddenly the ground beneath him trembled. He jumped to his feet and looked around – it wasn't his room anymore. He was back in the darkness of the cave!

The cave mouth glowed faintly in silver with shades of pink – most likely the moonlight was playing with the reflections of lava.

For several minutes Will stood in the darkness, listening. It was tranquil – no rain and no wind outside, only the constant low rumbling from the distant caldera.

He slowly moved along the wall, trying to keep his balance in the darkness. Hel must be asleep if it was night outside, but he had a burning desire to have a look at her castle, hoping to at least spot a lonely candle in the window.

The lava field outside was bathing in bright silver light, and it hurt Will's eyes at first as he slowly crawled out of the dark closer to the cave mouth. He had to stop several times to allow his vision to adjust. The light was too intense for moonlight and strange, even for a dream.

Will peeked outside and froze, grasping the wall.

The sky was cloudless with an enormous silver globe

occupying the whole celestial zenith. It was graciously embraced by a few sets of rings sparkling like diamond dust. Its light was as bright as the sun, but it had a ghostly silverish quality. Will went outside and still couldn't believe his eyes. His neck soon grew stiff, and he had to lie down – the view was stunning, and Will barely remembered to breathe.

Subtle streaks of red, yellow and royal purple mixed with the silver in the mesmerising display on the slowly floating globe. Three rings richly shone with gold, while the spaces between them glistened white.

An hour later, the burning desire to see the castle, which had at first been outshone by the silver light and the globe, returned with a new force, and Will stood up, still stunned by the view. He took the familiar path across the sparse grass with silver blades, brightly lit by the soft glow. Thin strands of fog stretched between strange the black shapes in the fields of frozen lava, creating an eerie impression of moving ghostly figures.

The volcano behind the castle still was spitting streams of flames, glowing bright red, and a dark spume rose like a black pillar high into the sky before slowly dissipating in the stratosphere.

The castle was dark and lifeless, but Will hoped that Hel was inside – the line of her dark knights stood guarding her rest.

He went as far as he could without alerting them and sat down on the rock, waiting. He didn't expect much – only a glimpse of some light in a window and, perhaps, her silhouette lit by a candle.

The sky was still dark and almost starless – the magnificent globe had outshone all lesser lights. Only a narrow band of purple in the eastern sky behind the volcano predicted the coming day.

Will silently waited in the middle of the lifeless field scattered with black basalt from the eruptions, between the hissing flow of lava and the silent knights guarding the castle, when a ghostly motion in the distance attracted his attention. A strange dark shape crept amongst the loose stones, and milky strands of fog looking like an apparition with only the sound of soft footsteps on the gravel and a stick scratching the rock revealed it as belonging to the material world.

Will looked around, but it was only him and that strange moving shape in the vast field. He grabbed a rock in his right hand and prepared to hold the defence.

The dark silhouette, still a hundred yards away, covered by the fog, slowly approached him under the shivering silver light of the globe.

"What do you want?" he asked, his voice crackling with growing agitation.

The silhouette stopped.

"I've brought you something to eat," was the slow response.

The voice was tired and breathless, as was the old woman in the dark robes leaning on her stick and clutching a bundle in her left hand. *Was it a trick?*

"I don't need anything," Will said.

"You haven't eaten for the whole week," the woman responded. "There's nothing edible among these rocks."

"I'm not hungry," he said firmly.

"Don't lie to your mother, Bryn," she said, resuming her slow approach. "You must eat something, or you'll starve yourself to death."

Why did they keep calling him Bryn in this dream? Will didn't dare to disappoint the old woman and tossed the rock aside.

She slowly carried her old bones, carefully stepping on the loose gravel. Will kept on sitting on the boulder and silently watched. She stopped twice to catch her breath before she came closer.

"Here," she said, handing him the package and sitting down next to him on the rock. "It's not much. I'm too old to carry anything heavier."

Will unwrapped the package. There were a few pieces of smoked meat, a chunk of cheese, three slabs of bread and a small flask of water.

"Why have you left home, Bryn?" she asked as he inspected the food. "Are you sure she's called you?"

"Are you talking about Hel?" Will shrugged having no idea about the matter.

"Shhh.." the woman looked around suspiciously. "Don't mention that name."

"Why? What do you call her then?"

"Don't you remember?" the old woman placed her stick on the ground. "Anyway, it's irrelevant for you now, I suppose. She's already seen you."

The old woman rubbed her aching knees before speaking again.

"Eat this," she told him. "You don't look healthy. Starving is no good for you."

Will didn't dare to object and started to chew the meat which had a strong smoky odour and a strange salty taste. He took a bite of bread along with it, and the taste became bearable.

"I know you can't fight it," the woman sighed. "You'll crawl around her and either die of starvation or end up as your father did – there!"

She pointed to the line of knights.

"My father?" Will nearly choked on the meat.

She turned to look at the knights, shading her eyes from the silver light.

"Yes. He's the last in the line, next to the flaming river. The one with the black beard," she frowned, trying to help her failing sight. "And your granddad is next to him."

She must be crazy. Will couldn't decide who was crazier, that dead girl or this old woman.

"Why don't you go and say hello then?" he teased her, chewing the cheese.

"Don't make fun of me, Bryn. I'm old but not mad," the woman cut him short. "They're dead to all living. They'd plunge those spears in my throat without hesitating for a single moment."

She was crazy without any shadow of a doubt. How could a dead man stand and guard the castle? Will sipped a little water and tucked into the remaining meat.

"I'm not angry with you," the woman muttered after a short silence. "I know you can't resist it. Gudula thought she could be stronger than her. She was mistaken. Now she's dead. Her father and your brother, Reuben, are dead too, Bryn. They never returned. It's a kingdom of Death, Bryn. No one stays here alive unless she allows it. And she only does that on purpose. She must have some plans for you, Bryn, or she would have killed you like she killed Gudula."

Was that crazy girl called Gudula?

"How could you know she's dead?" Will asked and stopped chewing. "I haven't seen any killings."

"I saw three sparkles on the Road of Gods three days ago," explained the woman, gesturing at the celestial globe. "Old people don't sleep at night. We have all our lives to remember. I warned Gudula so many times, but she was too much in love with you, Bryn. I knew this would happen, but nobody ever listens to the old mother. Death and love never walk together, and this is the kingdom of Death. Gudula had no place there."

Will raised his eyes to the rings – had she seen the sparkles there? The old woman must be fantasising, as myriads of scintillas played an intricate game of light around the silver globe. How could she know which spark was for Gudula and which for Reuben? It was pointless to argue. She was old, and her beliefs were too stubborn, too deep-rooted and too far from reality.

Will finished eating and drank the flask dry. He was surprised at how hungry and thirsty he had suddenly felt.

"Give me that," said the old woman and took the flask

and the wrappings. "I don't want her to know I've been here."

She picked up her stick and stood up.

"I have to go now. I'll bring more food tomorrow before dawn," she said, looking at him with tearful eyes. "Be closer to the cave, Bryn, if you can. It's hard for my bones to walk on the gravel."

He watched her silhouette slowly retreat into the kingdom of shadows. Minutes later, he was alone again.

Dawn was breaking in the east, and he watched the skies light up and turn pale blue. The silver globe faded long before disappearing beyond the horizon.

The castle stood tall and dark without any apparent movement. The knights did not stir either, and their spears pointed up at the sky. Will couldn't see clearly from a distance, but it seemed the slightest of fumes were escaping from the motionless spear tips. This might be an illusion too; he wasn't entirely sure if he could believe his own senses any more.

The morning was chilly, and Will moved closer to the flaming river. He climbed on top of one of the cliffs along the shore of the lava flow and sat there, trying to catch a better view. He was still hoping to spot Hel peering at him from one of the dark windows.

The hope was faint. He knew this but couldn't let it go. Will closed his eyes, and the image of Hel proudly riding away on her black stallion appeared, hurting him. He clenched his fists. *She was only teasing; she didn't mean to leave me*, the thought rolled over and over in his head, but it wasn't comforting. The pain and emptiness in his chest only grew stronger.

Will's eyes were moist when he opened them, and the castle seemed blurred. A sense of shame then sneaked into his boiling heart. Boys don't cry – he had been told that too many times and Will hastily wiped the moisture away as if afraid that she might see it. The rock was warm beneath him, but the chill in his heart had spread to the limbs, and Will hugged his knees unhappily as he stared at the dark windows of the castle.

Then he gasped and sprang to his feet when the line of dark knights stirred into motion. The gates of the castle opened widely, and Hel rode down the hill on her stallion. The knights moved in front of her like ghosts in an orderly formation with their spears ready to repel any attack.

They rushed along the shore of the flaming river without even noticing the lonely figure of Will standing on top of the cliff. The black stallion galloped at top speed down the slope and quickly disappeared in the west.

Will dropped down to his knees with moisture again uncontrollably pooling in his eyes and rolling down his cheeks. He felt utterly disappointed. Yes, he had seen Hel, but for a brief moment only. He had been hoping for a long talk and a cup of tea with her, longing for the precious time she smiled at him, laughing at his clumsy jokes. He would gladly have a long walk with her along the flaming river, or stand under her balcony looking at her lovely eyes. He was ready to beg her for this.

The nest was empty. She was gone, and he had no idea

when she would come back.

Nearly an hour had passed before the sorrow subsided. Will climbed down from the cliff and began aimlessly wandering around the field of frozen lava, waiting. Many times he looked back down the slope from where Hel had vanished with her knights, but not a shadow stirred between the black globes of basalt. Dark tumultuous clouds began to rise in the west instead, threatening rain.

The castle stood dark and empty, unguarded, and Will realised that he could wait for her inside. With the knights gone, nobody could stop him, and he would certainly at least have a chance to speak with Hel and beg her for forgiveness.

Will cautiously went uphill listening to the wind and the rumbling of the volcano. Nobody and nothing stopped him when he crossed the spot where the dark knights used to stand. He took the winding road with countless imprints of the hooves of her stallion on the gravel. Minutes later, he touched the open gate of the castle.

It was quiet here, no guards.

Will carefully peered inside. A large yard was behind the gate, paved with black stones. It was empty. Not even a dog or cat, not even a rat met his cautious gaze. The place was lifeless.

He slowly crossed the yard. The outside wall on the right was without any stairs or shooting holes. It seemed that nobody ever cared to think about any defence of the castle, and the walls here were to guard it only from the elements, not from intruders.

A large black door with a smooth surface was on the left, and Will hesitantly approached it, casting a few glances over his shoulder. He wasn't sure if he was doing the right thing by intruding into Hel's private space without an invitation, but he was even more reluctant to go back to the cave. Her life was hidden behind that door, and Will was determined to catch at least a brief glimpse of it if he couldn't wait for her inside.

The door was carved out of black oak with massive ornamental hinges. Will touched the surface hesitating. *Was this the right thing to do?*

He tried the door. It was unlocked, and Will sneaked inside carefully closing it behind him.

The big rounded hall inside was black and empty with only a steep staircase without any railings in the middle. The outer walls were as tall as a five-storey building with the only opening in the vault, letting through the stairs somewhere beyond. The dim daylight leaked inside through the several narrow windows stained with red glass that cast bloody shadows on the black marble floor. Will walked around. There was nothing there – no other doors, no furniture, no chandeliers. And not a living soul around. The ground continuously trembled and shook with every motion of the monster inside the volcanic caldera, but the floor and walls in the hall were even and smooth without a single crack.

Will took the stairs. The stone steps felt firm beneath his feet. Surprisingly, he couldn't feel any tremors here. It seemed as if the whole staircase was floating in the air, leaving the convulsions of the ground somewhere below it.

Never before had Will thought that he was afraid of heights, but now the lack of railings doubled his fear with each step he took. He tried to fix his gaze on the end of the stairs disappearing through the ceiling as a scary abyss opened on both sides while he continued to climb upwards.

Three times he had to stop climbing, close his eyes and calm his trembling heart before taking another step. When he reached the top of stairs, at last, he dropped to the floor and hastily rolled away from the opening. For a few moments, Will thought that he heard faint laughter from downstairs, but he wasn't sure. His body was still trembling, and he had to spend several more minutes, breathing deeply with his eyes closed, until the anxiety faded away. Only then did he braved to turn over onto his stomach and carefully peek downstairs at the hall below.

It seemed even darker than before, with only a few blood-red reflections from the stained glass piercing the dusk. It was quiet as well, not counting the continuous low rumbling sound of the volcano. Nothing moved there, not even shadows. *It must be my imagination*, decided Will.

He rolled away from the opening and sat up. The hall around was as empty as the one downstairs, only rounded and smaller with big clear windows around the perimeter and a clear glass vault, displaying the cloudy sky and the rising pillar of smoke to the east. The walls and the floor were made of smoothly polished black stone which reflected the skies when viewed at the appropriate angle. Will looked around. The emptiness was frightening – he saw no bed, no table, not even a single chair. *Where does she sleep at night?*

Will slowly went along the perimeter, gazing through the windows at the scenery outside. The dark green line of the forest was to the north, just behind the crest of spiking cliffs. Will spotted a few strands of smoke – probably a village with smoking chimneys – beyond the woods, but he couldn't be sure since the dark firs completely obscured the view. It was a strange place to live, but the whole of this dream was strange, and Will found himself becoming used to it.

The sky was still clear in the east, and the sun rose with a black stripe of volcanic ashes across its bright face. The volcano itself towered high above the castle with the red wound on the right side of its belly bleeding out blazing streams of molten rock.

The fiery flow was on the southern side and seemed very close to the castle – close enough to blow splashes of lava at the windows of the high tower, but none of the blue flames, hissing and spattering, ever got even close to the walls. A strange wind blew them away each time they approached the invisible boundary. Nothing ever hit the ground next to the castle walls.

The other bank of the flaming river was an endless field of frozen lava with another volcano and another fiery stream flashing along the horizon. Nothing but the black rocks were between the two lava flows. The sight was boring, and Will stepped a few more paces along the perimeter. Suddenly he froze, biting a nail. The cliff from where he had pushed those three bodies into the lava was perfectly visible, and he gasped, realising that Hel might have seen him doing this. *Was this the real reason why she had turned him down?* Will gasped as his heart slowly began to sink. *Damn Gudula! It was all her fault! Why couldn't she have just left him alone?*

He had to lean against the window as the sudden wave of fear left him weak at his knees. *Would Hel ever forgive him?* It must have been a very unpleasant sight to observe those burning bodies. It would have been much better to stash them deeper into the cave. Will could have lived with the stench of decomposition, but now he couldn't live without Hel.

The wave of weakness passed as quickly as it had arrived. Will beat his chest a couple of times in a bout of rage, circled the hall and absentmindedly glanced through the windows. *Damn stupid girl!* She thoroughly deserved what she had got! Will frowned remembering her constant whining and all those obstacles she had created for him. *Why did she do that?* He was glad she was gone.

It took some time for him to shake Gudula out of his head and calm down. He circled the place a few more times looking at the outskirts, but the scenery outside the tower was as monotonous and boring as the empty hall inside.

Dark clouds from the west passed over his head, but not a single drop of moisture hit the glass vault. Their heavy bellies seemed low, painted in pink and purple by reflections of the blazing river. The rain they carried was intended to water some distant lands in the east, not the black waste here. An hour later they were gone, leaving a dull grey haze covering the sky.

Will kept on pacing the empty hall wondering about Hel. It was a bizarre place to live, but still, she did live here. How did she manage anything surrounded by these bare walls? Did she sleep on the floor? Where did she prepare her food? Where was her kitchen? Will felt his tummy could use a biscuit or two or a small piece of cheese.

His stomach spasmed with a loud growl when he remembered food. Suddenly he felt starving, but there was nothing edible in plain sight, nor anywhere he could spot that might be suitable for hiding any foodstuff. Hel hadn't even left a breadcrumb for him. What had he expected by sneaking into her home – a cake on a silver plate with a letter of invitation?

Will circled the hall a few more times, searching for any stash or secret store – found nothing. His stomach growled in protest, but there wasn't much he could do. This was a dream, and he couldn't even have his usual protein bar. This place was empty. He looked outside at the erupting volcano almost ready to bite the glass as his stomach playing marches and demanding something edible and then Will remembered that old woman from his dream the night before. She had promised to bring some food, but he must return to the cave. She would never follow him to the castle, Will was sure. She was too superstitious for that.

Will felt sick just thinking about getting back on that scary staircase again, but there was no other way down. He could only blame himself. It had been his own silly desire to get upstairs. It had been pointless, though; he had found nothing there. Now he must return.

Will circled the opening several times before braving to set his foot on the first step. It was even scarier than climbing up had been, and he decided to try moving down backwards with his eyes fixed on the clouds above the transparent vault.

This helped for a while, but progress was slow. Will trembled and sweated profusely, forced to stop every few steps to calm down.

"What are you doing there?" came an almost inaudible whisper from the left during one of his stops halfway down.

His eyes almost popped out his head when he peered in the direction of the voice but saw nothing there.

"Who are you?" Will asked, doing his best to avoid looking down.

Soft laughter was the only answer to his question, but Will spotted a barely visible blurred motion among the shadows and reflections of the dim red light filtering through the stained windows.

"What are you doing there?" the voice asked again.

"Waiting for Hel," Will said.

"Has she invited you?" the question was strange.

"No," Will admitted. "I've been waiting for several days, but she's been busy with something else."

"Why do you need to see her? She's always busy with something else."

"Who are you?" Will asked again as he resumed his slow journey down without waiting for an answer.

"I'm Kanykei. You'd be better picking me. I'm younger and prettier than Hel."

"I can't see you," he said, carefully taking a few more steps down before stopping again. "You're just a voice in my head."

This time the laughter was slightly louder.

"Have you seen Hel?"

"Yes," Will finally braved to look down.

The ground was still too far away.

"Have you seen the *real* Hel?"

"She was real enough for me," he closed his eyes again, forcing the fear out of his mind.

"Real as this?" the smoky shape of a girl emerged from the shadows floating in mid-air. "Pick me. I'm younger."

Will shook his head. *Was he hallucinating?* Maybe the doctor had been right? *Was he ill?*

"Don't listen to her," another voice whispered on the right. "She flirts with everybody. Better pick me – I'm the real thing!"

The smoky shape of the real thing appeared as a curvy matronly figure, slowly floating towards the staircase. The ghost of a girl giggled.

"I am not dating spectres," Will said sharply.

"Better pick me, brother," the voice of a young man said behind him. "You'll need a helping hand and a friend you can trust."

"No! No! Better pick me!" more shapes were emerging from every corner like creepy swirls of smoke.

Will hurried down the stairs.

"I'll wait for Hel," he murmured.

The shadow shapes moved around, reaching out to him,

begging, laughing, flirting, even threatening.

"She gave you the flower, didn't she?" Kanykei asked.

"Yes," Will admitted. "But I've lost it."

"He lost the flower!" screamed the matron.

"I'm sorry," Will said watching the ghostly figures swirling in an insane whirlpool then dissipating.

"Then you're in trouble, handsome," Kanykei whispered and vanished too.

"I know..." Will murmured.

Moments later, the hall fell still and silent again.

Will couldn't remember how he had finished climbing down the stairs and rushed outside. The ground softly trembled, but he wasn't sure if this was due to volcanic activity or if his legs were still shaking.

As before, the yard was empty and lifeless. Will quietly crossed the black pavement to the open gate. The sky had cleared in the west, but the sun was setting, and Will's stomach reminded him of its rights again as he began his slow journey back to the cave. He hoped that the old woman would keep her promise.

He stopped several times and looked back at the black castle with its strange secrets. It stood dark without any motion again, without any life.

All the way back, Will thought about Hel. Why hadn't she told him how important that blossom was to her? He would have never let it slip from his grasp. It had just been a moment of weakness when he placed the flower in Gudula's hand. A moment he now deeply regretted, but there was nothing he could do about it. The blue orchid was gone forever in the flaming waves of liquid stone.

Will peered at the silver grass outside the cave, wafting slightly in the light breeze. There was little hope of spotting an orchid blooming somewhere there. He would make a bouquet for Hel – anything just to make her happy. But there were only blades of grass without one single blossom to be seen. He felt hungry and deadly tired, crawled into the darkness, and sat down leaning against the wall. Never before had a surface of rock felt so soft and comforting to him.

❧❧ ✿ ❧❧

It was early morning when the rising sun softly touched his cheek, dispersing the remnants of his dream. Will sprang out of bed with the chilling scenes of his nightmare still vivid in his eyes. What kind of secrets lurked in the dark castle – left unlocked and empty but yet mysterious? Hel had left him and hurried away and, without her, that dream was heading into strange territory where everything seemed to be slipping out of control and turning against him.

Will quietly paid a visit to the bathroom where for several long minutes, he looked at his reflection in the mirror. The skin was now pale as it used to be; only the whites of his eyes were still touched by redness. He felt a strong urge to rush to the gym and hide away from everything and everybody behind the dumbbells and the loud beat from his earphones. *Damn!* He remembered that his mother might have a different opinion. She would rather keep him in bed, waiting for the test results. But Will was sure – he was perfectly healthy. He felt as fine as he usually was. Did another day in bed lie waiting for him? *No!* His body needed some exercise, and his mind needed to get away from that dreadful loneliness that was permeating the dream. He still hoped that Hel would return and forgive him for that small loss.

Will peeked back into the hallway. The house was silent, and his mother still was asleep.

He quietly dressed, packed his rucksack and sneaked out. Will knew his mother wouldn't be happy, but he felt he was old enough to make his own decisions.

Bright sunshine greeted him outside. The weather was excellent, and this lifted his mood a little. Traffic was scarce at such an early hour as he walked downhill, keeping a healthy pace.

He stopped for a few seconds in front of the tattoo shop – it was still closed, and the giant skull still was missing. *Had they gone out of business?*

He fished the protein bar out of his pocket and chewed on it all the way to the gym.

There weren't many people in the gym, and Will stopped at the gate, searching through his pockets and trying to find his access card when a sudden bout of laughter hit him from the row of treadmills. Girls giggled as a strangely familiar voice was telling tales.

He froze as the sound of heavy feet on a squeaking treadmill stopped, and the lardy body in revealing bright red tights turned to face him.

"Hey, Willy!" Jill happily waved. "Come and join us!"

Will's heart sank, and two girls next to Jill nearly rolled on the floor in a hysterical bout of laughter. He hastily turned around.

"I'll track you down!" Jill firmly promised as he dashed back to the street. The gym was out of the question now.

Will was sure that she wouldn't run after him in those terrible tights. He was mistaken.

Luckily, the bus was waiting at the stop, ready to depart. Will jumped on without even looking at its number. He was immensely relieved when the door hissed and closed, and the bus began to move. Jill ran a few hundred yards after it, shouting something. She grabbed the attention of everyone on the street, but then ran out of breath, gave up and stood on the pavement.

The bus slowly hummed down the High Street, and Will finally succeeded in getting his agitation under control. He got out off a few stops later.

The day still was bright, but Will barely noticed the surroundings. He silently cursed at that mad woman who was making his life a misery. Will felt stuck and cornered, with everything slipping out of his control. Even his wonderful nightly dreams – with Hel gone – were empty and boring and slowly turning into nightmares.

Will went down the street, carefully glancing over his shoulder, then turned right and disappeared behind the rusty gates of the old park.

He had to find another gym somewhere, where Jill wouldn't be able to trace him – Will decided. The new gym must be far away and difficult to reach from there and require changing several buses. The idea looked like a solution, and he decided to do some research while he was at home. Will was sure he would be able to outsmart that mad woman.

He took a slow walk along the lane of magnificent trees, their branches twining into a green canopy above his head. It was peaceful all around with only occasional joggers running along the shady alleys. The hour was still too early for mothers with prams and noisy children, and Will did his best to try to relax and enjoy the moment of serenity. He failed.

He stepped onto the pavement like a shadow still deeply troubled by the persistence of Jill's attempts to get him into her bed again. That felt outrageous, and he silently cursed several times, trying to vent his anger. He failed again.

The alley ahead bent slightly to the left, then crossed a narrow stone bridge over a muddy stream and opened into the concrete-framed riverside esplanade with several benches dotted along the shoreline.

Will sat down on a bench. For several minutes his eyes wandered aimlessly among the seagulls and geese messing about in the slow-moving stream. Then he buried his head in his hands, unsure what to do next. He felt lonely like never before – now that emptiness in his chest had a name.

One more email from Jill pinged onto his phone which Will deleted without even bothering to open it. He longed for that black basalt field where he had drunk tea with Hel. It seemed so far away, in another life!

"What wonderful weather!" said a frail crackling voice in front of him.

Only then did Will's eyes focus on the elderly gentleman

leaning on a stick with a dog lead in one hand. He had probably already been standing in front of him for a while.

"Yeah," Will nodded.

"Do you mind if I sit on this bench with you?" the old gentleman asked.

"Go ahead. There's plenty of room," Will mumbled burying his head back into his hands again.

"My name's Alan," the gentleman nodded politely before lowering himself down. "And this is Jim. We named him after my brother."

"Did your brother approve of that?" Will briefly glanced at the dog. "I wouldn't like a dog to be named after me."

"My brother found it quite amusing," Alan smiled and placed the stick across his knees. "Jim, sit."

The dog squinted at his owner with his slightly smokey eyes and carefully lowered himself to the ground.

"How old is he?" Will asked.

"Older than me, if you converted dog years into human years," the man smiled sadly. "Sorry for bothering you. This was the favourite bench for my family to sit on, but then my brother Jim went first, then my wife, Pat. Now there's just Jim the dog left and me."

"It's a lovely place," Will said and added politely. "Sorry for your family."

"No need to be sorry," Alan smiled somehow sadly. "We had a very long and lovely life. Now I must finish this miserable remaining path alone and then I'll join her in heaven if I'm lucky. I've done a few bad things in my life."

They grew silent watching the geese messing in the

shallow water and searching for food. A soft breeze brought a few fluffy clouds and a hint of a chill. Will's phone beeped. He fished it out and made a face looking at another attempt by Jill to keep in touch.

"Women?" Alan asked and quickly added. "Sorry for asking. It's none of my business, of course."

Will nodded.

"She's not someone I'd ever be interested in," he said with some hesitation and surprising honesty.

"Let me guess," Alan smiled. "The one you're interested in is either unreachable, pays no attention to you or is too far away?"

"All of that," Will admitted sadly.

"That's bad," Alan shook his head slowly. "It was the same with Pat and me at first."

"What did you do?" Will asked with sudden interest. "I'm afraid to do anything. I don't understand her, and she's full of secrets. I'm afraid to get it wrong. I'm afraid that she might get angry and reject me entirely."

The old man smiled his tired smile again.

"I think it's always better to regret what you've done than regret what you didn't, young man. At least, you'll be sure that you tried," Alan said after a short pause. "I could tell you what happened between Pat and me, but it's a long story."

"I've plenty of time and would like to hear it, if you don't mind," Will told him, replacing the phone in his pocket.

Alan took his time looking at fluffy clouds,

remembering. Will didn't dare to interrupt his silence.

"It was in Normandy when I saw her for the first time. And it was wartime," he said finally. "We'd just had a bloody battle and moved forward near Ranville when I saw an unsaddled horse standing in the middle of the field. It was a beautiful dapple-grey mare, and we went closer to get a better look. Then I saw her for the first time."

"A horse?" Will was disappointed.

"No," Alan grinned. "She was on the ground next to the horse."

"Was she injured?"

"No," the old man shook his head. "She was clutching a dead body and crying. When she looked at me, I instantly knew I was in love, despite her face being covered in dirt and her dress stained by the blood of the man she was holding."

A shadow passed over the bench as a small cloud travelled across the sun.

"We had killed her husband in the battle, and she cursed us loudly in French. Even her voice sounded like the most beautiful music," Alan paused again. "Then I looked at the dead man. He was dressed in the *Wehrmacht* uniform. She was the wife of an enemy. In fact, she was the widow of an enemy."

"What happened next?" Will asked.

"It was wartime," Alan said, looking at the face of his dog. "The Nazis began shooting again and killed her mare. We had to fight back. That day was bloody in Ranville, and I had no chance even for a second glance at her. We went on fighting, and I lost her. Many men fell on both sides."

"Did you find her after the battle?"

"No, I had no chance to search for her. We had to move further inland, battles were still being fought everywhere," Alan frowned. "It was a bloody difficult time."

Seagulls shrieked harshly high above the calm water fighting over the small fish one of them had caught. Alan grew silent, looking at the sudden turmoil. Will waited patiently, but the silence went on for too long, and he began to fear that the old man had forgotten the subject.

"How did you find her then?" Will gently reminded him to continue.

They watched the river flow for some time as Jim lazily barked at a squirrel, not bothering even to stand up.

"That story is too long, unfortunately," Alan said slowly. "I'm not sure if I'd like to go through it now, young man. It's nearly time for my medication." He frowned standing up, then added. "Yes, I found her, but it was damned difficult. Maybe I'll tell you some other time. Sorry to disappoint you. I don't know your situation, young man, but I guess it's not as hopeless as mine was."

"It's entirely different," Will admitted. "It doesn't involve war, and I know her name and where to find her."

"Then what's holding you back?"

"I don't understand her," Will shrugged sadly.

"You'll never will," Alan sighed. "Don't even try. Accept her with all her strangeness and don't ever try to ask for explanations. She might give those explanations in a language you don't understand, and your inability to understand might anger her. Better accept everything as it is and give her time."

"I am patient," Will told him. "But she just ignores me all the time. I'm feeling bad about it."

"Then you must have already done something to anger her," Alan shrugged. "Try to undo that and wait until she forgives you."

"It's not an easy thing to undo," Will sighed.

"Unless you've killed her beloved cat, everything else can be solved, I guess," said Alan.

"I lost something she gave me," Will muttered. "I had no idea that it was significant."

"Well, look around then and try to find it."

"It's lost forever, I'm afraid," Will felt strange, talking about his dream so seriously.

"Look around again, and maybe you'll find alternatives."

"I doubt that," Will shook his head sadly.

"Then apologise and talk to her. Tell her how bad you feel that you've disappointed her."

Will shrugged. This might be easy to suggest, but Hel wouldn't talk to him. Will closed his eyes, and in his mind, Hel's black stallion proudly carried her uphill again, leaving him behind, crushed and unhappy. He distinctly recalled the feeling of emptiness which painfully squeezed his chest. He shook his head sadly – the task seemed impossible.

"You married your Pat," he said, attempting to get at least some tiny assurance about the reward which may wait for him at the end. "Was it worth all that struggle? Were you happy with her? Did you have any children?"

Alan sighed before answering.

"Life is long, my young friend," he said, looking at Will, "and you never know how things might turn out in the end. Yes, I was happy in love all my life. We had fights and quarrels – who doesn't – but now how I miss those fights. I miss her."

Alan grew silent and turned away, hiding the sudden moisture in his eye. "She lost her unborn child in that battlefield the same day she lost her husband." He said, his voice trembling slightly. "She couldn't have kids after that. I'm all alone, apart from Jim, the dog. But without a trace of hesitation, I would go through all those troubles again just to have one more look in her eyes. It was worth it – you can say. I've no regrets."

Will had his regrets for asking the questions which troubled the tender sores of the old man. There was no way he could undo it, and the silence grew uncomfortable.

Alan shaded his eyes and looked at his watch. "Oh, I'm sorry. I must go, I'm afraid. It's nearly time to take my pills."

"It was nice talking to you," Will said politely and watched as Alan gently tugged on Jim's lead.

"Don't lose hope, young man. Everything has its own time and purpose. I wish you luck and patience," Alan slowly went along the bank, leaving Will to watch the geese alone.

He sat on the bench, gazing at the flowing water, and the day around him slowly approached the noon. The park filled with children, screams and laughter, as young mothers walked around watching over their precious offspring.

It was time to return home. Will couldn't go back to the High Street and catch a bus without risking banging into Jill. He made a large detour through shady side streets, trying to avoid every red car. The journey was long.

"Where have you been?" was the first thing his mother asked as he closed the front door behind him. "In the gym again? You're ill, can't you stay at home? I was worried."

"I wasn't at the gym. I took a walk in the park to get some fresh air," Will assured her, and that was true.

She looked at him with suspicion.

"They called from the hospital today," the mother said.

"Am I fine?"

"No," her expression was concerned. "They said your liver tests were abnormal, so they've booked you in for a scan next week."

"Still, I'm feeling fine," Will shrugged with an uncertain smile.

"You must have the scan," the mother cut him short firmly. "I'm afraid and very concerned, Willy. That damned tattoo has made you ill! Why do you never listen to your mother?"

"Could I have a few scrambled eggs?" Will asked, meekly trying to navigate the conversation to calm waters.

"Sure," his mother was always happy to make him something to eat. "Wash your hands."

Will looked in the bathroom mirror as he washed – his skin was pink, touched by the sun, and the whites of his eyes were still bloodshot. He frowned, rubbing his face with a towel – his skin looked even rosier after that.

A large plate of scrambled eggs was waiting for him on the table.

"Do you want anything else?" his mother asked as she washed the pan in the sink.

"No thanks, mum."

Will ate everything that was on the plate and made himself a milkshake to help it down. Then he went to his room.

That call from the hospital had put him in a bit of a stew. *There must be some misunderstanding.* They must have mixed his blood up with somebody else's and taken the wrong readings. He felt fine, and the suspicion of some sort of mysterious illness seemed just plain silly.

He knew that he had no other choice but to go for that scan – his mother was too concerned and wouldn't calm down without getting the results. And he had to find another gym somewhere on the outskirts of town, out of Jill's reach.

Will dropped onto his bed and drilled into his phone. It was late afternoon when he finally finished clearing all the emails from Jill. He read some of them only to satisfy his curiosity, but most of her emails he deleted without opening. That woman was mad and desperate, begging him for a meeting!

He put the phone aside and closed his eyes, trying to give them a few minutes' rest. Moments later, somebody gently touched his shoulder.

"Wake up, Bryn," whispered a voice.

The old woman was crouching over him in the dusk of the cave. Will shook his head and sat up – the transition into the dream world was seamless and unexpected, and he stared with confusion at her wrinkled face looming in the shadows above him.

"I brought you some food," she said, holding out the package for him.

"Thank you," Will accepted it and began to unwrap it.

"I brought as much as I could," she said as if apologising.

"I know."

Several pieces of smoked meat, cheese, some bread and an apple were inside the wrapping. She produced a flask of water from her pocket and handed it to Will.

"Have you already seen her?" the old woman asked.

"Hel?" asked Will. "Yes, but she left days ago. The castle is empty now."

"The castle is never empty," the old woman whispered

and looked around with suspicion. "You must be very careful, Bryn. This place is dangerous."

Will put the apple and cheese into his pocket and began to chew the meat.

"I'll bring you more tomorrow night," the old woman said. "You're my youngest son, Bryn, and I've always loved you the most. My heart bleeds when I think of your destiny."

"What's so horrible about it?" Will asked without thinking.

"She's already stolen you from me," the woman whispered. "That's why you're here. She never forces you, but you'll give up your will to her, your soul, even your life. You'll get nothing in return, only an eternity of pain and false hopes. I fear for you, my boy."

The woman was rambling delusional.

"Why are you telling me this?" Will asked.

"Don't be angry with your old mother. I still have hope that you will listen and turn back before it's too late, Bryn."

Damn! This woman was talking the same nonsense as that crazy girl – Hel was kind, beautiful and well-mannered. The old woman had no idea what she was talking about, but at least she was bringing food.

"I don't want to turn back," Will said. "I think I'm doing the right thing."

"I know it's hard to fight her," she whispered and glanced at the cave mouth. "But you must give it a try. What has she promised to seduce you away?"

"She gave me no promises," Will admitted. "And I

haven't given her any either."

"Maybe, it's not too late?" it was only a self-deception voiced in a barely audible whisper.

The ground trembled, but Will was already used to it and didn't stop chewing the meat. The smoky taste felt tangy on his tongue, but it was filling. The old woman waited until the tremors had subsided and the dust settled before speaking again.

"I saw a sign yesterday when I was returning home," she quietly whispered while watching Will stuffing his stomach. "Thousands of crows black as death were circling the skies above the Tomb in Merthyr. Thousands of them were flying in complete silence. Then all at once, they turned towards the setting sun and disappeared. It was a sign from the Gods, and I don't think we have much time left in Merthyr, but I'm too old to flee alone."

She was insane. Crows never fly in silence – the old woman was simply deaf. Will was certain about that.

"You left all the crops in the fields, Bryn," she said after a few moments of silence. "But that's not important now. I'm not afraid to die and walk the Road of Gods. I've seen everything in my life. But you're too young, Bryn. You must save yourself. A great disaster is coming."

The warning sounded silly. Will wouldn't be scared by just a few crows. He was sure the biggest danger facing him was to wake up in a cold sweat. It was only a dream, after all.

"What kind of disaster?"

The old woman leant on her stick, and Will noticed her

eyes watering in the dusk of the cave. The earth trembled again before she was able to answer. Will shrugged, finished the meat off and fished the apple out of his pocket.

"No!" the old woman stopped him when he was about to take a bite. "Not the apple! Not yet! Save that fruit for the very last moment. I soaked the apple in a concoction of snakeflower roots. It will painlessly poison you to death. Eat the apple if you can't resist her any longer. I love you, Bryn, but this may be the only way if the Night Crawlers get here."

"Night Crawlers? What's so special about them?"

"You know," the woman squirmed uneasily.

"Why must I kill myself?" the mystery piqued Will's curiosity, and he decided to gamble with the old woman. "Let them crawl. Why must I die?"

There was a long silence before she finally answered.

"The Night Crawlers come at night and burn you with hellfire," her whisper was barely audible. "Painless death is better than flames, Bryn, and better than an eternity in the service of Death. I'll be waiting for you on the Road of Gods."

Her mumbling made no sense to Will.

"Of course," he said, replacing the apple in his pocket. "I'll eat it only in case of great danger."

The woman was as crazy as that Gudula. She sounded even more insane than the girl, but Will was keen to accept all her nonsense as long as she brought him something to eat. Was she indeed his mother? *No!* He secretly grinned – Will knew his mother was in her room or busy in the kitchen. It was only a dream.

"I know, son," the delusional woman said. "I brought you the apple as a precaution, just in case you could bear it no longer. I still have some hope that you'll be able to break free and flee, Bryn. She called you and then left you behind. Maybe she's changed her mind? Don't give up, son, resist the call of Death."

Will didn't answer. Her talk was annoying and meaningless. Of course, that crazy woman – mother or not – couldn't stop him from waiting for Hel to return. He hoped he would be able to persuade the woman of his dreams to forget that damned blue blossom. He only needed one more chance – one more try, but this time he would be more careful. He would never lose a speck of dust if it were important to her.

"I don't know how much time we have left," the woman continued her grim scaremongering, whispering in the darkness. "She's fled, leaving you behind. She doesn't care about you. Save your young soul, Bryn, but best you hurry. Now you're the only one left for me."

Will didn't feel too much obligation in exchange for a few pieces of meat and some bread. The woman was afraid of crows. It was her problem, not his.

"Hel will return, and I'll wait for her," Will told her firmly. "I must speak to her."

"I'm begging you, Bryn," she grabbed his hand. "Think about your old mother. I gave you life. Why are you listening to her? She might promise you everything, but there is only one thing she could give you."

Will didn't understand her. She was utterly crazy – that

woman didn't know Hel and kept talking about stupid things. Hel wasn't a liar.

"What is the only thing she can give me?" Will asked, withdrawing his hand.

Her touch was cold and uncomfortable, alien.

"Death," the old woman whispered.

"We'll all die anyway," he tried to comfort her. "Sooner or later."

But she saw no humour in his words. "Yes, we all are mortal, but I'd rather meet you on the Road of Gods than watch you serve eternity in her castle, Bryn," the woman said firmly. "I've lost enough of my family to her, but I don't blame you. I blame her!"

A sudden tremor shook the ground, and the old woman gasped pressing a hand to her mouth.

"I mustn't say that," she whispered. "I've angered her!"

She glanced around frightened, as all the usual tremors and rumbles of the ground were suddenly silenced.

"Hel is away, don't worry. She can't hear you," Will said, standing up. "I'll have a look what's going on."

He took a few hesitant steps towards the mouth of the cave. A strange noise came from outside like a strong wind shuffling through dead leaves, and he was curious. *Had Hel returned to the castle?*

"I'm sorry!" the old woman cried out in her frail voice.

The ground shook again.

"I must go, Bryn," she sounded desperate. "Be careful!"

She rushed back to the darkness of the cave as fast as her old bones could take her, leaning heavily on her stick. Will took another step, and everything grew quiet again. He put the food in his pocket and peered outside. The night was dark, with a hint of silver slipping through the thick clouds. The fiery river in the distance shone bright red, but the field between the lava and the cave was utterly black. Was something going on there, or was it just a game of shadows between the faint reflections?

Will carefully stepped forward, probing the way with his feet and trying to keep his balance. He hastened the tall pillars of stone, hurrying to have a look at the castle. *Had Hell returned?* The thought was exciting, rushing blood to his heart and making his feet move faster.

The castle was dark and quiet when he finally got a glimpse, and her dark knights were nowhere in sight.

Will collapsed on a rock in utter frustration.

Then it happened.

The ground began to shake like never before. Will desperately clutched the boulder he was sitting on, as it seemed like the entire field of frozen lava had started into motion. Rocks jumped and rolled around as the earth shuddered in convulsions.

The tall cliffs hanging over the lava river collapsed one by one with loud bangs, splashing into the fiery flow. Then everything calmed down again.

Will stood on his trembling feet. *What was going on here?*

Strands of thick smoke leaked from the castle. *Was Hel's home on fire?*

Will dashed forward unthinking, but he took no more than just two or three steps when the volcano behind the castle exploded, knocking him off his feet.

The solid ground around him started to move again like a raging river, and Will crawled onto the nearest rock using it like a liferaft. He covered his head, waiting for the shockwave to pass as flaming bright red boulders as big as a doubledecker bus tumbled across the field from the sky. The earth trembled and shuddered again, as deep, smoke-breathing trenches opened up.

Then another explosion hit the left side of the mountain expelling a cloud of burning gases that rushed down the slope like a fiery avalanche.

"Am I going to die?" – This was the only thought weakly pulsing through the fog of fear in Will's brain. The nightmare seemed so real that he did not doubt all the danger. "Please, I must wake up now! Please…"

Thick clouds of black smoke swirled around the dark castle. It seemed like the end of the world with flames threatening to consume everything. Another flaming boulder hit the ground just yards away from Will, and he screamed as a few bright splatters hit his back. The pain was sharp and drilled deep into his body, causing his muscles to arch in spasms.

When he opened his eyes, the dark fumes had filled the field and were swirling around him in a sickening whirlpool, flashing with occasional sparks. Will raised his head to have a better look, but all he could see was an impenetrable dark wall of smoke. The rock he was clutching seemed like an island of tranquillity, the eye of a storm within the crazy circling cloud of smoke and sparks.

"Get down and don't move," somebody whispered into his ear, but Will saw no one around. "There'll be another boom!"

Will closed his eyes. Then another even more powerful explosion shook the ground. The period of darkness took longer than he expected. The next moment somebody touched his shoulder.

❧⬥❧

"Willy, what's wrong?" the whisper was comforting.

He opened his eyes, trying to focus on the face in front of him. His mother was standing next to his bed with a very concerned look on her face.

"What happened?" she asked. "You screamed."

"It was just a nightmare, mum," Will said still feeling confused – was it?

She touched his forehead.

"Oh, Willy," she moaned. "Your head seems hot. I'll get the thermometer."

"I'm all right, mum," he began protesting, but his mother had already gone.

His reassurance wasn't entirely accurate. His back ached where the splatters of molten rock had burnt through his robes and hit his skin in the dream. Or was it his imagination playing tricks on him? The pain was real but wasn't great, and Will decided not to worry his mother any further.

A few minutes later, she returned with a thermometer

and stuck it firmly under his armpit. They patiently waited. The night outside was dark and quiet, and Will nearly jumped when the thermometer beeped. His mother took it out and looked at the reading.

"Strange," she said, touching Will's forehead again. "You seem quite hot, but your temperature's normal."

"I'm fine," he smiled, attempting to comfort her. "It was just a nightmare."

"I'll leave the door open," she told him. "Call me if you feel ill. Promise?"

"Promise."

For several minutes Will waited in the darkness until everything in the house became quiet again, and then he sneaked to the bathroom. His back still ached, and he was curious about what was going on with it. It wasn't easy to see, and Will had to use his phone and take a few pictures over his shoulder. The photos weren't impressive – three red spots had appeared just below his left shoulder blade. *Bugs?* He'd never had that problem before.

Will quietly returned to his room. He closed the door, switched on the lights and carefully inspected the bedsheets. Found nothing. His bed looked as it usually did.

Still, he wasn't ready to return to his nightmare. He sneaked into the kitchen and made himself a milkshake. He still felt that strange heat, and the cold drink pleasantly calmed his stomach.

Back in his room Will opened the window and let in some fresh night air. He kept rolling around in his bed, unable to find a comfortable position. Then he tossed the blanket off, still feeling the heat and let the cool waves of air roll over his naked skin, calming his soul and taking his troubling thoughts away.

❧ ❦ ✿ ❦ ❧

"I thought you were dead," there was a whisper ringing in his ears.

Will raised his head and had to shade his eyes – the whole field around was ablaze with lava splatters and red boulders as he lay on an island of black basalt no bigger than a king-size bed.

The transparent shape of a girl was sitting on the flaming rock in front of him.

"You can stand up now. The eruption is over," she told him.

"Who are you?" Will asked, getting to his feet.

"Don't you remember me? I'm Kanykei," she laughed. "We met in the Tower."

"Yes, I remember," Will admitted, glancing around. "But it's not so easy to memorise your features."

The dark castle on the slope of the mountain still stood unharmed, but a considerable chunk of the left side of the volcano was missing. The crater – once high on top on the right – was now low on the left with a lake of boiling lava spitting burning gas where the cave was. A new blazing river now made its way down the slope while the old stream had become darker and stationary, but still hissed fumes and emitted flames.

Will wondered if the old woman had managed to reach safety, but it was impossible to find out. He guessed she wouldn't be coming back with any food.

"What happened?" he asked. "I thought the castle was on fire. Why wasn't it blown away by that explosion?"

"It never is," Kanykei shrugged. "We're here to guard the Tower every time Patna threatens an eruption."

"You?"

"Not just me," she laughed, standing up. "There are billions of us in the Tower, stranger. We're here to serve Hel. Do you still believe in that shit about the Road of Gods? Forget it. Everyone ends up here. We're the dark power of Hel, but she will never acknowledge that."

Kanykei came closer, but her features remained indistinguishable. She was just a smoky silhouette, a shadow moving among the flames.

"Why have you saved me?" Will asked.

"I was curious," Kanykei crooned. "Where did you lose the flower that Hel gave you?"

"Why is that so important to you?"

"You're asking too many questions," the ghostly silhouette whispered. "I'm only curious."

"It's simply gone," Will shrugged.

"It couldn't just vanish. Not *that* flower," Kanykei sounded serious. "Tell me – was it a yellow daisy or a purple aster? Maybe a black tulip this time or a white rose?"

"It was a blue orchid," Will told her.

"A blue orchid?" Kanykei stopped. "That's something new. How exciting! Where did you lose it?"

"It's gone, forget it," Will shrugged. "I dropped it in the lava flow by accident. It's been burnt and gone forever."

"You're a strange man," the ghostly apparition came closer. "Her flowers don't burn. It must still be there. It's just been carried away. You must find it before someone else does."

Will's heart began to beat faster – if he could retrieve the blossom maybe Hel would forgive him? The thought was dizzying.

"But how can I find it in the flowing lava? Even if I would spot it floating on top of flames – that sounds crazy – I'd never be able to pick it up or even get close in that heat," Will's hope slowly died again.

"Indeed, you are silly and strange," the ghost said. "Look at Patna – now the mountain is spitting flames on the other side. The previous river is cooling down and soon will be hard and cold enough even for you. You can't imagine how lucky you are. Go down and follow the flow and find that flower!"

Will jumped to his feet, ready to run and instantly stopped with deep disappointment in his eyes. The field around him still was blazing with fire.

"I can't," he shook his head.

"Why?" the ghost seemed confused at first. "Oh! I see! It's only half a mile! I think we can fix this."

The silhouette of Kanykei vanished in flames, leaving Will alone. He sat down on the rock in the middle of his dark island and watched the sea of embers and sparks, facing the new fiery flow and wondering about the fate of the old woman. He would probably never find that out. The passing minutes seemed as long as hours, but nothing changed.

"Get down and keep low," Kanykei suddenly whispered in his ear.

Will dropped flat on the rock as a large black tornado passed in front of him and lowered on the embers slowly moving down the slope.

Flaming splatters rose in the air again, and Will rolled off the boulder and hid behind it afraid even to take a glimpse.

Moments later, Kanykei was back.

"You can get up," she said with laughter. "And you better hurry before it melts down."

Will peeked from behind the rock as long strands of blackness rushed past him, flying uphill over the flaming field and disappearing back into the dark castle.

"I'd like to have a look at that blossom if you do come back," Kanykei said. "I hope you'll pick me then."

She vanished before Will was able to answer.

"Thank you," he said but wasn't sure if she was able to hear this.

A road of black boulders thickly covered with snow now wound across the field of flames. Will hesitated for just a few seconds. The heat was already melting that snow, and he rushed forward trying to cover the distance as fast as he could.

It was like a winter's breath in the midst of a flaming hell – fragile and transient like a memory. The ground was slippery as Will ran down the sparkling white road amid the blazing fields of embers. He fell several times but managed to escape with just a few bruises, each time getting up and running again, trying to escape the heat.

He stopped when the road ended.

Only then did Will look back and allow himself a few minutes of rest. The dark castle was already out of sight, hidden behind the tall black waves of rock and flaming fields. The road he had passed was already black with no trace of whiteness, with a few dirty streams and strands of steam left, where only a few seconds ago snowflakes had glistened.

Will wiped away the beads of sweat from his face, catching his breath. The ground still trembled here and in the distance, the pillar of black volcanic ashes rose to the cloudy sky.

The new lava flow was heading north and disappeared behind the hanging cliffs, finding its way down. The old fiery river still glowed red but less was less hissing and less flaming. Will realised that it would take a few days to let it cool down sufficiently to approach it. If Kanykei was right and the blue orchid had survived the flames, it still might get trapped beneath the lava – even a tiny splash could bury it forever. Will cursed as the task seemed nearly impossible. But he had to try. He must wait until the flames turned to stone – it was the only answer.

A few miles down the slope Will spotted a line of low, crooked trees among the rocks and arched cliffs and headed there.

He looked at the distant woods – they seemed like a strange peninsula between the new and the old lava streams, with barely perceptible patches of green, still too far away and difficult to see clearly. He even wasn't sure if he was able to trust his own eyes. His throat was dry with a taste of blood on his tongue, and thirst kept on rushing him down the slope of the mountain, but he was glad to be alive and to be leaving that baking heat behind him. Life seemed to exist, just a couple of miles below, and maybe there was water too. Anyway, this was the only way left available to him – down the slope and into those woods. He kept his eye on the lava flow on the left, hoping to spot somehow that blue blossom floating among the flames. Will was sure that the entire venture was hopeless. It was just the weird advice of a ghost. *How could a fragile flower survive in such heat?* Kanykei said the blossom was indestructible. That statement sounded silly, but she had saved his life, and Will felt an obligation to at least try. He had a faint hope of meeting Hel on his way. This narrow land between the two flaming rivers was the only way for her to return to her black castle too.

He got as close to the flow as he could, where his body was still able to tolerate the heat, but all he could see were flames and red liquid rock. Maybe Gudula's body had been carried further down the slope? Her body had probably already perished, and just the orchid would be surfing the flames. *Where though?* Perhaps he was looking too close to the shore?

Will felt tired when he finally reached the crooked trees and thirst was driving him crazy. For some time he wandered among scorched and twisted trunks and charred branches without a single leaf. The trees were dead, burned in an eruption years ago. The blackened area was a few miles wide, turning to the right and disappearing behind the cliffs. Will had to cross it on his way.

It must be the usual state of affairs of a volcano. Will stopped and looked around. The new blazing river rushed down the slope and burning everything in its path as thick black fumes rose to the skies far away on the right. The old flow on the left seemed more peaceful with even a few dark islands appearing in the fading redness. Maybe tomorrow the surface would be hard enough to walk on, or it might still be too hot.

Further down the slope, there was a dark green wall of a forest. It looked more inviting than the crooked branches around, and Will decided to find a place to sleep there, as the day began to fade to the evening dusk. The woods looked more attractive than the frozen waves of the black basalt among the dead trees. And he might be lucky enough to find water there.

He was a halfway through the charred grounds when a mournful howl broke in the distance piercing the sky high above the woods. Will stopped. *Was it a wolf?*

Then another howl followed at a slightly higher pitch.

Will searched around and picked up a large stick. It was

next to nothing against a pack of wolves, but he didn't have any other means of defence. Nobody and nothing moved around, but the dark green forest now seemed a less attractive place to spend the night.

He stood listening, but no more howls followed.

Several yards down the slope, he found a spring and dropped to his knees grinning widely. The water was warm and tasted funny, but he drank his fill anyway. Then he stood up and looked around. The place was weird, and Will didn't feel safe facing the woods. That strange howling was still ringing in his ears, and he had a nagging feeling of being watched, but couldn't make out any spying eyes in the dying light. He spent nearly half an hour watching the dark firs in the dusk, but nothing moved there. Everything was quiet. Still, he decided against moving further.

Will moved closer to the lava flow and crouched under the hanging cliff, facing the distant forest. It was getting dark, and shadows began to play tricks on his imagination. The crooked branches of dead trees turned into shape-shifting monsters, and packs of wolves seemed to be hunting in the dusk, but nobody and nothing bothered him. He didn't notice the moment when he slipped into a dream, still clutching the stick in his hands.

He was back in his room, and the bed linen was wet, soaked with sweat during the night. Will tossed away the blanket and sprang out of bed, feeling chill on his naked skin – the window was open.

It was early morning, and the house was still quiet.

He peeked outside through the window – the sky was clear and pink in the east, heralding a beautiful day. A few of the brightest stars were still fighting the approaching daylight, but their brightness was already fading.

Will had spent the night next to the heat of molten rock, and this morning chill seemed refreshing and inviting. He felt an urge to stretch his muscles. Will knew his mother would object, but the temptation was too strong to resist.

He quickly packed his rucksack and quietly sneaked outside while his mother was still asleep. It was too early for anybody else to be about. Hopefully, it was too early for Jill too.

Everywhere seemed deserted, but Will took a side street anyway, preferring to remain on the safe side just in case Jill thought about stalking him again. That woman was crazy, and he expected almost anything. He went down the shady street, feeling the refreshing chill on his skin. That strange howl he had heard in his dream still rang in his ears. Sometimes the sound seemed too real, and Will looked over his shoulder trying to spot the source. All he saw was a girl jogging on the other side of the street with bright red earphones shielding her from the real world. Will smiled at her, but she paid no attention and quickly vanished behind the corner.

Several cars passed down the road, none of them was red.

Will crossed a few more streets before he reached the gym about the same time as the morning sun finally touched the ground. For several minutes he wandered in front of the window carefully peeking at the row of treadmills – it was empty. It was too early even for such a mad woman as Jill.

He widely grinned opening the door and greeted the receptionist who was quietly sipping his coffee in front of the computer.

"Looks like I'm first today," Will said.

"You are," nodded the guy and turned back into his screen.

Will quickly changed and put his earphones on, heading to the free weight corner. He didn't reach it.

Somewhere in front of the treadmills a sharp pain suddenly pierced Will's left shoulder, and the world suddenly began spinning and shaking. He dropped onto the ground, passing out before he hit the floor.

The silver light of the enormous globe shone in his face making him blink when Will raised his head in an attempt to have a look around. He felt the ground around him, trying to find his stick – it was gone. At least a dozen spears were pointing at him out of the shadows, but all he could see behind them was just dark shapes.

"What's going on?" Will mumbled making no further attempt to move. His left shoulder was still aching, probably bearing the mark from a spearhead.

The silence was the reply before a few silhouettes moved closer. Will frowned, trying to get a better look, but their faces were hidden behind bizarre and frightening brown-red masks. He gasped as several spearheads touched his chest but didn't pierce the skin. The scene was like that from a bizarre pantomime as his captors didn't make a sound. The spearheads lifted a little, and dirty hands emerged from the dark and unceremoniously grabbed him.

"Stop that!" Will began protesting, but moments later, he had been tied up and lifted to his feet. "Why are you doing this?"

Nobody answered him.

"I'm not going anywhere!" Will struggled trying to break free, but was prodded with a spear and had to shut up.

Shadowy silhouettes silently dragged him down the slope along the bank of the flaming river. One of the captors went a few paces ahead, and Will was forced to follow him as several spearheads pricked his back. Two of them held the ends of the rope, which was tied around Will's wrists. Another four or five dark shadows followed them with their spikes ready. Will had no other choice but to watch his steps in the ghostly light and follow the lead.

It was a scary experience. He had been hurried along among the crooked branches and twisted trunks, among black pillars of stone and strange rocks resembling skeletons of long-extinct monsters that seemed alive in the swirling and flickering lights of silver and red. There was no road or even a narrow path here, and Will kept stumbling on loose boulders and lost his balance and fell a few times. He was immediately dragged back on his feet with a tug of his ties and was then pushed forward with the spears.

They passed the dead woods, and the way became even more challenging and eerie as his captors pushed Will into the dusk among the living firs. The hard needles of the resilient branches stung his skin, and tangled roots tried to twist his ankles.

It was much darker here. The fog was rising and filling the woods with even more shadows, and Will just kept stepping forward, with no idea where his captors were taking him. They had left the flaming river and its bloody reflections behind, and the only light between the firs was occasional rays from the silver globe reaching the moss through the scraggy branches.

Several miles later the woods stepped aside in front of what looked like a dark lake in the silver light. His captors turned left to the clearance on the shore where even lines of thick shrubs framed the sandy beach. A row of wooden cages appeared, placed a few feet above the ground on thick wooden poles.

The captors cut Will's ties and shoved him into one of the cages.

"Why are you locking me up?" he asked as soon as the door was shut.

The captors remained silent with their faces hidden behind their masks. They left, moving along the shore without dropping a sound.

"Let me go!" he cried out to the retreating shadows.

"Shut up," said a calm voice from the nearby cage. "They won't answer."

"Who are you?" Will asked, peering at the neighbouring cage but unable to make out who was talking.

"The same sort of jouster as you," the voice explained. "We'll fight to the death in sixty nights when their holy silent fasting is over."

"I'm not fighting anyone," Will cut in fiercely. "They've got the wrong person."

"They won't care," the voice remained calm and indifferent. "We'll both die in that tournament. You may die fighting or die later sacrificed in their sacred Lifeless Pond."

"What is that?" Will gasped.

"You'll see it later quite clearly," the voice chuckled. "We're right in front of it."

"That pond?" Will pointed to the dark water they were facing. "Why is it called Lifeless Pond?"

"You'll see that later too."

For the first time, Will felt truly scared in his dream.

"You seem to know a lot," he observed.

"I've been here for a while," the voice chuckled.

"How did you manage to survive the tournament if it's inevitably fatal?"

"I haven't," the voice said. "The Rybbaths hold the holy feast only once in a decade after six months of silent fasting. I was unlucky enough to be wandering around at the time when they needed combatants. Probably, the same as you."

"What will happen to us now?"

"Relax. You still have sixty days to live."

That didn't sound very encouraging. Will couldn't believe he had been so easily trapped. Kanykei hadn't mentioned any dangers, and he could easily have avoided this by staying closer to the new flaming river to the north. With him in this cage, his mission to find the blossom for Hel might become next to impossible. So first, he must find a way to escape.

Will moved closer to the door and got a good grip on the bars with both his hands.

"It's useless," the voice observed. "The bars are really strong."

"You're in a different cage," Will cut the voice short and began to shake the bars with all his might.

Minutes later, he dropped back exhausted.

"I told you," the voice observed calmly. "Relax and get some rest. They feed the combatants twice a day, but that's the only advantage. Nobody will come here until tomorrow morning."

"Will they bring food tomorrow?" Will asked retreating to the back of his cage.

"They'll bring you food, but don't expect much. They won't give us any meat."

"Maybe I'll get a chance to break free when they open the cage?" Will didn't realise he had spoken aloud.

"They don't open the cages," the voice said with a yawn.

Will lowered his body onto a loose bunch of straw. The pale silver light remained outside of the cage, and here he was covered with darkness. It was quiet.

He looked to the left at the neighbouring cage again, but there wasn't too much to see – only dark shadows loomed there. None were moving.

"We're stuck with each other for a while," Will addressed the shadows in the neighbouring cage. "Maybe, we should get introduced? My name's Will."

Then one of the shadows turned red glowing eyes on him.

"I am Qu Sith," the voice said. "Don't waste your energy. Better get some sleep."

Will felt a chill looking at those glowing eyes, but he couldn't make out anything else in the darkness.

"Are you human?" he asked, feeling his voice slightly trembling.

"No, I am not," Qu Sith answered. "Do you have any problem with that?"

"No," Will shrugged, feeling not so sure. "Who are you?"

"You'll see tomorrow," the shadow said and closed its glowing eyes.

Did that mean the conversation was over? Probably...

A sudden bout of dizziness struck Will's head. He gasped, looking at the walls of his cage floating around and fading.

❧❦ ✿ ❧❦

"He's back," a male voice stated somewhere beyond his field of view as his wandering eyes attempted to gain focus.

Will was in an ambulance which was speeding down the street, loudly wailing its siren and flashing blue. A line was attached to his vein, dripping a clear fluid from the plastic bag above him. His chest was bare with electrodes attached, and two concerned paramedics stared at the equipment.

"What happened?" Will attempted to ask, but his tongue felt swollen and funny.

His head was fixed to a rigid plastic collar, and all he could move were his eyes.

"How do you feel?" the male paramedic asked, checking Will's pulse.

"Funny," Will's tongue felt lazy with consonants. "What happened?"

"You lost consciousness and went into a seizure at the gym," the paramedic explained. "Have you taken any drugs or illegal supplements? Any steroids?"

"No," Will said firmly.

"Have you had any recent traumas?"

"No."

"Strange," the paramedic observed. "Your body is covered in bruises."

"I've no idea," Will sighed with his tongue still failing him.

"Don't worry," smiled the girl in a green uniform. "We're taking you to hospital."

"Can you feel this?" the man asked, touching Will's bare feet with a needle.

"Yes," Will chuckled. "It's ticklish."

"Can you move your toes?"

"Yes," Will attempted to nod. "I can move my arms and my feet. I'm fine. Can I go now?"

"Let the doctors decide if it's safe," the girl said. "You had a bout of seizures and lost consciousness for more than an hour. That's not normal. You'll need a few tests to find out what's going on with you."

"Okay, if that'll make you happy," Will mumbled.

Will's phone began ringing in his pocket.

"I have to pick it up," Will said but, in fact, he wasn't very enthusiastic about answering the call.

"Best, you don't move," the man stopped him. "You might have some internal damage."

"I could answer it for you if you trust me enough," the girl said.

"Go ahead," Will nodded. "Please…"

The girl took the phone out of his pocket.

"It says – mother," she announced and answered before

Will could manage to stop her.

Mother will be angry – Will did not doubt that. He watched the girl as she spoke on the phone and silently cursed. He had a big problem.

The girl hung up and put the phone back in his pocket.

"Your mother's really worried," the girl announced. "She's coming to the hospital."

"I bet she is," Will sighed. "But I think it's a lot of fuss about nothing. I'm fine. You better let me go before she arrives."

"You can't," the male nurse said with a serious expression. "Normal people don't blackout with seizures. You need some serious tests. Don't play the hero."

Will bit his lip and was silent for the rest of the way. The ambulance ceased its wailing and a few hundred yards later stopped in front of A&E.

"Don't move," the girl told him. "We'll wheel you out."

The clear blue sky flashed above him as the pair carefully lowered the trolley and rushed him inside the hospital.

"You're lucky," the male paramedic remarked. "This place is almost empty at this early hour."

"Don't move," warned the girl as she parked the trolley in the corridor. "We'll just go and book you in."

This was silly. Will felt fine, just a little tired. That's why he had fainted; he was sure. That crazy dream began to wear him out, but he was still happy to have some gateway from his otherwise dull everyday life. There was a sense of adventure in that dream. Will caught himself staring at the ceiling and thinking about Hel, how to break free from that cage and where to begin looking for that blue blossom, and who was Qu Sith?

The nurse wheeled him into a large room with fancy equipment and several beds lined along the perimeter and separated by pale green curtains. Another two nurses came to help her, and they checked the intravenous line before transferring Will into bed.

"Good luck," the male paramedic from the ambulance waved at him, wheeling his trolley away.

Will frowned as he gazed at the three junior doctors bustling around the bed, eager to begin with their examinations, and strengthening their collective knowledge by looking through the records that the ambulance crew had given them.

Then a seemingly endless interrogation followed. Will answered mainly in monosyllables, hoping that the torture would end at some point.

"He's a little drowsy, don't you think?" the girl with shiny black hair who was orchestrating the event addressed her colleagues.

"Are you sure you haven't hit your head?" the blonde girl asked, turning her full attention to the patient in the bed.

Will just wearily shook his head. He wasn't sure about anything. He simply needed some rest.

"Let's order a CT," the male junior offered from behind. "It's unwitnessed trauma and witnessed seizures. We need to investigate this."

"I'll go and fill the request form," the blonde girl nodded

and left.

The leading brunette returned to her questioning without even raising a brow. They measured his blood pressure, listened to his heart and lungs, and felt his belly. What they were looking for – Will wasn't sure. He felt fine.

"Radiology has approved it," the blonde girl beamed a victorious smile. "We only must check his blood in case they need contrast."

Finally, they stopped torturing Will with their silly questions and rushed out of the room to make the necessary arrangements. But the moment of peace was shortlived.

Another nurse came in with several packets and phials in her hands.

"We need another line for Radiology," she explained as she began digging at the veins in Will's right arm.

That was painful, but he didn't say a word. When the catheter was in, at last, she filled three phials with his blood.

"That goes to the lab," she explained marking the labels on the phials.

"Great," Will shrugged. "They'll find nothing. I'm fine."

"I'm sure you are," she grinned and left.

Will was left alone listening to the soft beeping of equipment around him. The place was unpleasant and alien, and he felt the urge to jump out of bed and run home. But he had tubes in his veins and that clear liquid dripping into his left arm. Will was afraid to touch the tube, afraid that he might bleed to death if the tube left a gap in his blood vessel. Nurses must have some proper technique for removing those tubes. Will was afraid to try.

The trio of juniors returned a few minutes later, and the peculiar interrogation continued. They checked his reflexes and looked at his tongue.

There was a short awkward pause, and several confused looks crossed between them when they finally ran out of options from their mental checklist and still hadn't arrived at any conclusion.

"Look at my pen!" the blonde junior doctor waved her pen in front of Will's nose in her very own lightbulb moment.

"No nystagmus," the black-haired girl observed calmly.

Will wasn't sure if that was a good or bad sign. He felt fine and just wanted to get out of this strange place as fast as he could.

"We're ready to go," the nurse announced, peeking in from the corridor.

The announcement created visible agitation as the junior doctors stepped aside, trying not to touch the tubes and wires as nurses took Will's bed and wheeled it into the corridor.

Will pulled the sheets up, covering his chest up to his chin, as his bed began a steady journey through the maze of hospital corridors. It was a long way, and the bright beams of luminescent light passing over his head from bulb to bulb hurt his eyes. Will closed them, feeling helpless. He only hoped that he would be able to run away as soon as they'd finish that damned examination. This place seemed frightening.

They came to a halt in front of a white door with a red

bulb glowing above it. Inside, something softly hummed.

A few minutes later the sound stopped, the door opened, and a guy in dark crimson scrubs wheeled out a skinny old lady who was hiding her bald head under a badly fitting wig and gazing at Will with her apathetic colourless eyes.

"Just a minute," the guy stopped the nurse who had already sprung into action and begun to push Will's bed inside the room.

He slipped back into the room where the machinery was and returned shortly with a few sheets of paper. The list of questions he asked wasn't long, but Will had already been worn out by the junior doctors and answered in short monosyllables and nods only. On a few occasions, he had no idea what the guy was talking about and merely shrugged.

The situation felt awkward.

The guy quickly finished his questions, wheeled Will into the room and helped him to get onto the scanner bed. The doughnut-shaped machine hummed softly behind him, shimmering with green and yellow lights. The guy in crimson silently messed with the lines and that silence made Will even more nervous. He cast a few glances around like a frightened bird, but there was no way to escape – he had to go through with this examination.

"Don't be afraid," the crimson-clad guy told him at last. "You'll just need to get into the machine a couple of times and then we'll be finished."

"I'm not afraid," Will said proudly, but barely believed his own words.

The guy smiled but did not comment. Will hoped that his anxiety wasn't too obvious, but the cheeky machine attached to the electrodes on his chest began to beep faster.

"Don't move," the guy said and left the room, closing the white door behind him.

Will could see him through the large window, busy behind several computer screens. Seconds grew into minutes, but nothing happened. Will frowned impatiently.

Finally, something softly clicked, and the doughnut-shaped machine began to hum at an increasing pitch while the table Will was laying on stirred into motion. The sensation was weird, as he moved a few times through the doughnut. Will tried to keep still, but his eyes flashed around like frightened bunnies.

"You might feel a little hot now," the guy told him through the speakers hidden somewhere inside the machine.

Shit! The line in his hand trembled with tension as streams of clear liquid poured into his vein. Now the doughnut-shaped machine sounded like a jet plane taking off, and Will shuddered as the table began to move again. Suddenly it grew unbearably hot. He squinted around trying not to move his head. *Was he on fire? Was he going to die?*

He felt a strange metallic taste in his mouth and the unbearable urge to pee. Then a flash of sickness passed as quickly as it had come, and the table moved out.

"All done," the guy in crimson said, appearing through the door.

"Have you found anything?" Will asked. It was a pointless question – he was perfectly fine; he was sure. They were wasting their time with him. "Can I go home now?"

"It's not up to me to decide," the guy said, busy disconnecting the lines. "The doctor will have a look at the images and will let you know."

That sounded complicated and would delay Will's freedom. He unhappily frowned as he transferred back to his bed.

Nurses wheeled the bed down the endless corridors again and delivered him back into the hands of the junior doctors.

"How do you feel?" the guy asked, checking his pulse, while the girls discussed something, paying little attention to anybody.

"I'm confused and have no idea why I'm still here," Will complained. "I feel perfectly well. You're wasting your time on me."

"We've nobody else here to waste our time on at the moment," the guy admitted with a smile. "It's sometimes good to have a healthy patient. Just for a change."

Will shrugged but managed to smile back.

"Ben is the name," the guy said, releasing Will's wrist. "How was that CT?"

"Scary," Will admitted. "It was sweltering when they flushed something inside me."

"Still feeling that heat?" Ben looked a little concerned.

"No," Will shook his head. "It passed quickly. I'm feeling fine now."

"I think we need to get more fluid into you to get that dye flushed out a bit quicker," Ben decided and left.

The girls were still mid discussion using an abundance of words which Will couldn't understand when the sounds of some turmoil reached them from the corridor.

"Where's my son Willy?" was the loud question demanding immediate attention. "I want to see him right now!"

Will bit his lip, expecting public humiliation – he had left the house ignoring his mother's request to stay in bed. Wasn't he big enough to make his own decisions?

"The doctors are examining him at the moment. You must wait," he heard a nurse's attempt to explain.

He knew perfectly well that this wouldn't stop his mother. Seconds later, she rushed wearing a very concerned look and eyes full of tears.

"Oh, Willy," she pushed the leading junior doctor aside and grabbed Will's hand. "Why don't you listen to your mother?.."

The question was a rhetoric accusation and required no answer. Will pulled his blanket up as if trying to hide. His mother touched his cheek lightly as she brushed her tears away. Then she turned her full attention on the junior doctors.

"What happened to my boy?" she asked, unceremoniously breaking into their discussion.

"I just fainted," Will muttered.

"He lost consciousness for over an hour and had several bouts of witnessed seizures," the leading junior doctor with black hair confidently translated Will's murmurs into that strange language of doctors. "We're investigating this."

His poor mother gasped, covering her mouth and looked back at Will.

"Willy? Why is that?" she demanded. "What happened?"

"Nothing, mum," Will shook his head. "I only wanted to go for a bit of a stretch after that nightmare. You were still asleep when I left, and I didn't want to wake you up."

The blonde junior doctor quickly marked something in her notes.

Unexpectedly, the room began to shake, and Will looked around in surprise. Nobody else seemed to notice this, as junior the doctors were still quietly discussing something, and his mother was holding his hand. Will could even see a nurse in the corridor sipping coffee from a paper cup.

Then the room blurred and darkened. And it wasn't a room anymore.

❧❀❧

Will was back in his cage, and the ground around him was shaking.

"What's that?" he asked, frightened.

"The late evening show," a quiet voice from the neighbouring cage said with a yawn.

The dusk was still and windless, but a low rumbling sound filled the place as the ground continued its crazy dance. The waters of the lake in front of the cages hissed with angry steams and splashed in random ripples.

Will grasped the bars trying to take a better look. The sky was dark, covered with low clouds. Far to the right, their bellies were painted red by the fiery flow. The woods surrounding the area were black.

Distant fires flickered on the other side of the lake, and their reflections seemed like a tremulous bloodied path across the raging waters. Invisible drums beat insane rhythm, and strange shapes danced around those fires, casting long shadows across the water. The cage was still vibrating, and sometimes it seemed that those shadows were dancing their way across the lake on the path of red reflections. It was just an illusion; Will was sure about that.

The beat was hypnotic, and soon Will's heart raced in unison with the drums as he looked at the shadows dancing across the troubled water. Then unexpectedly everything ceased – the drums, the dancers and the ground tremors. The surface of the water cleared with the reflections of distant flames playing upon it with silver shadows. Will looked up – there was a rip in the clouds just above the lake where the silver globe glanced through the gap.

"I'd advise you to move away from those bars," Qu Sith observed.

"Why?" Will glanced at the shadows in the neighbouring cage but was still unable to make out the silhouette of the creature.

"Just do it... Now! Hurry up!"

There was a note of terror in the voice of Qu Sith, and Will rushed to the back wall of his cage. The night was still and silent with the reflections from distant fires mixing with silver flickers on the tranquil surface of the dark lake as a few ripples hit the shores. Nothing else was happening.

"Why..." Will began to complain, but his voice was interrupted by a sudden rumble in the depths of the lake.

The surface remained still for only one more moment as a monstrous column of boiling water and steam erupted from the depths with such a blast, reaching high into the gap between the clouds and obscuring the silver face of the celestial globe.

"Shield your eyes!" Qu Sith hissed. "Some of that water

will come down on you!"

Will curled away at the far end of his cage, burying his face in his hands, waiting. He heard the distant sound of drums through the deafening roar of the stream, whose direction had now reversed and boiling water was pouring back into the lake. Hot showers hit the cage in waves. Luckily, the rear section of the cage had a shelter built from dry branches and leaves which deflected most of the hit, but the front of it became soaked with boiling water.

This lasted for only a few seconds, but it seemed like an eternity to Will. Several heartbeats later he was abruptly hit by deafening silence – all sounds ceased, except for occasional drops softly splashing onto the sand below the cage.

Will's heart still raced like crazy. He closed his eyes, trying to calm it down – the danger seemed to be over. Strangely, moments later the insane lub-dub, lub-dub in his chest was quietly joined by a high-pitched electronic beeping.

"Did you hear that?" he asked Qu Sith, but the creature wasn't there.

❧ ❦ ❁ ❦ ☙

"He's back," a loud female voice announced.

Will glanced around – he wasn't in the cage anymore. Two concerned nurses and a senior consultant were staring at him. His mother and the junior doctors were quietly talking at a distance. Will looked at his body with wires and tubes strapped everywhere and sighed – this was no better than the cage in his dream. Again he felt trapped.

"How are you feeling, young man?" the consultant asked.

"Strange," Will replied without thinking.

His mother rushed back to his bedside.

"What happened? Can I go home now?" Will demanded.

"You had another seizure," the consultant explained. "I'd like to keep you in for a while. We need to find out what's wrong with you."

"I'm fine," only Will's assertion didn't sound so certain this time.

"Let's make sure that you are," the consultant replied

seriously. He left, heading to the corridor, shuffling some papers on his way. The junior doctors stormed out after him, leaving Will entirely in the hands of the nurses.

"You frightened everybody, Willy," his mother grabbed his hand with tears in her eyes. "Was it painful?"

Will's gaze wandered around, still in confusion. There must be some mistake, some misunderstanding. It was only a dream… He felt perfectly healthy.

But, for the first time, that dream began to frighten him. It had flooded his mind in broad daylight twice now without any warning, taking him out on the way. That must have some scientific or medical explanation, but Will wasn't ready to discuss it with anybody. If the doctors had some way out to stop that dreaming, he wasn't prepared to take it. He still hoped for Hel's forgiveness. He must find her blue orchid.

"Willy?"

He only then realised that his mother was still waiting for his answer.

"No, mum," he shook his head. "I feel no pain. I think I'm perfectly healthy. I just need some rest."

"You were unable to rest at home, Willy, but now you'll have the perfect chance to rest here," his mother still looked worried as she held his hand. "Remember what the doctor said? They'll find out what's wrong with you and fix you in no time."

"I don't think it's necessary…" Will began protesting. "I don't need any fixing."

"Willy!" the mother interrupted his moaning. "Don't you dare contradict the doctors. They know better. You're staying here. Is this clear?"

"Yes, mum…" Will felt humiliated, but he knew that any further arguments would only bring further embarrassment.

Several cries from the corridor suddenly ignited another turmoil. Everybody rushed outside, leaving Will connected to the beeping machines and his mother clutching his hand.

Minutes later, the commotion rushed into the room as somebody loudly moaning was wheeled in on a trolley. Will pulled his blanket up and silently watched all the running and shouting. They moved the trolley past him to the far right side of the room where strange machinery lined the wall. Moments later, the nurses drew the curtain, blocking themselves and that sick moaning person from Will's view.

They watched nurses rush back and forth with bags of blood and clear liquid, bringing tubes, syringes and more equipment to the screened-off corner. Something terribly wrong was going on there as the turmoil intensified and the moans waned.

"Oh, God," Will's mother gasped. "Somebody's dying!"

"Everything will be fine," Will reassured her, staring at the green curtain. "This is a hospital, isn't it? They'll fix it."

His mother clutched his hand. "I'm so afraid for you, Willy…" she whispered suddenly looking very fragile.

"That's ridiculous," he attempted to grin and ease the tension. "I'm not dying. I'm perfectly healthy, mum. Don't worry. We could go home right now."

She squeezed his hand.

"You scared me, Willy," she was looking away. "I can't

even think about losing you. Let's get everything checked as the doctors said. Promise me; you'll have all the tests which doctors think are necessary. This is very serious, son."

"They'll find nothing," Will mumbled.

"Just do it," she cut him short firmly.

They were interrupted by two guys in green uniforms who casually released the brakes of Will's bed and began wheeling him towards the corridor.

"Where are you taking him?" Will suddenly sensed a rising panic in his mother's voice.

"To the Cheerful Sparrows," said one of the guys.

"Are you kidding me?" his mother grabbed the side of the bed, stopping them.

"No, ma'am," one of the porters shook his head with a serious expression. "It's the real name of the ward, and in my humble opinion, I think they should rename it. We have to explain it every time."

They slipped out, leaving the monitors displaying flat lines, frantic electronic beeping and the subsiding turmoil behind.

The porters navigated Will's bed through the long maze of corridors in silence with his mother following them a few steps behind.

"Where are these Cheerful Sparrows then?" she asked impatiently.

"Top floor," said one of the guys stopping in front of the lift.

"Closer to God," mumbled the other, pushing the bed inside the lift.

They covered the rest of the way without another word. Will felt trapped. He closed his eyes and surrendered to the hectic flow of events. What else could he do? He knew his mother wouldn't let him out of that bed without having had those stupid tests.

"Are you okay?" his mother gently touched his fingers while the porters chatted casually to the nurses in the ward. "You look pale..."

"I'm fine, mum," Will looked at her just briefly. He knew that any discussions or arguments would be useless.

The place was spacious, with six beds lined up against the walls and a large window on the left. All the beds were empty. He kept his eyes closed as the nurses steered him to the bed at the side of the window. Will couldn't bear the situation that was unfolding around him. Everyone was pretending that he was extremely ill, but the comedy had already gone too far. He was in the hospital! *Why?*

Will silently stretched his muscles and then slowly relaxed a few seconds later. It felt normal. What was all the fuss about?

He opened his eyes just in time to see the nurses leaving. His mother was staring at him, and Will instantly realised that he must pass through all this hell before he was able to regain his freedom.

"I'm fine, mother," he attempted a small smile. "You don't need to worry."

"I'll stop worrying when your doctors say so," her gaze was tight. "You're frightening me, Willy."

"They'll kick me out before lunch, I'm sure," he

shrugged. "I'm not their man. I'm feeling perfectly healthy."

"Then why are those things happening to you?" she came closer, gently touching his hand. "I'm so afraid of losing you, Willy. You're hiding something, I know it. I can feel it. Please, tell your mother."

"You don't need to worry..." Will repeated with a fading smile. "I'm not hiding anything."

His mother shook her head, disbelief still in her eyes.

"I have to go now," she said, still holding his hand. "I need to take care of your sister too. But I'll check on you later. Promise me, Willy, you'll do all those tests the doctors think necessary. Promise me, you won't say no to anything they might request."

"I'll do whatever's necessary to prove I'm healthy," Will nodded. "I hope they find that out pretty quickly."

"I'll be back this afternoon," his mother released his hand.

"I'll be fine," Will assured her. "I'll call you if they decide to kick me out sooner."

"Don't rush things, Willy," she warned him. "I'll see you later."

He looked after her, suddenly feeling lonely and abandoned, caught up in a silly misunderstanding. The only hope was that it wouldn't last long. There wasn't too much for a healthy young man to do in a hospital bed.

Soothed by the thought, Will turned his gaze to outside the window. Out there people were going about their business unaware of somebody looking across their rooftops. Will followed a few lonely birds passing the blue sky in the distance. Everything was peaceful and quiet, and he smiled, forgetting his problems just for a brief moment. He would be able to get through all this mess, he was certain.

An hour or two passed merely gazing out the window.

The ward was filling up with sick people, but Will barely noticed this as his imagination still wandered around the cage in his dream. *How to get out? How to find that missing orchid? What kind of a creature was sitting in the cage next to him?*

"How do you feel?" the question woke Will from his semi-dreaming. One of the junior doctors stood at the foot of his bed. *What was his name? Ben?*

"I'm feeling great," Will flashed a tight smile with bare irony in his voice. "I don't understand what I'm doing there."

"No need to be sarcastic," Ben said softly. "They're trying to help you. Normal healthy people don't drop to the ground with seizures."

"Did the consultant send you to spy on me?" Will mumbled glancing through the window again.

"No. Nobody knows I'm here," Ben admitted. "It's my free time, and I've decided to check how you're doing instead of devouring my lunch."

"That's some sacrifice. Why?"

Ben seemed lost with that simple question.

"Could I take a seat?" he asked, indicating the chair next to Will's bed. "I won't annoy you with any examinations, I promise. But I'd like just to ask a few questions if you don't mind."

Will rolled his eyes – more questioning!

"And then you'll get an excuse to keep me here," he spat disdainfully, but that didn't seem to affect the determination of Ben. The young doctor moved closer and took a seat.

"What is it?" Will's voice sounded impatient.

Ben looked at him intensely before answering.

"I watched your last seizures – they were quite unusual, not like any ordinary *grand mal*," he said softly at last. "I've seen that type of seizure before with another person, and I know the exact cause of them. Your situation might be similar if the cause is the same."

"And you're now trying to outsmart the others, aren't you?" Will looked at the guy, frowning.

"No, not at all," Ben ignored Will's gaze and whispered. "I'd like to help you. I think you're in danger."

"I'm in the hospital," Will chuckled. "What kind of danger could be here?"

Ben's face reddened. The question made the young doctor look at his shoes trying to hide a wave of embarrassment and Will suddenly felt sorry for the guy – he had said he wanted to help.

"What is it you wanted?" Will demanded in a more gentle voice.

Ben looked Will in the eyes before answering.

"You mentioned some nightmares," he said. "I want to know more about those nightmares."

"Forget it," Will shook his head. "I've got nothing to tell."

"It's not for the papers," Ben calmly reassured him. "This won't go on your medical records or affect you in any way."

"No!"

Ben stared at him for a few seconds. The guy was clearly hesitating.

"I'll try to help you anyway," he whispered at last. "I just need to be sure that you're the right person. May I have another look at your tattoo?"

"Well, you promised there would be no any examination, but if you insist…" Will couldn't think of any quick way to get the young man to go away and simply lifted his T-shirt.

Ben looked closely at the image without touching it.

"It's not complete," he concluded at last.

"*What?!*"

"It's missing a few large cliffs on the left and, a little further, a gaping cave surrounded by silver grass," Ben whispered before casting a few glances around at the other occupied beds in the ward. "The castle is missing as well, and there should be a line of dark knights at the foot of the volcano if Hel is at home. Am I right?"

Will gasped suddenly feeling dizzy. *How did he know that?*

"Is this some kind of a trick?" Will's tongue felt numb as he asked this.

"No," Ben kept his face straight. "Is this the nightmare you keep seeing every night? Did it drag you in during those fits too?"

Will silently nodded, keeping his eyes on the young man. *How could Ben know about his dreams?* The thought was silly, and Will nearly burst into laughter in an attempt to hide his embarrassment.

"Did that humming doughnut-shaped machine show that?" Will asked.

"No. It's nothing to do with the CT," Ben kept his voice low. "But I knew when I saw your tattoo and your seizure. Are you in some kind of trouble in that nightmare? It seems that your dream is slipping out of control."

"It's only a dream," Will attempted to wave it away. He felt strange discussing it, but Ben was persistent.

"It isn't," Ben's soft voice again dropped to whisper, but his face remained serious. "Your mind transfers to that world at night. It's real. I must warn you that if you die in that world, you'll be dead here as well."

Will pulled his sheets up suddenly feeling a wave of chill. *This guy wasn't serious, was he? How was that possible?* Ben's statement sounded ridiculous, but the dream indeed was strange – too real to be waved away as nonsense. *Was Ben right indeed?*

"I don't understand..." Will kept shaking his head. "You're kidding me. But how you know about my dreams?"

"I don't know about your dreams," Ben admitted. "But I know about the world your mind is visiting. It's a dangerous place, and I thought to warn you, despite it being strictly forbidden for us to interfere."

"Us?" Will popped his eyes. "Have you told someone else about that dream?"

"No, of course, not!" Ben's eyes flashed with anger at the implication.

"Good…" Will sighed with visible relief. "Keep it secret, please. I'm not ready to be cured and give up that dream yet. I need to speak with Hel."

"You don't understand," Ben whispered, casting a careful glance into the corridor again. "There is no cure. You can't stop visiting that world until you die – either in that world or here. There's no way out!"

"Excellent!" Will exclaimed grinning. "I like that state of affairs. It's kind of entertaining."

Ben sighed, but his eyes flashed his firm intention to get the message through.

"You don't understand how dangerous it is," he insisted, looking directly into Will's eyes. "If you get hurt in that world, your body here suffers the same injury as well. It's very serious. The cycles alternate most of the time seamlessly, but when that world drags you back during the daytime here, it usually means you're in trouble there. Are you in trouble? I can't interfere, and you must find the way out by yourself. Being in the hospital might help, giving you some flexibility, use it wisely. You're in a dangerous place there. Don't get yourself killed."

"It's only a dream," Will began, waving the thought away. The things Ben was implying sounded absurd.

"No, it isn't," Ben repeated firmly. "I can't believe you haven't realised that yet. Look at those scratches and bruises on your body – you can't get any like those in a gym. There is trouble on the other side, and it is not a dream. Regard it as a warning, or you'll find that out the hard way. It might be too late then. Never take safety for granted, even here. Your place is not here. You must find the Sanctuary. Until then, your life is in great danger."

"How do you know all this?" Will asked, hiding his confusion behind a silly smile. "Where is that Sanctuary?"

"We're involved in this," Ben whispered. "I've never been to that world, but I knew someone who had. That's how I know. And I've no idea where that Sanctuary is. You need to find out. It's the only safe place for you."

"You're tricking me, aren't you? It's some of that fancy equipment you use, isn't it? Where are those girls? They can come in now and laugh at me."

"No," Ben patiently shook his head again. "It's nothing to do with the hospital. Just stay away from any danger, and you'll get back to normal and out of the hospital. If you keep getting into trouble, our consultants will want to investigate the physical manifestations, and that'll keep you in a hospital bed. Is that clear?"

The question hung in the air as Will stared at the young doctor still unable to believe his words. *Did that mean that Hel was a real person?*

"Am I healthy?" Will managed to ask at last.

"You are," Ben acknowledged hesitantly. "But you'll have to pass all the tests to prove that before you'll be able to leave the hospital. I'm sorry about your situation. You're in the most precarious part of that world, and you must learn quickly. Just keep away from anything dangerous and learn to survive. Remember, that world *is* real."

Will stared at Ben with evident mistrust in his gaze, but the guy knew too much about that peculiar dream. *Could he be right?*

"Where did you got that tattoo inked?" Ben asked. "I suppose you began your visits shortly after that?"

"Visits?"

"Dreaming," Ben explained patiently with a serious expression.

"No, it wasn't immediately," Will mumbled. "I couldn't sleep the night after I had it inked."

"I see..." Ben's gaze wandered away for a moment. "Where you got that tattoo?"

"It was at Custom Tattoo & Piercings," Will shrugged. "But it's closed now. I didn't even get to thank the man properly."

"We'll investigate this," Ben said quietly still looking away.

"We?"

Then Ben slowly turned his head to face Will with his gaze suddenly empty and unfocused.

"We?" Will demanded.

The young doctor remained silent for more than two full minutes. His face was expressionless, and his eyes were fixed on Will.

"Are you okay?" Will asked carefully, drawing the blanket to his chin.

Another minute passed before Ben answered.

"Sorry about that," he said as his face regained its agility.

"What was that?" Will asked unsure how to react.

"A long-distance call," Ben was clearly embarrassed, but his answer explained nothing.

"I didn't see any phone," Will observed dryly.

Ben shrugged with a quick smile.

"I must go now," he said, standing up. "I'll catch up with you later if I can. Be careful and don't do anything stupid if you want to outlive your mother. Be careful."

Will said nothing, just followed Ben with his gaze until he disappeared into the corridor. The guy was weird and talking daft, but Will couldn't get rid of the memory of Ben's empty gaze staring into his face. It was scary.

"It's a dream. It's only a dream," he repeated several times bluntly but couldn't force the strange guy from his mind.

The day was busy. Nurses and junior doctors rushed around like angry ants, coming to his bedside with their questions, examinations and tests more often than to the other beds in the ward. Several times the self-important faces of consultants glanced in his direction too, giving short orders to their entourage of juniors while moving along the other beds with sick people. Will was given something to eat and to drink but had to bring back samples of his pee and stools from the loo in return.

Ben had said that Will was healthy, he just had to prove this, but the process of substantiation was lengthy and irksome, and Will had to suppress his temper more than once to carry on. During those brief moments when he was left alone, Will kept thinking about that strange young doctor. Ben said he was telling the truth, but it was a weird truth he could scarcely believe. How could he know about those bizarre dreams? *It must be that machine that had hummed around his head; it must have shown the pictures* – Will decided. There was no other explanation. And the guy was playing jokes on him, probably secretly laughing somewhere around the corner – Will was certain about that too.

He was angry to have let him hook him in so easily. He felt like a fool.

The day slowly turned into a lazy afternoon, and Will gazed through the window again at the red rooftops drowning in the crowns of dark green trees. All life was teeming out there, but he remained stuck in his bed, unable even to have a glimpse outside. He had been taken to the hospital by mistake, Will was sure, now he had to prove that in every step of his way out.

"How are you, Willy?" the question shook him out of his daydream.

"I'm fine, mum," he answered, bravely meeting her worried eyes. "You don't need to babysit me."

"I know you, you're a little bastard," she managed a small smile. "You'll sneak away as soon as you're left alone and will get into trouble somewhere."

"No, mum," Will smiled back. "You know that won't happen. I've promised to prove to you that I'm healthy. Those doctors just need to do some tests, and I'll be out in no time. You don't need to worry."

"A mum's job is to worry about her kids. Have you had any more of those fits?" she asked, getting closer.

"No," Will's smile waned. "And I'm not lying, mum. I only want to get home."

His mother took a seat in front of him. Will looked through the window expecting a long list of accusations to be addressed to him, blaming him for things that had led to his current miserable position in a hospital bed, but it didn't happen. His mother stared silently at him with a sad smile, saying nothing.

"How was your day at home?" Will asked, trying to lift her mood.

She responded in a quiet voice as if waking from some absentmindedness. This was unusual, but Will was afraid to ask anything else, letting her go with the flow and listened to how she had spent time preparing breakfast for his sister, then did a bit of cleaning, drank some cups of tea and waited for his sister to come home from school. Will listened to her voice until it trailed off and fell silent.

"Oh, Willy," his mother shook her head, suddenly turning her wet eyes away. "You're frightening me. I hope the doctors don't find anything serious."

"They won't," Will told her firmly.

For the first time, Will noticed the tiredness in her face, poorly hidden behind the nervous smile.

"I'm perfectly healthy, mum," he mumbled, taking her hand. "You don't need to worry. Those doctors can do whatever tests they like. They'll find nothing. You don't need to visit me, mum. I'm a big boy and can take care of myself. You have more important things to do than look at your lazy son playing sick in a hospital bed."

She wiped her tears away and quickly nodded as she stood up.

"I need to go," the mother said. "I have to keep an eye on your sister."

She leaned forward and quickly kissed his forehead.

"Don't worry about me," Will said, embarrassed by the kiss. He hoped nobody had seen it.

She hurried out without casting another glance at him. Someone quietly moaned a few beds away, but the dark green curtains barred the view. Will could see the nurses going behind those curtains and then hurrying away with tubes and basins in their hands. The scene was disturbing, and Will rolled onto his side, turning all attention to the rooftops outside the window.

Later in the evening, the moaning stopped, and all the turmoil subsided. Will kept his eyes on the rooftops with stubborn persistence, until the night consumed the city, spitting out the ghostly yellow lights of the streetlamps shaded by the trees. His mind wandered away with the darkness a few moments later.

⁂

He was back in the cage. No wonder – the dream was still the same.

It was a quiet morning with strands of fog slowly rising from the still surface of the Lifeless Pond. The other side of the Pond disappeared in the greenery beyond with several straw rooftops poking through the crowns of the trees. It was quiet there, as well.

Then he remembered Qu Sith and glanced at the cage on his left. The creature didn't move, but Will flinched, gasping. Its dark body was nearly twice as big as Will's – massive with bulging muscles underneath black skin that was covered with short fur. The figure resembled an overgrown lion with four muscular limbs and clawed paws resting on the ground and a tail that ended with a tuft of black hair. Qu Sith was looking directly in front of him. His face was dark but with human features that had a long mane of black hair and a black beard framing it.

"Who are you?" Will asked with a failing tongue.

The creature turned his head to face him.

"I told you my name yesterday, but I guess you're not interested in my name. It seems you've never seen a sphinx before," Qu Sith said, a smile exposing his pointed fangs. His black eyes lacked any whites, which made his gaze uncomfortable and eerie.

"No," admitted Will. He hadn't even noticed when he had backed as far as he could until the bars of the cage stopped him.

Qu Sith chuckled.

"Don't be afraid. I won't hurt you," the beast said, still looking at Will. "But don't get too fond of me either. We'll fight to the death in a few months."

"No, no, no… That's crazy," Will shaking his head in disbelief. "That can't be the truth. I'm just dreaming."

"No," said Qu Sith turning his black eyes back to the Pond in front of the cages. "It's not a dream. And our breakfast is coming."

Will followed his gaze. The thin fog rose above the still water, and he had trouble spotting the two dark figures at first. They slowly moved along the shore, both dressed in long black cloaks that covered their entire bodies. Their faces were hidden behind those bizarre red and brown masks, and it was impossible to tell if they were men or women.

"Sit still, don't speak and don't move," Qu Sith whispered, observing the Pond. "Or they'll go without leaving any food."

Will backed to the far end of the cage and sat down on the straw den keeping his eyes on the approaching silhouettes. Indeed, they were carrying trays plaited out of thin willow branches and lined with broad leaves. The morning was quiet, and the figures moved silently like two ghosts among the thinning strands of fog.

They stopped in front of the cages.

Will quickly glanced at the neighbouring enclosure. Qu Sith was silent, and not a muscle moved in the body of the sphinx as one of the figures stepped forward and pushed the tray through the slit in the bars. The other cloaked shape stopped reluctantly, having most likely spotted the movement of Will's head. A few seconds passed, and then Will lost his patience.

"Please, let me out," he moved closer to the bars, begging. "I need to find that damned flower!"

A pair of grey eyes calmly observed him through the slit in the mask as the figure backed a few paces and put the tray on the ground.

"Please..." Will whispered.

The pair that brought the food turned around silently and returned to the village the same way they had come – along the shoreline of the Pond. Will's tray remained on the ground several paces away from the cage, and he could only look at the three carved pumpkins that lined the tray as his hungry stomach already gurgled loud protests.

"I warned you," Qu Sith observed, getting closer to his food.

"Damn!" Will helplessly cursed as he watched the sphinx burying his face into one of the pumpkins. "That's not fair."

"Life isn't fair," Qu Sith mumbled, chewing. "I can't

help you with the food, and it's entirely your fault that you're starving hungry. They'll come again at dusk, and you'll get a chance to eat if you're wise enough to keep still and silent."

"What's in there?" Will asked, watching the sphinx devouring the contents of the pumpkin.

"Nothing fancy," Qu Sith sighed. "It's just mashed parsnips with some strange roots. No meat. Not even a dead mouse! But it's filling. Anyway, it's a pity you decided to skip the meal."

Will rattled the bars screaming with rage, but this didn't change anything – he remained locked in, and his breakfast teased him from just several paces away, unreachable.

"That won't help either," the sphinx calmly observed. "They might decide to starve us both if you get too noisy."

"Why are they so obsessed with this?" Will asked in a quiet voice.

"It's their religion," Qu Sith explained, burying his face in the last pumpkin. "For six months, the Rybbaths can't let make a single sound, even if they're dying or suffering. They starve themselves, only briefly breaking the fast each night with the first rays of light from Wyrna. And they don't even do that on cloudy nights when the light can't reach them to bless their food."

"Silly people," Will grunted with disdain.

"No," Qu Sith said, finally lifting his head from the pumpkins and sitting down again. "Not silly. Rybbaths have a very strong faith and an iron will. This is why we're here. Our death will allow them to celebrate their faith and their will. They will eat the loser as a gift from Gods and will sacrifice the winner to Gods in the Lifeless Pond."

This was a chilling observation, but it couldn't be true. Will shook his head in disbelief. It was only a dream – *his dream!* It must play by his rules too! That cage was just a silly obstacle that he must find a way out. There was a way, Will was sure. He must find it even if the dream resisted his efforts.

"Are they going to force us to fight? What if we refuse?" Will asked.

"Then they will sacrifice both of us to their God," Qu Sith sighed. "We'd then be boiled alive in that scalding water. I'd prefer to die in a fight and on land."

"I'd prefer not to die at all," Will mumbled, sitting down on the floor.

"That's not an option in our situation, I'm afraid," the sphinx glanced at Will with his black eyes. "These cages are too well built. We can't escape. We'll have to fight, and I hope you succeed in killing me."

"Why do you say that?"

"I can't swim, and sphinxes are terrified of water," Qu Sith looked at the Pond again, but Will couldn't read the expression on his face. "I'd rather die on land."

"Do you want me to kill you?" Will gasped.

"Yes," Qu Sith said calmly. "I'll jump around a bit to keep the Rybbaths excited, but won't move a muscle if you begin to cut my throat."

"The water can't be *that* bad," Will shrugged looking at the slight ripples on the calm surface.

"Yes, it can," the beast didn't move as he spoke. "You saw the geyser eruption yesterday. There won't be a single bit of meat left on your bones when that scalding water passes through your body. Face reality."

"It's not reality," Will shook his head with a laugh. "It's a bad dream. It's a nightmare, and I can't wait to wake up."

"Why do you keep saying that?" Qu Sith wondered.

"Isn't it obvious?" Will spat the words at him. "I can't think of a more ridiculous situation. I'm forced to sit in this stupid cage and wait until those stupid starving people make me kill a sphinx. I don't have time for this!"

"Don't rush things, my friend," Qu Sith observed. "You've missed the point that you'll soon dead too, straight after you've finished killing me. Yes, I agree; the situation is pitiful. We're both too young to die."

Will cursed loudly looking at his breakfast still steaming on the ground outside the cage and rattled the bars a few more times with all his might. The wood didn't even crack.

"It's useless. I told you that already," the black eyes of the sphinx looked at him without compassion. "We have no way out. We must concede to the circumstances and die with dignity."

"That's not an option!" Will cut in impatiently.

Qu Sith only shrugged and kept staring at the water. The fog cleared, and Will could see some figures slowly moving on the other side of the Pond, but the light morning breeze didn't bring any sounds or odours. No smoke rose from the chimneys he could see peeking above the tree crowns. It was a strange place, indeed.

"You mentioned a flower. You need that flower for a woman?" asked Qu Sith, still watching the water. "Was that the reason that brought you to this perilous place, and the reason why you ended up in this cage?"

"Yes," Will admitted. "It's her flower I'm looking for."

Qu Sith chuckled.

"What's so funny about that?" Will frowned.

"I've always been amused by the strange mating rituals humans have," the sphinx said grinning. "Do they work?"

"What do you mean?" Will frowned as the sphinx's question sounded strange. Was the beast trying to make fun of him?

"Well..." Qu Sith took his eyes off the Pond at last. "Those rituals might seem strange to an outsider. I'd like to get an insider's opinion. You have to give her flowers if you're trying to mate with her, do you?"

Will shrugged but slowly nodded.

"You go and collect the best plant genitals you can find. Does that make her excited?" the sphinx seemed genuinely curious. "Have you tried animal genitals? Would that work better?"

"That's disgusting!" Will cut him. "You've got it all wrong."

"Which part of it is wrong?" asked Qu Sith. "You're not giving her the roots or leaves, are you? It's only the blossoms that work. Which plants work best? Have you tried to get her excited with animal genitals?"

"Stop it!"

"Are you going to kill me in ignorance?" Qu Sith

narrowed his eyes.

"Shut up, or I'll leave your death to that water!" Will cried out, pointing at the Lifeless Pond. "It's nothing like that. She's different. It was her who gave me the blossom, and I lost it."

"I understand," the sphinx sighed and turned to face the water again. "She got mad at you because you lost the flower so couldn't get excited. I never thought that a female could initiate the rituals."

"Don't you dare to speak that way about her!" Will exploded. "You don't know her!"

The sphinx flashed a glance at him and then turned to face the Pond.

"Of course, I don't," Qu Sith said quietly. "I've never been interested in human females. Can you stop shouting? The Rybbaths might leave us without any food if they hear you. Two months is a long time…"

Will's face grew red, but he managed to hold back his temper. He followed the sphinx's gaze across the water and gasped. Several dark figures stood on the distant shore of the Pond gazing at them or maybe listening.

"Sit down," Qu Sith squeezed through his teeth quietly. "Don't do another blasphemy."

Will carefully lowered himself onto the straw den. The morning was still, and his shouts had probably heard across the village. He bit his lip – two months of starvation was indeed a long time.

Will sighed with relief when the figures finally turned around and returned to the village. "It was a stupid idea to shout," he admitted. "We're lucky they've gone."

Qu Sith cast a fierce glance at him.

"We'll only know about our luck this evening," he spat out. "It will be entirely your fault if we're forced to live our last days eating flies and cockroaches."

"I'm sorry," Will apologised. "I hope they'll bring your supper."

The sphinx turned to gaze at the water again without saying another word. Will watched the Pond too as the sun was slowly climbed towards its zenith. It was a kind of small torture. With too many things waiting to be done and little hope of seeing Hel again, Will was pinned to the straw den like those strange insects are pinned to dark velvet in museum displays, feeling utterly helpless.

"I can't just sit here," he complained. "I must find that blue orchid."

"What orchid?" the sphinx didn't bother to take his eyes away from the Pond.

"The one Hel gave me," Will explained.

"Hel? *That* Hel?" whispered Qu Sith.

"Yes," Will nodded. "The one who lives in the castle on the slope of that volcano."

The sphinx was silent for too long.

"Well..." Qu Sith said at last. "Then you have a very good reason to break free, but that won't impress the Rybbaths, I'm afraid. They need a contestant to sacrifice, and they don't care if that contestant is on an important mission or not."

Will stood up and went closer to the bars looking at the

black eyes of the sphinx. Qu Sith returned his gaze calmly, keeping his face expressionless.

"We need to find a way to break free from this insanity," Will said.

"We're in separate cages," Qu Sith reminded him.

"But we can still act together in coordination," Will said with a persistence that was unusual for him. "I'll free you if I manage to somehow get out."

"And I'll do the same…" Qu Sith let the sentence trail off with a small smile playing on his lips.

They looked at each other for a few moments smiling like two kids. Then Qu Sith became serious again.

"We'll need a miracle to break free," he observed, looking at Will. "Do you have any powerful magic artefact or a secret army lurking in the bushes and ready to save you?"

"No," admitted Will. "But we'll find the way. Let's keep thinking."

"I can't share your hopeless optimism," Qu Sith turned his face away, fixing his eyes on the Pond again.

"We've nothing else to share," Will insisted. "Only a hope that this nightmare will end and we'll wake up before we're forced to fight."

"It's not a nightmare, may I remind you," the sphinx said without changing his posture. "You can't wake up from reality."

"It *is* a nightmare," Will mumbled, not so sure this time as he sat down and leant against the bars.

Qu Sith couldn't be right. He was just a creature of a

dream, the same as that pond and the village of Rybbaths with their religion, fasting and the crazy festival in two months. *Was it?* The doubt was disturbing, and Will shut his eyes firmly, ordering his mind to change direction and plunge into something peaceful. A few minutes later, the bittersweet odour of decaying flesh hit his nostrils, and Will opened his eyes.

Nothing had changed.

The pond still leaked thinning strands of fog, and the bars barred him from his breakfast. And the sphinx in the cage next to his own still was calmly observing the village of Rybbaths on the other side of the Lifeless Pond.

The light breeze brought another wave of that foul odour, and Will nearly choked as his stomach churned in convulsions splashing acid into the back of his throat.

"Move closer to the front," Qu Sith advised calmly. "That might help a little."

"What is that smell?" asked Will, crawling forward.

"We're in the burial grounds, my friend," Qu Sith said with a sad note in his voice. "The Rybbaths regard us as half dead. And we will be dead in fifty-nine days unless you will find that magical solution to get us out of here."

"Burial grounds?" Will squeezed through his teeth, suppressing another wave of nausea building in his guts.

Qu Sith chuckled. The odour didn't affect him.

"Take a closer look at that greenery behind your cage," the sphinx uttered. "Do you think they're shrubs?"

Will looked back, frowning. Several rows of green broad-leaved shrubs were lined behind their cages, and the dark wall of the forest was a few hundred paces away. A wooden pole peeked out through each of them – this didn't seem surprising to Will. Some of the shrubs were scattered with dark crimson blossoms, and some were just a dull green. It looked like just another greenery planted by the villagers, but something didn't feel quite right. The smell and buzzing flies added a macabre tone to that eerie sensation, and Will again gulped down the rising acid when he spotted a human palm protruding through the leaves of one of the shrubs.

"Why don't they bury their dead properly?" he managed to ask.

"This is the proper way for the Rybbaths," Qu Sith explained. "Don't worry, whatever remains of us after that combat and sacrifice will be buried in exactly the same way. There are a few empty spots closer to the forest."

"Why do they do that?"

"It's their *religion*," Qu Sith said disdainfully. "They believe a soul would suffocate forever if the body were covered with earth. So instead they tie their deceased to a pole and plant a few suckle vines around it."

"How do you know this?" asked Will, still having trouble settling his stomach down.

"I saw a funeral here a week ago," the sphinx told him. "The palm of that poor woman is still sticking out through the vines, and I saw her jaw fall off only yesterday. She's the one making that smell, but it will stop in another week or two. Now you can only hope that the wind changes direction."

"That's disgusting."

"Indeed, it is," Qu Sith agreed without changing his posture.

They were silent for most of the day. Either the wind had changed, or Will had got used to the smell as it wasn't bothering him quite so much. He glanced a few more times at the palm sticking out through the leaves as a grim reminder of their fate but didn't say anything. Qu Sith was silently observing the calm surface of the water and the Rybbathan village across the Pond. That drove Will insane because nothing at all changed in the scenery and staring across the water seemed pointless. But he couldn't find any topic for another chat either.

Will carefully inspected the perimeter of his cage, testing every bar and every joint. Everything was rigid and didn't move one bit, no matter how vigorously Will shook them. Qu Sith squinted at his efforts a couple of time but didn't say a word.

Will fussed around his cage until he felt entirely exhausted and dropped down on the floor, leaning against the bars. The Lifeless Pond was still in front of him, and suddenly Will realised that those fifty-nine days before the ceremony might be all he had. That thought seriously shook him up. He tried several times to brush it away with his simple "it's only a dream" mantra but failed at each attempt. The world around him was too complex in the smallest of detail, and his mind refused to accept it as a dream.

The sphinx wasn't very helpful either. Most of the time, Qu Sith simply ignored him. He reminded Will that the time was ticking a few times but still accomplished nothing. Will's vague statements about being stranded in a dream were met with scornful laughter.

Later in the afternoon, Will lay on the floor in frustration, not sure what else he could do to regain his freedom. Then, another chilly thought sneaked into his mind, which freaked him out. He didn't remember much that the strange young doctor, Ben, had told him – his talks were thick and sounded like gibberish, but he did recall the warning about staying away from danger in his dream. He was now head deep in danger without any possibility of escaping! Would this be dangerous in his real life too? Ben had implied that it would, and Will gasped as doubts writhed around his heart like a swarm of angry snakes.

"Thank Gods. Our dinner's coming. I'm so glad that they didn't decide to starve us because of your blasphemy," Qu Sith announced assuming his sphinx pose. "Don't speak and don't move this time, and you'll get something to eat."

Will sprang to his feet. Two dark figures were moving along the shore of the pond carrying trays with carved pumpkins. Will cast a glance at Qu Sith and assumed the same pose as the sphinx at the back of the cage. This was ridiculous, but his stomach was already rumbling loudly and begging for food, so he had to obey the strange rules of the dream.

Two figures in the same outfits and the same masks approached along the shore, but it was impossible to tell if they were the same ones who had brought the breakfast – anything identifiable was covered and hidden.

As before, they stopped in front of the cages. Will looked at them unblinking, with not a muscle twitching in his body. He was sure Qu Sith was doing the same. The dark-robed figures pushed the trays through the horizontal slits of the cage, then turned around and left without even bothering with a second glance at their prisoners or at the trays they had left earlier.

"Now," Qu Sith whispered diving into the first carved pumpkin.

Will picked the pumpkin up and cautiously inspected the pale slop inside. The odour was neutral, not as repulsive as he had expected from the appearance, and he tasted it carefully.

"It's mashed parsnips," the sphinx mumbled, briefly lifting his head and glancing at Will. "Nothing fancy but fills your stomach well."

"It'll make you fat," Will observed plunging two fingers into the slops and then licking them.

"That won't matter in fifty-eight days," Qu Sith muttered with his mouth full of food. "I guess you've not discovered any magical solution for our situation."

"Not yet, but I'll keep trying," Will promised.

Will was still in the middle of his first pumpkin when the sphinx had finished dealing with all three of his and had backed up in his cage.

"I don't want to spoil your appetite," Qu Sith said, wiggling his butt between the bars. "But nature is calling, and I can't hold it any longer."

Will looked away as the foul-smelling brown stream hit

the nearest grave.

"Oh," Qu Sith sighed, sitting down again. "I never digest this properly."

Will chose not to comment and ate silently facing the Lifeless Pond. The slops in the second pumpkin were slightly bitter and spicy, and he found a few oddly red roots, probably responsible for the taste. His mouth was burning when he had finished, and Will quickly dived into the third pumpkin and only realised half-through it that the last portion of the mashed parsnips was sweet with a fruity taste and a vague smell of lemon.

It was dark by the time he had finished eating. The sphinx in the neighbouring cage was silent, and they sat leaning against the bars looking across the Pond where fires were lit, and the hypnotic rhythm of drums reached them across the rising fog.

Will watched the flames reflecting on the calm surface of the Lifeless Pond and long shadows dancing among them until the ground began its gentle tremors.

"Back off!" Qu Sith said from the neighbouring cage.

The drums stopped, and an enormous wall of boiling water and roaring steam shot into the sky. Will crouched in the corner shielding his eyes and waited, but all that came down were just a few sprinkles. The major splash hit the other shore.

"The wind must have changed," the sphinx mumbled in his corner.

"Probably..." Will agreed, stretching his body on the straw. "Can we go to sleep now?"

"Yes," Qu Sith whispered. "Happy dreaming. At least there you'll be free."

Sleep didn't come easily to Will. He kept staring at the dying flames across the pond and thinking about how sitting in this cage might affect his real life. The sphinx had patiently accepted his fate, counting the days until his death. Will wasn't ready to give up, but he was stuck in this crazy dream, and that was the main problem. Dreaming another dream could be a quick solution for this situation, but Will saw no way how to do this. His mind was firmly fixed on Hel, and he was sure that was the reason why it kept allowing this nightmare to bounce back in. But Will wasn't ready or willing to forget her.

What if he could somehow take a break from this dream? He could return two months later when that stupid festival of the Rybbaths and the sacrifice would be over, and he could calmly resume his search for Hel's orchid. The lava fields would be solid and cold by that time too.

Will smiled. It sounded like a plan, but he had no idea how to implement it.

Only then did the voice of that young doctor, Ben, raise objections in his head, crushing his plan into dust. He had spoken strangely but knew a lot about that dream. He knew about the cave and the castle, and even mentioned the knights who guarded Hel. *Maybe Ben could advise him?* Perhaps he could give Will some pills to keep that dream away for two months?

Will allowed the thought to circle his brain several times. Yes, it was based on assumptions, he could see that, but otherwise, the plan was flawless.

Will smiled, ignoring the putrid smell that wrapped around him along with the cool night air. It didn't matter. He had a plan to escape the holy festival of Rybbaths, the fight with Qu Sith and that painful sacrifice in the Lifeless Pond. All he needed was a small pill. Will was sure; Ben would be able to provide it. The young doctor would just need a little persuasion.

❧❦ ✿ ❧❦

Somebody touched his shoulder.

"What would you like for breakfast?" the question required some input from Will. The transfer to reality was abrupt, and he frowned, looking around the ward until his eyes focused on the nurse smiling in front of him.

She handed him a list, and Will pointed to the first option without thinking about it too much. He wouldn't be here for long anyway.

A bright day was breaking outside the window, and Will quickly stuffed down his breakfast, hoping all his problems would soon have a similar clear solution. He stretched his muscles before getting out of the bed.

"Where are you going, young man?" the nurse stopped him in the corridor.

"I need to find Ben, the doctor," Will mumbled uncertainly.

"I don't know any doctor named Ben," the nurse barred his way. "Please, stay in the ward."

"He works in A&E," Will stopped. The nurse was even

worse than his mother.

"A&E is no longer taking care of you, young man. We are," she told him seriously. "You've got a few tests scheduled for this morning, and the doctors will want to speak to you after that. Please, go back to your bed. Don't make me chase you around the hospital."

"I need to see Ben," Will protested.

"You can do that this afternoon," she was adamant. "When all your tests and visits have been done."

There was no way around her, and Will reluctantly returned to his place at the window. Cheerful Sparrows wouldn't let him go that easy; that was clear. He must pass those tests. He had promised that to his mother.

Will slipped back under the covers, pinning his dissatisfied gaze on the distant rooftops outside the window again. The morning had been spoiled.

Will went through endless questioning and tests again with the same disgruntled attitude. Strange people kept visiting him – some joking and trying to be friendly, some frowning and alienated. They inspected Will's chest, touching it, feeling it. Then one matron dug her fingers into his armpits and shook her head. Will wasn't sure if she had found what she was looking for, but the expression on her face was as dissatisfied as his own.

"Let's take an ultrasound of that," she noted to the nurse, pointing at Hel's face on Will's chest. "I don't feel that there's anything wrong, but those muscles are too hard to palpate and may be hiding some deeper collection or a foreign body. Let's do it just to be sure."

The nurse took Will to ultrasound an hour later. The smiling doctor operating the fancy machine kept grinning and joking about going to the gym and muscles. Will smiled politely, feeling a little embarrassed, but the real humiliation came when the doctor poured some disgusting slime on Hel's face and placed a probe on her eyes.

The next ten minutes went by in silence. The doctor frowned, turning a few knobs and pressing lightly glowing buttons while staring intensely at the screen. The pressure from the probe on his chest varied from a light touch to an almost painful squeeze, and Will began to worry that the machine might damage his precious tattoo.

"I can't see anything wrong there," the doctor admitted at last. "Do you feel any pain in your chest?"

"No," Will assured him, shaking his head. He was keen to get out as fast as he could.

"Fine," the doctor said, placing the probe back in its holder. "I'll report it as normal. You can go back to the ward now."

He gave Will a few sheets of paper to wipe the slime from his chest.

"Thank you," Will quickly thanked him and rushed back into the corridor before the doctor could change his mind and think of some other investigation.

The nurse was nowhere in sight, and Will grinned at being left on his own at last. He had the opportunity to sneak into A&E and find Ben before returning to the Cheerful Sparrows.

The corridors were long and tangled, but the red arrows

on the walls with "A&E" on them helped with the navigation. Before long, he found himself in the same waiting area as he had been when he was admitted. It was crowded and busy. Nobody paid any attention to him.

"Excuse me," Will stopped the nurse rushing by carrying a few packets in her hands. "Have you seen doctor Ben?"

"Ben?" she popped her eyes. "I don't know any consultant called Ben. Sorry."

She rushed away without casting another glance at Will. He stood helplessly in the midst of the commotion looking around in a desperate bid to spot any familiar face. Ben was nowhere in sight, but a familiar face finally wandered into the waiting area. Will put on the widest of smiles as he approached the young blonde doctor who examined him together with Ben on admission.

"Hello," Will said when she finally lifted eyes from her notes and noticed him standing in front of her. "I'm looking for Ben. Do you know where to find him?"

"I remember you," she ignored his question pointing her finger at his chest. "You're the one with epilepsy we were examining yesterday."

"Yes," Will nodded happily. "Do you know where Ben is?"

"He's on study leave today," she said, eyeing him with suspicion. "Why do you want him? Ben's boyfriend is missing. Leave him alone!"

"It's not that," Will blushed unexpectedly. "He gave me some advice, and I need to ask him a few more questions."

"Oh. What kind of advice? Maybe, I can help you if it's urgent?" the blonde girl bit her lip trying to hide her confusion. "Otherwise Ben will be working here tomorrow morning."

"I don't think you can help. It's a long story, and I wouldn't like to waste your time. Thank you, I'll try to find Ben tomorrow," Will said, wiping the smile off his face but the blonde doctor had already rushed away, barely waiting for his gratitude.

Will spat a silent curse but wasn't ready to give up. There was no use wandering around A&E any longer. He might try his luck again tomorrow.

He slowly went back to Cheerful Sparrows wandering through the long corridors again and trying hard to remember what Ben had said during his brief visit to the ward. *Damn!* He should have been more attentive! All he could remember was the doctor warning him to stay away from any danger and avoid any injuries in his dream. Ben hadn't said how to stop dreaming that dream. Will wasn't ready to abandon it entirely – he still had hope of finding the orchid – but a few months' vacation would be quite nice since the idea of the imminent fight with Qu Sith and sacrifice in the Lifeless Pond had begun to feel unsettling.

He went through the corridors again, trying to retrace his way back to the ward. Will wondered why hospitals were built like tangled mazes, resembling multistorey anthills with distinct parts dropped into the labyrinth of corridors without any apparent logic. The people he met were busy going about their business, and he didn't dare to ask for directions. Will had probably circled the hospital twice before he managed to reach the familiar staircase that led to the Cheerful Sparrows Ward.

His mother was waiting next to his bed.

"Where have you been, Willy?" she demanded. "I've already been waiting here for half an hour."

"They did an ultrasound," Will explained, sitting down on his bed. "And I had some trouble finding my way back."

"You always find trouble even when there is none," she sighed, passing a card to him. "Your sister asked me to give you this."

It was a small card with a cute ginger kitten and the words "Get well soon!" in bold golden letters. Will smiled, suddenly feeling grateful for being remembered. He didn't expect that.

"How was the ultrasound?" mother asked, taking his hand. "Did they find anything?"

"No," Will gave her a small smile. "The doctor said everything was normal."

"That's a relief," she said and added with concern still apparent in her eyes. "Have you had any more of those fits?"

"No, mum," Will kept smiling. "Not a single one. I'm fine like I told you. I'm hoping I'll be out of here tomorrow."

She smiled too, but suspicion hadn't left her face. They talked a little more, mostly about home. Then his mother stood up.

"I must go, Willy," she said. "Your sister will be back from school soon, and I need to take care of her. Do everything the doctors say, Willy. Don't object. I want you back home, but I want you healthy. And then we'll have a serious talk about your future plans, young man. It's time to grow up."

Will didn't like the idea, but forced a smile back and nodded. She left without saying another word.

Will found himself still clutching the card with the cute kitten and put it into his pocket. He stretched his muscles on the bed, scanning the distant rooftops through the window again. Nothing had changed since he'd looked at them last time. The place was boring, but it did give him time to think about more pressing issues, about his dream that he used to enjoy and to brush aside the apparent dangers it involved (it was a dream, after all). Still, a shadow of fear appeared and wandered around deep in his mind spoiling everything. He had no idea how to address it.

Will ate a few snacks looking at the dying day outside. He found no way of resolving his doubts, and those fears only became more deeply rooted in his mind instead of fading away. A few beds in the ward now had different occupants, but Will barely noticed that with all his thoughts already back in the cage, searching for any weak spots where he could apply his strength and break free.

$$\mathcal{C}\mathcal{S}\mathcal{O}\circledast\mathcal{C}\mathcal{S}\mathcal{P}$$

He didn't notice the transfer. Will closed his eyes only for a moment, but the still surface of the Lifeless Pond was in front of his eyes when he opened them. As expected, the sphinx was in the neighbouring cage on his left, still sleeping.

The morning was early, and Will stretched his muscles, enjoying the light breeze from the Pond which carried the stench of the burial grounds away. The village on the other side was quiet, but he could see a small fire flickering there. *The Rybbaths were preparing parsnips for their prisoners.* Will flinched at the thought. He didn't like to regard himself as a prisoner, but the truth remained unchanged – strong wooden bars stood firmly between him and his freedom.

Will sighed, stood up and began the inspection again, touching every bar, every joint, every plank.

"Lovely morning," Qu Sith observed as he completed his third round.

"Yes, indeed," Will mumbled without interrupting the search.

"Found anything?"

"I'd have been outside already if I had," Will told the beast. The question was inane.

Will carried on without looking at the yawning sphinx. He was facing the burial grounds when there came a sudden warning.

"Get down," Qu Sith whispered. "Our breakfast is coming."

Will dropped onto his belly without a word assuming the same pose as the sphinx. The two dark figures were still quite far away, and he hoped they hadn't noticed any movement or heard a sound.

Qu Sith let out a sigh only when the trays had been put inside the cages, and the figures went back to the village along the shoreline of the Lifeless Pond.

They ate in silence.

Will pushed the tray and the empty pumpkins out through the same slit they had come in, and they fell next to his first breakfast which was gathering dust on the ground. He shook the bars again with sudden rage looking at the freedom he couldn't reach.

"That's hopeless," the sphinx observed calmly, wiggling his butt and aiming at the graves.

"I know," Will had to agree. The situation in this dream did seem hopeless, indeed.

Will sat down on the floor, leaning against the bars. He must get out of that cage at least, or get out of this dream entirely until it was too late. Still, he had fifty-eight days to find a solution. Will was afraid even to think about what would happen if he failed.

The thought was at first merely annoying and unsettling but soon became frightening. He closed his eyes, trying to recall what exactly Ben had said about this dream and blaming himself for not being attentive. *Avoid danger...* That was good advice, but had come too late – Will was already sitting in the cage.

The most insane thing Ben had said was that any injury he suffered in his dream would be reflected in real life as well. That did sound crazy.

Ben must be wrong. Usually, when somebody chopped your leg off in a dream, you just woke up to find both your legs still there, then you would turn on your other side and get into another dream. Why should this dream be any different?

Will grinned. *Ben must be wrong! That simply couldn't be true.* And that was easy to test. He didn't have to chop his leg off, but a small wound inflicted in this dream would be sufficient proof. Will looked around the cage with a victorious smile on his face, but nothing there caught his eye.

"I hope they give you a spear or a sword," Qu Sith said, looking at the pond. "Or a knife, at least. Your teeth aren't strong enough to tear my throat."

"I wouldn't like to bite anybody anyway," Will observed wryly.

Qu Sith chuckled.

"Probably no point in asking but have you found a magic way out of your cage?" the sphinx looked at him grinning. "No? Then better prepare to die. We could discuss a few best options to make it quick and least painful."

"You can die if you want to," Will said, inspecting the sphinx's fangs. "That's not an option for me. I must find my way out or risk being boiled alive in that stupid pond."

"Ponds are not stupid," Qu Sith observed, erasing his grin. "It's stupid to…"

"Are you poisonous?" Will cut the sphinx's tirade short.

"I beg your pardon!" Qu Sith jumped to his feet, his eyes flashing with anger. "How ignorant are you?"

"Yes or no?" Will demanded.

"Of course not!" Qu Sith hissed through his teeth. "That was the most insulting. Why did you ask?"

"I need your help," Will whispered, then stood up and went closer, ignoring the incredulous gaze of the sphinx.

"I won't help you to die," Qu Sith said firmly. "I need you to kill me."

"I don't want to die," Will assured him. "That's why I asked about whether you were poisonous. And I apologise for insulting you. I didn't mean to."

"Apology accepted," Qu Sith mumbled. "What is it you need?"

Will felt embarrassed having to voice the silly idea for the first time. Anyway, it was only a dream.

"I need a small wound on my finger," he said at last. "I've nothing suitable in my cage. I thought if you could just bite me a little?"

"That might impair your ability to fight," Qu Sith observed. "Are you trying to trick me into something?"

"No, it's not a trick," Will said firmly. "I wouldn't ask

you if I could do it myself but, as you said, my teeth aren't sharp enough. I promise I'll kill you the way you like if things get that far. But I hope we'll be able to escape the fighting."

The black eyes of Qu Sith showed no emotion, and his face remained serious.

"I still don't understand how this can help you to escape," the sphinx said at last. "What kind of magic is that?"

Will couldn't explain his true intentions to him. Qu Sith would never agree to cooperate if he knew the real purpose of that wound. It was Ben's theory being tested and, if Ben was wrong, Will just had to find a way to dream another dream, and the Rybbaths would have no sacred festival. Nobody would die if Will left his cage empty! It was a perfect plan. He only had to persuade the distrustful sphinx.

"Only a small wound, that's all I'm asking," Will gripped the bars looking at the beast. "It will heal in two months and won't impair my ability to fight. And I promise to plunge into your heart whatever weapon they give me. A direct strike, and you will die peacefully without any suffering."

"A direct strike, you say…" Qu Sith licked his lips. "Sounds great, but I still don't understand why you're willing to accept suffering in the Pond?"

The question caught Will unprepared, and he struggled to produce a prompt answer.

"Well…" he trailed off with uncertainty. "I hope it won't take too long to die in the Pond. I've heard that certain suffering purifies the soul."

"So, that's religious," Qu Sith barked, and Will couldn't make out if it were approval or disapproval in the sphinx's voice.

"You can call it what you want," Will said firmly. "I'm not afraid of that pond. And I'm willing to help you to avoid it, but I need a little favour first."

Dark eyes hid the sphinx's soul, but hesitation was apparent on his face.

"A favour for a favour?" he asked, staring at Will.

"Yes!" Will nodded happily.

"I think, we could agree on that," Qu Sith slowly nodded. "What do you want me to do?"

"All I need is a small wound," Will grinned. "If I could put my little finger between your teeth, can you bite it just enough to pierce the skin, not bite the finger off? Do you think you can do that?"

"Easily," Qu Sith was grinning too. "And I'd love that taste of blood on my tongue after all those parsnips."

"Oh! Don't overplay this," Will gasped.

"Don't worry," the sphinx still was grinning. "I know my limits. Which finger do you want me to bite?"

"The left little finger," Will decided firmly.

"Go ahead. Place it between my teeth," Qu Sith said, pressing his head against the bars of his cage and opening his mouth.

Will frowned, inspecting the sphinx's molars and fangs and decided to stick with the smallest looking incisors. He extended his arm out as far as he could, barely reaching the neighbouring cage, and placed the tip of his finger between the teeth.

"I'm ready," Will whispered, closing his eyes.

The pain was sudden and sharp, and Will cried out, quickly retrieving his arm. The fingertip was absent, and the wound was bleeding. Will cursed wrapping it with the edge of his shirt. The wound was too big, and it was bleeding too much, but it was what he had asked for.

"That was delicious," Qu Sith observed. "And you're welcome."

"I didn't ask you to bite it off!" Will complained.

"You put your finger there. I only squeezed my jaws together," the beast grinned. "Don't blame me. And I hope you've achieved what you wanted. Still, I don't understand why you needed this."

Will pressed the cloth against the gaping wound and cursed. It was too painful, and he hadn't expected such consequences. But it was only a dream, and Ben's silly theory must be wrong. Later, when the bleeding had stopped, he managed a victorious smile finally and thanked the sphinx. It had been his idea, and he couldn't blame Qu Sith for its poor implementation. Will had got what he wished for, and he could just shrug off the pain, carry on and hope he had proved Ben's words to be wrong.

The day was hot, and Will spent the rest of it in the scant shade of the branches that covered the roof of his cage. They were intended to protect him from the scalding water from the Lifeless Pond but were neither big enough nor thick enough and were lousy protection from the direct sunlight too.

Will was sweating profusely, but a grin lit his face as he stared at his little finger with its missing tip. He couldn't wait to wake up in the ward and have a look at his proof. He had everything under control.

Later in the afternoon, when the heat had subsided, they watched the fire being built and smoke rising from the village across the pond.

"Food is coming!" Qu Sith announced spotting two figures with trays approaching along the right-hand shore.

He sat down and stilled his body. Will did the same, again assuming the same pose as the sphinx. There was no use attempting to speak with those people again, waste that parsnip mash and go hungry through the night. Will was sure that they wouldn't be concerned even if he waved his severed finger at them.

They waited until the trays with the pumpkins had been pushed inside their cages, and the figures had turned back. The food was still warm, and they ate in silence, watching the day dying over the Pond.

"Not as delicious as those few drops of your blood," Qu Sith observed wiggling his butt between the bars. "Not even remotely."

"We'll become weak eating this food," Will muttered, still slurping the pale slop. "It's got no protein."

"Protein? What's that?" the sphinx asked, as he again defiled the nearest grave.

"Meat," Will explained, stuffing the remnants of the mash into his mouth and pushing the tray out of his cage.

"We'll get weak without any meat."

"That is exactly my point," Qu Sith nodded. "But maybe the Rybbaths want us weak?"

"Maybe…" mumbled Will looking at the strands of fog slowly rising from the water.

His finger was throbbed, but not too much, and Will sat leaning against the bars waiting for the dusk and the usual evening eruption of the geyser. Qu Sith was already asleep on his den and farting loudly from time to time. It was a peaceful evening, and Will stared dully over the treetops waiting for the geyser eruption. He didn't want to get scalded, even in a dream.

Then Will's eyes focused on something moving in the southern sky high above the treetops. The shape was white and constantly changing, making its way against the light breeze. It was big – much bigger than any bird could be, and its long body with a pair of white wings resembled a snake rather than any member of the avian world. The creature was magnificent but too far away to see clearly. It surfed the wind with its unmoving wings spread widely, then turned to the west and descended behind the distant trees.

At about the same time the drums began to beat in the village of the Rybbaths, and the long shadows of dancers began to dance over the tranquil surface of the Lifeless Pond. Will shaded his eyes, but the creature didn't show up again. Soon it became too dark to see anything but the reflections of the distant flames on the water.

Will backed away as the stream of geyser shot high into the sky silencing the drums of the Rybbaths. The wind blew it to the left with only a few sprinkles landing on the cage. Qu Sith didn't even bother to raise his head.

Will lay down on his den looking at the distant fires dying in the village. The night was quiet, with only a few distant cries of owls piercing the silence. Will closed his eyes, giving them some rest. A few minutes later, somebody touched his shoulder.

༄ৎ৩ ❀ ৫৩৶

"What *is* that?" the voice was female, and it carried a note of terror that demanded an immediate answer.

Will blinked shading his eyes from the morning dawn. He was no longer in the cage.

"What happened?" the nurse demanded, standing at the foot of his bed and pointing at his left hand.

Will gasped, glancing at the bloody stain around his palm and the severed tip of his little finger lying next to the wound.

"I've no idea," he mumbled suddenly feeling ashamed for not having listened to Ben's advice.

"Let me have a look at that," the nurse lifted his hand. "I don't remember us doing any surgery yesterday."

She frowned as if unable to believe her eyes.

"I'll be back in a few minutes," said the nurse as she turned away. "The bleeding has already stopped, but you still need it bandaged."

She rushed out.

Will looked at his hand. The wound was precisely the

same as he remembered it from his dream, and the thought made his heart to skip a few beats. He couldn't understand how it happened, but it was firm proof that the dream was slipping into dangerous grounds, and he didn't like the thought of that at all.

The nurse returned with bandages and a junior doctor, who paled at the sight of Will's hand.

"How did that happen?" she asked, cautiously approaching Will and leaving the nurse aside.

"I've no idea," Will shrugged with a straight face. "I've been asleep."

"But didn't you feel any pain?" she frowned, staring at the severed fingertip.

"I did," Will admitted. "But I thought it was just part of a dream. I didn't wake up."

"That's very strange, I told you," said the nurse handing the junior doctor bandages. "What do you think?"

"It can't have been an animal," she said firmly. "Any animal would swallow what it had bitten off. It must be some sick joker."

"Are you implying that someone sneaked into the ward and cut his finger?" the nurse paled at the thought.

"I see no other reasonable explanation," the doctor placed some ointment on the wound and wrapped it in a bandage.

"That's ridiculous," the nurse muttered. "We need to check the CCTV."

"And you'll need to change the bed linen," the doctor added.

They rushed into the corridor, creating a small turmoil that slowly seemed to spread with notes of surprise and even horror being expressed in hushed voices. Will stared at the sky outside the window as deadly fear gripped his heart for the first time in his life. The wound proved that Ben had been telling the truth and that he now had less than two months to live with a painful death awaiting him in the boiling water of the Lifeless Pond.

He didn't pay much attention when the nurses changed the bed linen. Later, when consultants and hospital managers gathered around his bed, questioning him about the severed finger, he only kept shaking his head.

"I don't know anything," Will repeated stubbornly at every question. "I was asleep."

"Didn't you feel the pain?" they kept wondering.

"I did," admitted Will, repeating his story with stubborn persistence. "But I thought it was a part of a dream."

"We'll need to investigate this…"

A wave of weakness passed through Will's head as he realised that his stupid idea of biting his fingertip might keep him in hospital for a few more days. *Damn!* Why hadn't he waited to do that experiment until he got home?

Ben was right. Damn, Ben was right! The thought kept rolling around his brain, suffusing everything with fear. Will hadn't been listening to what the doctors were telling him until he realised that they were waiting for his approval.

"More tests?" he asked in an uncertain voice. "Yes, let's do it. I have to prove I'm healthy."

"It won't take long," one of the doctors said. "We just

need to find out why you didn't respond to such a painful stimulus. And we'll check the surveillance to find out who did this to you. The police will speak to you at some time, so don't go too far."

Ben was right. I must speak to Ben as soon as possible. The thought raised a little point of sanity that broke through the whirlpool of fear raging in Will's mind. Yes, he must see Ben!

Will frowned, looking at the gathering around his bed. They were talking amongst themselves, barely looking at him – one of the doctors was dictating a long list of examinations he wanted for Will, the others were immersed in a strange discussion, most of which he couldn't understand. They used some unknown words and expressions, and all Will could make out was their uncertainty as to whether thalamic or cortical lesions could cause such anaesthesia. It looked like he was doomed to spend the rest of the week here.

The unsettling crowd began to move towards the corridor, and Will sighed with relief but, before he was able to get out of bed, two nurses hurried in bringing trays with tubes and syringes and began the bloodletting, sample collecting, pricking and injecting him with great enthusiasm on their faces.

"Don't go anywhere," one of them warned Will before leaving with his blood. "You'll have a busy morning."

"I need to find doctor Ben," he told them. "He'll be in A&E this morning."

"I don't think you'll be able to make it this morning,"

one of the nurses smiled, shaking her head. "You've got a very long list of urgent procedures. Maybe, later this afternoon…"

They left. Will cursed behind their backs but didn't dare to disobey.

The morning was indeed busy. Will was rushed around the hospital for countless procedures and consultations. He had a few injections, and his finger was unwrapped for inspection on several occasions.

"Your fingerprints will be different now," the surgeon joked, putting a few stitches on the gaping wound.

"I don't care," Will said sadly.

He managed to have a snack between his travels, and then he was rushed across the hospital for another examination.

"Wait here until they call you," the nurse told him, indicating a chair in the waiting area.

Will sat down with a sigh and looked around. The area wasn't crowded, and he felt a bit uncomfortable with his bulging muscles among those frail, skinny grandmothers. He lowered his head and fixed his gaze on the floor. Still, he remained aware of eyes silently watching him. Will waited, but the feeling was still the same ten minutes later. Someone was blatantly staring at him.

Will blushed before he lifted his head. The grandmother in front of him was barely alive with an oxygen tank sitting on her left and a sleepy nurse on her right. Her hands kept shaking as her pale grey eyes stared unblinkingly at Will. It was an embarrassing moment, and Will attempted to smile, but the grandma's expression remained unchanged. Her eyes still drilled into his face, and that gaze felt threatening, almost physical.

Will shifted in his chair and looked through the window, but the old lady didn't give up. He quickly stole another glance at her face – no, she didn't look at all familiar.

"William?" The nurse saved him. It was easy to spot him as he was the only guy towering over those old ladies.

"Yes," he raised his bottom off the chair.

"I'm sorry," the nurse apologised. "We can't do your examination. There's a note on the system that you have some sort of implant in your body. We can't verify its suitability for this procedure, so that's why we need to reject it. We've already phoned the ward. Please wait here, and they'll come to fetch you."

"Implant?" Will popped his eyes. "I know nothing about that."

The nurse shrugged.

"Strange," she told him. "They usually tell patients, and you're young enough to remember. Anyway, there's a note on the system, and we can't ignore it. Sorry."

She smiled and left him again under the death stare of that strange grandma. Will studied his feet, doing his best to ignore her eyes. He was glad when a nurse from the ward finally came to collect him fifteen minutes later.

Will ate his lunch gazing sadly through the window while another nurse impatiently glanced in from the corridor where two police officers were waiting to question him. And even more tests were waiting for him in the afternoon.

Suddenly, Will felt nostalgic about his previous life, when he had not had very much to worry about. Life had been a lot easier then. Pumping iron was strenuous but rewarding, and he missed those furtive glances at his muscles from the row of treadmills. Here, he was just another patient.

The chat with the police officers was brief. Will only repeated the same thing he had said many times before. Of course, he didn't mention his dream and Qu Sith's part in the severing of his fingertip. They wouldn't have believed this anyway. He needed Ben to have that sort of discussion.

When they had left, another nurse took him on one more journey around the hospital. The tests, questioning and examinations that followed seemed endless, and Will felt exhausted when he was finally able to drop onto his bed. The nurse who had stopped him from his mission that morning came in a few minutes later bringing the news.

"One more examination," she said with a small smile. "And then you'll be able to go and look for that doctor in A&E."

"Thank you," Will managed a smile as well.

"Let's go," she said. "I'll take you to the examination room."

Will grinned and sprang out of bed. Finally! They went through the long, brightly lit corridors and then took the stairs down simply to enter into another maze of long and brightly lit corridors.

"Here," the nurse opened the door letting him in.

The place was dark with the only illumination coming

from a few screens attached to a strange machine. Will flinched as the door shut behind him, leaving him in the darkness.

"Have a seat, please," a voice came from the left, and only then did Will notice a table there with a single chair in front of it. The voice was male.

Will went closer. He saw only a shadow on the other side of the table.

"Sit down please," the man repeated.

Will took a seat. Indeed a man was sitting across the table. Will was sure when his eyes had finally adjusted to the dusk. The man was flanked by two smaller silhouettes – most likely women – silently staring at Will.

"I'm William," he felt he should formally introduce himself.

"We know," the man cut him short. "Our names would mean nothing to you."

"What kind of examination is this?" he asked with increasing agitation. Will wasn't afraid of the man or those smaller silhouettes – he was far bigger and stronger and could defend himself with ease, but the situation was nevertheless unsettling.

"This isn't an examination," the man told him in a flat voice. "But we do advise you to cooperate."

"What do you want?" Will asked.

The question was left hanging in the darkness since nobody bothered to answer. Will squirmed in his chair, but the silence uncomfortably extended into minutes.

"Can I go now?" he asked at last. "I need to find doctor

Ben in A&E."

"You won't find doctor Ben in A&E," the man said.

"Why? He's supposed to be working today."

"Doctor Ben is dead," the man told him calmly.

"That can't be true!" Will sprang to his feet.

"Take a seat, please. We haven't finished yet," said the man from the shadows, tapping the table. "Doctor Ben was very inattentive when he ran across the road today. An accident happened."

A small screen lit under his fingers, and he passed the tablet to Will. It bore the image of a heavily distorted and bloodied body under a heavy lorry. The body had Ben's face.

Will returned the tablet to the man and slumped back in the chair, shaking his head in disbelief. He suddenly felt like he was waist-deep in quicksand, totally losing grip on solid ground.

"You don't need to worry," the man said. "Ben had broken the Code, but it wasn't your fault."

"Was he killed deliberately?" Will gasped.

"It was an accident," the man placed the tablet on the table and repeated. "It wasn't your fault."

"It can't be my fault anyway," Will muttered. "I've been in the hospital all the time. I don't need to prove my innocence."

"You won't be accused of anything. You don't need to worry," the man told him quietly. "There's an overwhelming opinion that your proceedings in Rehen are fascinating. The Code's already been broken by Ben, so there's no further risk of anything illegal. That's the reason why we agreed to meet you here."

This conversation was turning into a farce. These people were freaky and crazy.

"Rehen?" asked Will, unsure of what they were talking about.

"That's the name of the world you visit," the man told him. "Usually, we don't deal with Sleepers directly, but your unfinished proceedings would result in much frustration."

"What proceedings?"

Will's muscles grew stiff as he sensed a shadow of danger lurking in the man's words. Ben was dead, and Will had a feeling in his gut that the poor doctor was helped with that accident.

He stared silently at the three dark silhouettes across the table. Three sets of eyes, barely visible in the dusk, stared back at him from the shadows and again the silence extended into uncomfortable minutes. Will stirred in his chair ready to spring to his feet at any moment but froze as the man raised his hand.

"We've made a decision," he announced indifferently.

"What decision is that?" Will demanded.

"We're going to put you to sleep," the man said in the same flat voice.

"What?" Will jumped to his feet and leaned forward, trying to make out the man's face. Was he joking? "What do you mean by that? I don't need to be put to sleep like a sick dog! You can't do that to me!"

"Please, sit down," the man didn't move, nor raise his voice.

"I'm not playing by your rules!" Will put all the anger he had in this statement. "I'm not a sick dog!"

"You're right," suddenly the man agreed. "You're neither a dog nor sick. Still, you need some help since you seem unable to juggle both lives effectively. We can't help you with the cage, but we can put you to artificial sleep and give you more time in Rehen. Probably, you can figure the way out by yourself if given more time."

The statement left Will gasping, and he leaned across the table.

"The *cage*?" he asked, feeling a knot in his throat.

The man simply nodded in response.

"What do you know about *that* cage?" Will demanded, his voice trembling slightly.

"You'll die if you don't get out in time," the man said. "And the sphinx won't help you out. You must find your own way."

"There is no way out," Will clenched his fists, then relaxed. "I've already looked."

"Then you'll die," the man said bluntly. The women on his either side kept staring in silence. "You must know that we'll only help you once. Then you must go and find a safe place."

"A safe place?"

The man sat in silence.

"A safe place?" Will repeated the question.

"You'll be forced to if you won't comply," the man said absently.

Will slumped back on the chair as his limbs refused to

hold him up properly. He didn't understand a thing the man was saying, but the situation seemed threatening.

"Is there any way out of this dream?" he mumbled the question as he looked at the figures across the table. "I want my life back."

"Death is the only way out," the man told him. "This is why you need to try harder with your search. We'll help you only once, and I must assure you that this decision does surprise me. I don't remember any other such interference before. Take this opportunity and use it wisely. Take your time to do a thorough search. A cage built by savages can't be flawless."

Will shook his head, feeling a wave of fear locking his limbs. How could he get out when he had checked every inch of the cage several times already? There was no way he could have overlooked anything! Will felt doomed with the clock slowly ticking towards death in the Lifeless Pond. Would some additional time make a difference?

"Probably, I've no other choice," he mumbled, staring at the man.

"Good. We expected your cooperation," the man said in the same flat voice, and Will couldn't make out if he were smiling in the gloom. "We'll put you to sleep right now."

Will gulped. "What do you want me to do?" he asked.

"Undress and lie down on that bed," the man indicated behind Will's back.

Will looked where the man's finger pointed but still couldn't make out anything in the dark. "Will you drug me out for the entire two months?" he asked in a shaky voice.

"No," the man said. "We'll reverse your coma as soon as you're out of the cage and able to resume your quest. Bear in mind, that if you don't get out within a week, you may find yourself with a tracheostomy."

"Trache... What?" the word sounded frightening to Will. "What's that?"

"A tube inserted through your skin directly into your airways," the man explained. "It might be dangerous for you in Rehen."

The statement sounded even more alarming.

"Why?" Will asked quietly.

"You might be suffocated by your own blood," the man shrugged. "There'll be no doctors in Rehen to stop the bleeding. Be out before that happens."

Will cursed loudly and stood up. The three figures behind the table remained seated.

"It seems, I don't have any other choice," Will uttered, heading into the darkness until he stumbled on the bed.

He stripped and folded up his T-shirt, trousers and socks.

"You must undress completely," the man observed from the other side of the room without getting up. "We'll need to put a catheter into your bladder."

"Why?" Will asked, dutifully taking off his underwear.

"To stop you from wetting the bed," the man explained.

Will shrugged. He got under the sheets, wondering what it would feel like to be put to sleep. Then he gasped suddenly remembering.

"What will you tell my mother?" he demanded. "She'll

be worried."

"That's none of your concern. She already knows what she needs to know. We had taken care of that," the man assured him. "Officially, you'll be in an artificial coma following one of those fits to prevent damage to your brain. That explanation won't be too far from the truth, don't you think?"

There was some shuffling in the darkness, and suddenly the room became brightly lit. Will blinked and frowned as it hurt his eyes. Then he glanced at the table. The man was a middle-aged grey fox with faint blue eyes and a narrow mouth. His features were average – nobody would ever give him a second look when they met him in the street. He sat at the table motionless and stared at Will with unblinking eyes. The two nurses left his side and became busy across the room, preparing tubes, needles and syringes.

"It will hurt a little," one of them warned him, spraying his arm with antiseptic.

Will said nothing, closed his eyes and prepared for the journey.

It felt like a small sting as the needle entered his body then a warm wave rolled over him, knocking him unconscious.

He was back in the cage when he opened his eyes again.

The night was clear, and the magnificent silver globe claimed the larger part of the sky, but Will had no time for the view. He touched his throat, recalling the grim warning about a tracheostomy and stood up.

The Lifeless Pond was still and dark, sweating thin strands of fog. The village across the water was dark too, as silent and as lifeless. Will grinned as he sneaked along the perimeter of his cage. The silver light was sufficient for his search, and he went through all the bars again, trying to spot any weakness, taking a good grip of the wood and shaking it with all his might. His body in Rehen was weaker than his usual physique, without all those bulging muscles he was proud of but was still strong enough for sufficient pull.

"What are you doing?" Qu Sith asked from the neighbouring cage. Will had probably woken him up.

"Trying to find a way out," Will mumbled, shaking the bars.

"You've tried that before," the sphinx reminded him,

yawning.

"I know," Will said and took a grip of another bar.

"You'll wake the Rybbaths," Qu Sith warned him. "Can't you wait until tomorrow?"

"I can't," Will said firmly. "I've got less than two months to live if I stay here."

Qu Sith chuckled.

"You knew that before," the sphinx looked at him with red reflections in his eyes. "Why the sudden rush?"

Will stopped for just a few seconds wondering how to satisfy Qu Sith's curiosity. He wasn't prepared to share the story of the artificial coma and tubes being poked into various holes in his body, but nothing useful crossed his mind. He shrugged and went on to shake the next bar.

"Have you checked the floor?" Qu Sith tried to be helpful.

Will stopped. The sphinx was right. He had circled the walls for maybe the tenth time already but hadn't looked at the floor or roof. Perhaps the way to freedom was hidden there?

"Good idea," he gratefully nodded to the sphinx with a grin and began relocating his straw mattress to another corner of the cage. "I'll start looking now!"

A braided mat was under the straw, fixed to the bars with ropes. It would need just a few strokes of a knife to cut the mat loose, but Will had no knife. He sat down instead and began undoing the knots, cursing each time his fingers slipped. Will even tried using his teeth by lying down flat and biting the funny tasting rope. He managed to untie two there were still over fifty keeping the mat in a position.

"Could I just point out," Qu Sith observed, "that you might find nothing under that mat? It might be entirely useless. But if it keeps you amused…"

Will cursed.

"At least, I'm doing something," he barked at the sphinx with a sense of hurt pride. "While you're just waiting for your death!"

"As far as I can see, you're just wasting your effort," the sphinx's eyes flashed red on the remark. "Of course, it's your personal preference for how you spend your last days. You can dig your nose into that moulded mat, or you could simply enjoy your time here as much as you can."

"Shut up!" Will raised his head at the creature.

"As you wish," Qu Sith dropped head on his crossed paws and closed his eyes.

Will managed to loosen three more knots before dawn. All this time Qu Sith slept and raised his head as Will dug his teeth into the fourth knot in a row.

"I'd advise you to take a little break from those knots," the sphinx told him, yawning.

"Why?" Will stopped chewing on the rope.

"They're already making our breakfast," Qu Sith indicated the rising smoke on the other side of the pond. "I doubt if your troubles with that mat will make them happy."

"I'll just finish this one," Will said, sinking his teeth into the rope again.

"You don't have time for that, I'm afraid," Qu Sith observed calmly.

"Why?"

"They're already on their way," the sphinx sat down in his usual pose waiting for breakfast.

"Shit!" Will jumped to his feet. Two lonely figures had just left the village stepping along the shore of the pond, and he had to cover his mess up quickly or risk starving. He only hoped they were too far away to notice any movement in the cage.

The straw was back on the mat in a minute, and Will sat down in the pose of the sphinx, waiting. The Rybbaths had barely covered half of the way by then.

"Thank you for the warning," he whispered, but Qu Sith didn't answer. He was calmly gazing at the approaching silhouettes.

The Rybbaths left the trays of mashed parsnips without casting a second glance at the messy straw in Will's cage and, as always, left in silence. Will's gaze followed them until they were too far away to hear or see anything. Then he tossed the straw aside, exposing the mat again. It felt like an obsession. *Why was it secured with so many knots?* He was sure those savages had hidden something under that mat. A few cracked planks, perhaps?

"Wouldn't it be better to eat first?" Qu Sith asked him, lifting his head from the carved pumpkin. "There's a lot of flies here. They might spoil your appetite."

Will looked at his tray with hesitation. The rows of untied knots urged him to begin, but his empty stomach began protesting at the sight of food, and Will had always listened to his stomach.

He dug into the first pumpkin, stodging the mash together with his fingers. The taste was bland, and Will cursed doing his best to gulp the parsnips down faster, almost bypassing his mouth, straight into his throat. Qu Sith was mumbling something with his head already inside the second pumpkin.

The breaking morning was clear with a cloudless sky, promising the day would be long and hot. Will swallowed the mash unhappily observing the calm of the Lifeless Pond where, somewhere deep beneath the surface, lay his own death. The thought was unsettling, and he gritted his teeth hard, trying to calm his fluttering heart. *He must find the way out!* There was a way; Will was sure about that. That's why those people had granted him some extra time. To find the way, to find the way out!

Qu Sith had finished his meal and retreated to the back of his cage, answering the usual call of nature. He wiggled his butt between the two bars with a silly expression on his face and aimed at the nearest grave then the foul stinking stream was suddenly interrupted by a loud crack.

Will froze with a mouthful of parsnips, then sprang to his feet.

"Damn," Qu Sith said sadly. "I've shit on my heels."

Will gulped the mash down, gripping onto the bars of his cage.

"Do that again!" he said.

"What?" the sphinx asked with an element of astonishment in his voice. "My gut's already empty. I can't do that again until tomorrow morning."

"Wiggle that damned butt!" Will roared.

"Be quiet. You'll anger the Rybbaths," Qu Sith whispered. "I got the message."

The sphinx carefully fit his butt into the same space between the two bars and strained. The wood cracked again bringing a small smile to Will's face.

"Try harder…" he whispered to the sphinx.

Qu Sith wiggled his butt once more, and one of the bars moved an inch aside, splitting in the middle.

"Yes!" the grin couldn't get wider on Will's face.

"I still won't fit through that hole even if I was able to push that bar outside," Qu Sith didn't share Will's optimism. "The slit is too narrow."

"You need to check everything!" Will was bursting with enthusiasm. "You may find two weak bars in a row, and that could make a hole big enough for you to get out then you can let me out, and we'll run away!"

"Sounds like a plan," the sphinx said flatly. "Where do you want me to start?"

"Try the next space between those unbroken bars," Will pointed from his cage. "Maybe that would make the hole bigger!"

Will watched Qu Sith fit his butt into space with the broadest smile firmly fixed on his face, but the feelings raging in his heart weren't that straightforward. Their prison did have weaknesses, but he was in the wrong cage. Will was worried that the sphinx would leave him behind as soon as the beast sensed freedom. He kept quietly urging Qu Sith on just to keep him progressing along the perimeter of the cage. The bloody creature constantly complained of tiredness, weakness and sores on his butt, but he kept moving.

It was late in the afternoon when they finished checking the perimeter of Qu Sith's cage. The sphinx had found three more cracked bars, but they were all on different walls and too far apart to be useful.

"Now what?" Qu Sith asked disdainfully. "I've checked my cage. There's no useful way to escape. My ankles are smelly, and my butt is aching. Now what? It can't be any clearer – we're going to die here."

Will bit his lip. He wasn't ready to give up.

"We might still work out something," he said, attempting to reach the sphinx's cage with his right hand. He got a decent grip, but his arm was fully extended, and all he could do was to shake his body, rattling both cages.

"You're trying to do what I've already done," Qu Sith stretched out on the straw. "Anyway, it would be more helpful if you tried shaking the bars next to the one that already has a crack."

Will withdrew his arm and went closer to the back of the cage where one of the cracked bars was. Here his grip was even weaker – the cages were a little closer at the front but too far apart on the back, and Will could only get hold of the bars with his fingertips.

"All that effort has been useless. You've wasted the whole day on it and achieved nothing," the sphinx observed. "There's no way out."

"There must be," Will said with stubborn persistence.

"We just haven't found it yet."

He kept shaking the bars while Qu Sith watched him indifferently with his black eyes. An hour passed, but Will still found nothing – no other bars were cracking. He sat down on the floor, feeling exhausted entirely.

"Our food is coming," Qu Sith announced, gazing across the Pond. "You better sort your mess out."

It only took a few seconds for Will to toss the straw back on the mat and sit down to observe the two dark masked silhouettes approaching with trays in their hands. From a distance, they looked like two strange bugs crawling along the rocky shore of the pond.

"Do you think they'll be able to notice our attempts to escape?" Will asked quietly.

"I hope not," Qu Sith mumbled, casting glances around his cage. "I don't think those cracks are noticeable."

"We'll see quite soon," Will chuckled and straightened his face instantly as the Rybbaths came close enough to overhear them.

Will looked at the grey eyes behind the mask as the Rybbaths came closer. He didn't move a muscle, following them with his gaze only, and those grey eyes were fixed on him as well; they never left his face or slipped down to inspect the cage. The face was hidden, and Will caught himself wondering if it was a man or a woman bringing him food. It didn't make any difference, but he saw no fear or aggression in those grey eyes. Will watched the tray being pushed inside his cage through the same slit which was barely big enough for the carved pumpkins.

The dark figures backed a few steps away, still watching the prisoners. They looked like two ghosts between the milky strands of evening fog, already leaking from the surface of the Pond. The grey eyes still watched him, and Will dared a tight smile. The Rybbaths turned around, carefully stepping along the rocky shore. A few paces later the one who had brought Will's diner glanced back at his cage – this had never happened before, and Will gasped, ready to jump in defence of his food, but it wasn't necessary. The silhouettes kept moving, and that glance slipped away but, before it did, Will thought he had caught a spark of compassion in those grey eyes.

Qu Sith was already feasting, but Will kept following the two silent figures as they made their way back to the village.

"Aren't you going to eat?" the sphinx asked with a mouthful of parsnips.

Will silently moved closer to the tray and dug his fingers into the first pumpkin. The mash was tasteless, and he gulped it down almost without thinking. Qu Sith mumbled something with his face deep in the third pumpkin on his tray. Will wasn't listening. He ate and watched the dusk slowly descend upon the world. The sky was covered with clouds, and the rising fog obscured the village, with only the monotonous sound of drums and the flickering reflections of flames indicating its presence behind the milky wall. Qu Sith retreated to the back of his cage, leaving the empty pumpkins on the tray.

"I'd advise you to move back," the sphinx said from the dark. "The eruption is near."

"You should stick your heels out to wash that shit off," Will grinned, quickly stuffing the remaining contents of the second pumpkin into his mouth.

"That's my shit on my heels," Qu Sith observed dryly. "I don't want my ankles to get boiled."

Will grabbed the third pumpkin in his hands and pushed the tray outside. He sat down at the back of the cage, leaning against the bars. It had been a busy day, and his muscles were slightly aching as they did after a strenuous workout in the gym. That seemed so far away, almost in another life.

"I feel utterly exhausted," Qu Sith complained. "The day was a complete disaster."

"But now you've got four cracked bars in your cage," Will said, placing the pumpkin between his legs and digging into the mash. "A few more days at that pace, and we'll be free by the end of the week."

Will watched the shadows dancing over the pond in the flickering light of bonfires and listened to the hypnotic rhythm of the drums. Then the evening breeze brought the foulness to his nose – Will wasn't sure if the stench was from the dead bodies behind them or the sphinx's heels, but the parsnips began to taste funny too.

He dug his fingers deeper into the mash, trying to reach the still warm layers and nearly cried out when his finger was suddenly cut by something sharp! Will cursed sucking blood from a small gaping wound in his thumb. It wasn't very big or too painful, but whatever had pierced the skin still was hidden in the mash and was waiting to be found!

Will carefully lowered the fingers of his other hand into the mash, gently probing. There was something hard at the bottom of the pumpkin, something elongated. The drums in the village stopped abruptly, and the ground began to tremble as he grabbed that thing and pulled it out of the mash.

"Careful!" Qu Sith roared from the next cage, and Will curled into the corner covering his head as the water came down in their direction.

Will squeezed the finding in his fist, waiting for the streams of hot water to ooze through their soggy shelters. The dry branches placed on the roofs had stopped only part of the spate, and Will was instantly soaked down to his last thread. The water wasn't scalding after travelling all that distance in the atmosphere but was still uncomfortably hot.

Qu Sith was softly whining, but at least, his ankles were now clean.

Will rolled onto his back on the damp straw. He raised the thing he had retrieved from the mash and tried to have a better look in the failing light of the dying flames across the pond. It looked like a curved knife, probably used to carve pumpkins. The blade had been sharp enough to cut his finger, and Will didn't risk testing it again. He shook his head since large drops were still splashing down from the leaking roof, but a wide grin split his face. Some joints of the cage were fixed with oiled ropes, too strong for any teeth, but he was sure they would be unable to withstand the nick of a knife.

"You never mentioned you'd got a knife," Qu Sith

growled.

That sounded like an accusation.

"I hadn't," Will said, sitting up. "I found it in my mash! But how can you see in complete darkness?"

"I just can," Qu Sith chuckled. "And it's not complete darkness. There's something big glowing in the north. I can see the reflections of the flames on clouds. A big fire, maybe."

"Where?" the sky was completely dark to Will's eyes.

The sphinx was silent for a few seconds. "Turn your head to the right a little and look at the sky. Even you should be able to see it."

Will did as he was told. It was utterly dark at first, but he kept staring. Then a faint red flickering appeared at the edge of his perception. He would never pay any attention to small things like that shimmering.

"Do you see it?" Qu Sith asked quietly.

"Yes," Will whispered. "It must be just a lava flow."

"Lava is flowing in the south from here," the sphinx said disdainfully. "It must be something different."

"Do you see anything like that in the south?" Will asked, keeping his eyes on the flickering.

Qu Sith was silent for too long.

"Well?" Will demanded.

"No," the sphinx finally admitted. "That's very strange."

Will slipped the knife into his pocket. Anyway, it was too dark to cut anything, and he was afraid to lose the only key to his freedom.

"There's nothing strange in that," Will said after a pause.

"There was a huge eruption shortly before I got here. The northern slope of the volcano blew off, and now there's a new lava flow down the northern slope. And the old flow has cooled down. You've been sitting here for too long, Qu Sith. You've missed all the fun."

The sphinx snarled in the darkness.

"It wasn't from choice," he growled. "You know that perfectly well."

"Don't get angry," Will stretched his body out on the wet straw and placed an arm under his head. "I meant no offence."

"You're a very strange man, Will," Qu Sith mumbled in the dark. "All day you've been shaking those damned bars without a single second of rest. You seemed unable to stop. Now you've got a knife, but you're still lying down watching the skies. Aren't you going to cut some ropes?"

"It's too dark for me," Will sighed. "I don't want to risk losing the knife."

"Maybe you're right," the sphinx chuckled. "Still, we've got nearly two months at our entire disposal. Why rush, indeed. At least, they're feeding us."

"We'll run away tomorrow," Will promised and closed his eyes, but sleep didn't follow. He felt tired, but his mind was stuck in this world, and Will realised that the artificial coma those strange people had promised him was holding him firmly in the cage.

He stirred uneasily, unable to find a comfortable position, then sat up leaning against the bars. The pale red aurora still danced on the clouds as Will watched it slowly moving left down the slope of the mountain. Then it stopped.

Will waited for a few minutes, but the faint flashes of distant flames were pinned to the same place, as the low bellies of heavy clouds moved without stopping.

"That's strange," he said, standing up and going closer to the front of his cage to have a better look.

"What?" Qu Sith asked in a sleepy voice.

"Look at those reflections," Will pointed at the sky.

"I showed that to you, remember?" the sphinx yawned. "What's so exciting about it now?"

"It's stopped moving," whispered Will with his gaze fixed above the dark wall of the forest.

Qu Sith didn't bother to get up. "You said, it was a lava flow," he mumbled, closing his red glowing eyes. "Maybe it reached the lava lake. Get some rest. You'll need all your strength if we're going to break free tomorrow. The Rybbaths will send a hunting party after us, have no doubt."

Will ignored the advice. He was unable to sleep and watched the faint flickering reflections instead. There was nothing else he could do.

The village across the pond was silent, and Will listened to the distant cry of an owl somewhere in the dark woods. It echoed in the night, and Will gasped as those strange reflections on the clouds began to move again, this time heading back up the slope of the volcano. It couldn't be lava! Maybe Qu Sith was right – it could be just distant wildfire spreading across the forest, pushed by the wind.

Will didn't dare to wake the sphinx and ask him again.

He stood, watching the sky until his legs got tired. Only then did he return to the back of his cage and laid his body on the wet straw waiting for the dawn.

It was the most useless night Will had spent in his entire life. Thick clouds still covered the sky, and all he could do was wait. Now and then he checked the precious knife in his pocket, afraid to lose it. The blade was still there, and he grinned each time tracing its edge with his finger.

Several times Will got up to look at the faint aurora in the night sky. It was a strange wildfire – each time it flickered in a different location, and Will wondered if the wind on the northern slopes of the volcano had gone entirely crazy. It wasn't windy around the Lifeless Pond, and Will frowned each time the light breeze brought the stench of decaying bodies.

Qu Sith was soundly asleep all this time or, at least, silent.

The sky began to clear only when the first light of dawn appeared in the East. Will patiently waited, leaning against the bars of his cage until the darkness turned to grey twilight, still barely enough to see. Then he got to his feet and began inspecting his cage again. This time it was different. He didn't shake any bars. Will slowly went along the perimeter of the cage stopping at every joint that held the walls together, touching the oiled ropes which were tightly wrapped around these joints, inspecting them, planning.

The construction was simple. Four large logs had been ground deep into the soil, forming the base of the cage. Will had no idea how deep they were set, but the logs felt firm and solid, and he ditched any thought of touching them. Four smaller logs were attached to the base a few feet above the ground, forming the floor of the cage. Two joints were carved into the base and didn't even need a rope to hold them together. The other two were wrapped with the thick rope and moved a little when Will tried to push them with his feet. That seemed promising. The walls and the roof were attached to each other in the same way, and this looked promising too. With the blade in his hands, the ropes held the key to his freedom. He only had to decide which rope to cut first.

"I would advise not to rush this," the sphinx snarled at his back. "Breakfast is coming, and you won't be able to escape in time."

"I'm not going to cut anything yet," Will glanced over his shoulder.

Two dark silhouettes had already left the village, carefully stepping along the shore of the pond with trays in their hands. Will wondered if it would be the same well-wisher who had brought him the knife and sat down at the back of his cage waiting for the Rybbaths to get closer.

"Take that stupid smile off your face," Qu Sith whispered. "That might make them suspicious."

Will dutifully wiped the grin away. When the two figures stopped in front of their cages, he dared to look at the weird mask in anticipation of meeting those grey eyes again. The eyes looked back calmly, but they were dark brown, almost black.

The savages pushed the trays inside and left without casting a second glance at their prisoners. Will waited until they had covered half their way back before getting the knife out of his pocket. The sphinx's head was already buried in the first pumpkin.

Will decided to begin with the back wall. The upper joints seemed loose enough, and by just holding onto the ropes, he was sure he could loosen them even further.

"Are you cutting already?" Qu Sith asked with a mouthful of mash. "Don't you think it would be a good idea to eat first? Nobody's waiting for us in the woods with freshly baked pies."

Will stopped, replacing the knife in his pocket. Cutting through those ropes seemed like an easy task which could wait a little. Anyway, he didn't need a big hole – only a slit, sufficient for him to get through.

Will sat down in front of the tray. This must be his last meal in the cage, and he decided to enjoy it to the full. As had been rightly pointed out by the sphinx, nothing but mushrooms and berries were waiting for him in the woods.

The day was breaking with a clear blue sky and a gentle breeze from the Pond pushing the stench away. Will dug his fingers into the first pumpkin and licked them clean – this time even the mash seemed to be less tasteless than before.

He was in the middle of his second pumpkin when Qu Sith had finished gulping all three portions of his mash and, as always, went to the back of his cage to shit on the graves. Suddenly, he stopped in the middle of the process.

"You are you going to free me as well, aren't you?" the

beast asked cautiously.

"Of course," Will nodded and licked his fingers. "I won't leave you behind."

"I was counting on that," Qu Sith grinned, resuming his dirty job.

"Where are you going after we break free?" Will asked as he dug his fingers back into the mashed parsnips.

"I don't have any particular destination in mind," Qu Sith yawned. "Maybe I'll go south. I'm sick of these barbarians already."

"Why did you go north then?" Will asked, stuffing another portion of mash into his mouth.

"It was personal business. Sightseeing, you may call it…" the sphinx answered vaguely, staring across the Pond.

"I don't believe you," Will said with a grin. Qu Sith flashed an angry glance at him but said nothing and turned his head to gaze at the water again. Will quickly finished eating the parsnips from the second pumpkin, then tossed it aside.

"I'm nearly full," he remarked, taking the third pumpkin into his lap.

"The third one is supposed to be sweet," the sphinx reminded him flatly. "Eat it. We won't be able to hunt until we get far enough away from the village."

"What makes you think we'll be going together?" Will asked.

"As I understand it, you'll go down the mountain?"

"Yes. Down the mountain by the *old* lava flow," Will nodded. "I need to find that blossom."

"That means you're going south, down the slope," Qu Sith grinned exposing his rows of sharp teeth. "I'm going south too. We could keep each other company for a while at least."

Will shrugged. He dug into the mash with a contented smile, but his fingers hit something just below the surface.

"What's that?" he exclaimed as he lowered the pumpkin to the floor.

"Another knife?" Qu Sith frowned. "We don't need another knife!"

"Doesn't feel like a knife…" Will suddenly felt hesitant about taking another dive into that mash.

"What is it?" the sphinx sprang to his feet. "What is it?"

Will moved the tray closer with his foot and then carefully scooped out the contents of the carved pumpkin.

"What is it?" demanded Qu Sith again.

There was something beneath the mash. Will fished the knife from his pocket and carefully poked the thing out.

"Lucky bastard!" Qu Sith exclaimed before Will gasped, realising.

It was a human hand, severed at the wrist. Will pushed the tray away, gulping in a desperate effort to keep his breakfast in place.

"Aren't you going to eat it?" the sphinx asked as he licked his lips.

"I'm not a cannibal," Will forced out, fighting with the convulsions in his stomach.

Qu Sith chuckled. "I didn't ever think you were that sensitive. You could pass it to me," he said expectantly when

Will's spasms finally subsided. "I'm not a human, and it won't be cannibalism."

"No!"

"Why waste a good piece of meat?" the sphinx sat down in front of Will with nearly begging eyes.

"No one's going to eat that hand!" Will said with a burst of anger.

"Are you going to sit there and stare at it until it begins to stink?"

"No," Will said firmly, then stood up and grabbed the tray. "It's a burial ground down there. It can go where it belongs!"

"Wait..." Qu Sith's voice trailed off as he sadly watched the palm flying out of the cage in a cloud of mash.

"Consider, I had eaten it," Will told the beast, tossing the tray away.

"Such a waste," the sphinx said vexatiously.

"May I remind you that we're getting out today, and you'll get the chance to hunt for fresh rabbits," Will said, still feeling upset. "Or would you rather stay behind and wait for another body part that the Rybbaths decide to offer you?"

The dark eyes of Qu Sith flashed with anger.

"I have one condition if you want me to release you before I go," Will said, calmly studying the expression on the sphinx's face.

"What's that?"

Will stepped closer before answering. He took a grip of the bars between him and the sphinx and stared into the black eyes of the creature.

"What is that?" Qu Sith demanded, returning the gaze but with less fierceness.

"You must make a vow to me," Will told him. "Swear on the holiest and most sacred thing you know, that you'll never eat human flesh again."

"If you so wish…" the sphinx mumbled uncertainly.

"Do it, or I'll leave you behind," Will furrowed his brow.

"I swear on my life that I won't taste human flesh," Qu Smith said. "If I break this oath, I will guard the gate at the Tower of Whispers for eternity like the worst guard dog, serving as a shadow among the other shadows until the last stone in Rehen crumbles to dust."

They looked at each other for nearly a full minute in silence. Will couldn't decide if the oath sounded serious enough, and Qu Sith simply waited.

"Good," Will sighed at last. "Now I won't be afraid to turn my back to you."

"I am no threat to you, dear. You're the one with the knife," Qu Sith murmured, sitting down. "Start using it, or my oath will be meaningless if we stay here for too long."

"Right…" Will nodded and took the knife out of his pocket. "Let the fun begin."

He went to the far left corner of his cage and kneeled in front of the lower joint of the back wall. It was greasy business, and Will had to tear a piece of cloth off his shirt to wrap around the slippery surface.

It wasn't as easy as he had expected. The rope had been hardened by extended exposure to the elements, and Will had to press with all his might to cut through just a thread.

Half an hour later, he felt exhausted but had managed to cut through a single rope. The joint itself was still holding.

Qu Sith silently observed as Will sat down and leant against the bars, gasping.

"I need some rest," Will felt as if he was apologising.

"Take your time," the sphinx told him with a note of disappointment in his voice. "We still have almost two months to do this."

Will cursed, looking helplessly at the Lifeless Pond which seemed serene and tranquil in the light of the morning sun. An imaginary clock loudly ticked in his ears and, five minutes later, he was again vigorously digging the resistant ropes.

Fifteen minutes later, Qu Sith coughed behind Will's back.

"I would advise you to stop," the sphinx whispered. "Something's going on down there."

"Where?" Will glanced at the creature and stopped cutting.

Qu Sith silently indicated the Lifeless Pond.

Will quickly slipped the knife into his pocket and sat down, shielding the cut ropes with his body.

Something unusual was indeed going on at the other side of the pond.

Four rows of masked figures in dark robes, six in each, were silently approaching the pond from the village. The inner rows of the figures carried a wooden floater with a large bundle on it covered with a white cloth.

"What's that?" Will whispered.

"I think it's a live demonstration of what will happen to the winner of the contest," Qu Sith observed, keeping his eyes on the bundle. "I wonder what dummy they are using for the body."

The procession didn't stop at the water's edge. The outer rows split aside with ropes in their hands and continued moving along the shore while the inner rows carried the floater into the pond and lowered it onto the surface then picked up their ends of the ropes from the back of the floater and walked ashore.

It was an eerie silent pantomime. Will watched, holding his breath realising that two months later he would be fixed to that floater if he didn't manage to escape.

The white bundle, supported by the web of ropes, slowly floated towards the middle of the pond. The setup looked like a giant spider waiting for its prey. Will gasped as the spider stirred in silence.

"Someone is alive on that floater," Qu Sith whispered. "And that someone is injured. See those red stains on the cloth?"

Will gulped imagining his own body under those sheets. "Shut up!" he hissed to the sphinx, as two Rybbaths stopped just a few yards away from their cages.

The floater slowed and stopped in the centre. As if by some silent command, the Rybbaths raised their arms to the sky, holding the ends of the ropes with both hands. It seemed like a prayer from Will's perspective, but not a sound came from their mouths, and whoever was under that white sheet didn't scream or moan either.

Will watched the scene unfold with increasing horror, painfully realising that each passing minute was a wasted opportunity to cut the ropes, which also brought him closer to a similar floater. He even considered letting the sphinx win their fight rather than lie under that white blanket waiting for death.

The Rybbaths stood unmoving, hands and faces raised upwards, for nearly half an hour. Then again, as if by silent command, they lowered their arms and dropped on their knees, fixing the web of ropes to the wooden poles that stuck out from the mud along the shore. A few more minutes passed before they raised to their feet again and returned to the village. No one looked back at the floater or the cages. In just a few more minutes, they were gone.

Will jumped to his feet, squeezing the knife in his fist. He must get the job done! He must cut through those ropes. He must do it as quickly as possible.

"I wonder who's under that sheet, and what the crime was?" Qu Sith mumbled under his breath.

"It is the one who gave us the knife!" Will offered, already working on the third rope. "The one who's hand I found in the mash this morning! Is it punishment for trying to save us?"

"Why haven't they searched our cages then?" Qu Sith demanded.

"I don't know," Will shrugged. "You're the expert on their beliefs. You tell me."

"I'm no expert," the sphinx spat out fiercely. "They just happened to capture me before their silent months, so I got a few explanations, at least."

"How long have you been in the cage?" Will stopped working and glanced at Qu Sith. "Four months?"

"Five."

"And you did nothing to escape?"

"I couldn't hold a knife in my paws even if I had one," the sphinx explained flatly. "And I'm probably not as handsome to the human eye as you are to get any help on the side."

"I'm not handsome," Will cut him. "Didn't you think about using your teeth?"

"That oil they use on the ropes is terribly bitter," the sphinx moaned. "And we'd tested the hold of those bars already."

"I get the picture..." Will mumbled, returning to his work. "Could you watch the Rybbaths, at least?"

"I will," Qu Sith said harshly, casting Will an angry glance.

Will worked without raising his head. The stubborn ropes around the joint gave way with great difficulty. Only twice Will sat down breathless and leaned his aching back against the bars of the cage looking at the grim reminder of his fate in the middle of the Pond.

"Could we save that poor soul if we got out?" he asked the sphinx on one of those occasions.

"You won't make it in time," Qu Sith observed. "You're struggling with one rope. The floater is held by twenty-four ropes, and you'd have to release at least two-thirds of them to get the floater ashore. And I'm sure someone in the village would be watching over this. There's no way you could do it before the eruption."

"Shit!"

"Calm down," the sphinx said. "You can't save the world if the world doesn't want to be saved. Look after your own skin. How's that rope looking?"

"Still holding," Will sighed sadly. "I hope I'll be able to free that joint by dusk."

"Don't get stressed," Qu Sith muttered. "You'll have to cut the ropes on my cage too."

"I know," Will sighed, taking up the knife again. "Unless we find another way to open your door."

It was late afternoon when he finally cut the joint loose. The back wall gave a little – he could pass his arm through the slit, but nothing bigger than that. It was a small victory – too small to be excited.

"Better camouflage it now," Qu Sith advised, peeking through the bars. "They'll be bringing our meal shortly, so it's best not raise any suspicion. You might need to cut another rope or two before you're able to get out."

Will sighed. "And I'll have to cut even more ropes to set you free," he said, carefully hiding the loose ends. "All in one night. We won't get a second chance."

"So you're not leaving me behind?" Qu Sith smiled widely. "Are you?"

"I don't ever leave my friends in trouble," Will said simply. "I guess you're my friend now."

Was there some sudden moisture in the sphinx's eyes? Will couldn't be sure.

"It's a great honour to be the friend of a strange human," Qu Sith said seriously. "I might be useful for you in your quest to find that lost flower."

"Thanks," Will said and sat down at the next joint. "We need to get out first, though."

The rope here was rotten and weakened in places, and Will was able to cut through it before Qu Sith warned him about the Rybbaths approaching. The two dark figures began their usual journey along the shore of the pond with trays in their hands.

"I wonder what kind of surprises they'll bring us this time," Will mumbled and glanced at the white shape floating in the middle of the pond. "Has that poor thing stopped moving yet?"

"Yes," Qu Sith slowly nodded. "But you better hide your work in case these two get too close."

"Oh…" Will gasped. "Too late for that, I guess."

"Do something!" Qu Sith squeezed through gritted teeth, assuming the usual pose.

The two Rybbaths were probably only a dozen steps away, and Will had no other option but to try to shield the loose ends of the ropes with his body. He froze, pressing his back to the bars and hiding his right hand with the knife behind him.

When the two dark-robed figures in masks stopped in front of the cages, Qu Sith suddenly exploded with a roar and jumped to his hind feet shaking the bars. The Rybbaths shuddered and dropped their trays on the ground. One more roar from the sphinx was addressed to their retreating backs.

"You've left us without our food," Will observed.

"They were looking at you too intensely," Qu Sith explained and sat down. "We needed a distraction. And I hate those parsnips anyway."

"Now we'll be starving," Will observed and got up, clutching the knife.

"You promised me I could go hunting tonight," the sphinx said, licking his lips.

"Don't forget, that we might be hunted too though," Will mumbled quietly and got down on his knees in front of the next joint. The ropes there were tight.

Will worked with his knife holding the sticky oiled ropes with a piece of cloth. The clock was loudly ticking in his ears, and he did his best to focus on the cut, ignoring everything else. Then the hushed mumbling of Qu Sith cut through his concentration.

The sphinx was visibly upset, standing on his hind legs and leaning on the front of his cage. *What was happening?*

Then a gory scream pierced the evening silence.

Will looked back. The village of Rybbaths was on fire. Or so it seemed at first glance. Monstrous flames engulfed the straw roofs that were clustered on the other side of the pond, and dark figures jumped around in desperate attempts to escape the fate. Someone screamed again.

Will stood up, placing the knife in his pocket. *What was happening?*

Qu Sith gasped, but Will ignored him, looking directly at the village. The flames were acting strangely. The houses were catching fire one by one as if a mob of arsonists was running uphill through the village and seeding the horror. The woods behind the houses were aflame as well and, at first, it looked like the wind was urging the fire on, but when the stench of death hit his nostrils, Will realised that the flames were moving against the wind and uphill.

"Look at that!" Qu Sith exclaimed.

The flames moved aside as something bright emerged, shining like a midday sun. That something moved like a flaming river, consuming whatever got in its way – trees or houses.

"Is it lava?" Will asked. That seemed obvious.

"Why is it running uphill then?" Qu Sith responded quietly, his gaze fixed on the flames across the pond. "I don't know what it is. Usually, everything that is good for us is bad for our enemies, but I don't think this is the case now. It scares the hell out of me."

The flaming stream went from house to house swelling on its way, growing bigger and brighter, and then it rose high above the roofs and treetops, taking shape, remotely resembling a viper. It froze for just a few long moments, turning its head around and looking with its flaming eyes as if searching for prey. Then it dipped down, and the earth trembled as the creature began its hunt.

That was a messy carnage. The dark silhouettes of the Rybbaths raced away from the flames, but their efforts were in vain. The viper had already encircled the village with its body of fire, blocking all ways of retreat. The monster watched them unhurriedly, clearly enjoying the view. Now and then the flaming head rose in the sky and then dunked down, grabbing someone. Sometimes the Rybbaths died with a heart-piercing scream, but most of them took the strike silently, as their entire village was bursting with flames.

"Cut the ropes! Now!" Qu Sith roared, and Will rushed back to his interrupted work, hastily slashing at the hardened ropes with his knife. "We're next!"

"We'll never make it in time," Will mumbled under his breath. "No way…"

"Do it!"

Frantically Will scratched the knife across the slippery knots, trying hard with all his might, but his hands were shaking, and most of the slashes simply brushed the oil rather than making any real cuts. He glanced over his shoulder a few times at the village. The carnage continued, but not too many people were left alive to entertain the viper.

"Get to the back of the cage!" Will hissed to the sphinx. "We won't make it in time. We must hide!"

"There's nowhere to hide," Qu Sith said slowly but retreated to the back of his cage anyway. "We're doomed if you can't cut those ropes."

Will checked the slit he had made again. He could push his arm through, but it got stuck at his shoulder – one more joint was barring his way to freedom. He cursed aloud and shook the bars with rage, but that didn't help to make the slit any wider.

"Be quiet," the sphinx whispered. "Don't attract its

attention."

Dark wings of dusk descended on the world as the village of Rybbaths collapsed, embraced by the flaming creature. There were no more screams – the Rybbaths were all dead or were dying in silence.

"Hurry..." Qu Sith whispered, watching the flames across the pond. "The night is falling, and the fog is rising. We might succeed!"

Will's hand hurt as he pressed on the knife, slicing thread by thread, but he was still not halfway through the whole thickness of the rope. He quickly glanced at the village and froze. The flaming viper was staring directly at them!

"Close your eyes!" Will hissed to the sphinx. "They're glowing..."

"Too late," Qu Sith cut him off with a flat voice. "It's seen us. You won't have time to save me. Get out and run."

Damn!

Will redoubled his efforts. The ropes were still holding.

"It's our turn now," the sphinx said and lay down on the floor.

The flaming creature was making its way along the shore when Will glanced over his shoulder. There wasn't much he could do now. The ropes were too strong.

He cried out in a rage and began shaking the bars violently.

"You won't scare it away," Qu Sith said sadly. "No need to bother."

An excruciating wave of heat rolled over the cages as the

flaming creature stopped in front of them and then lowered its head to have a look inside. It looked like a viper with amber eyes and a long forked tongue. It stuck its tongue out several times, touching the wooden bars and straw roofs of the cages. Flames and smoke began swirling around, and it seemed that the cages jerked at the contact.

Qu Sith jumped to his feet and roared with all his might.

The viper stirred with interest but didn't back away. The ground trembled under its body as it raised its flaming head high above the cages, preparing to strike.

Then the ground shook again, and an enormous wall of water suddenly erupted high into the cloudy sky behind the viper. The flaming monster turned its fierce gaze upwards, but before it even had a chance to react, the water came down on the cages in a colossal hot stream, flooding everything.

Will crouched and covered his head just before the water hit. Those few seconds under the scalding stream seemed like a painful eternity.

The silence was deafening when everything was over. Will hastily brushed away the moisture from his face and looked around. It was dark, except for the still glowing embers at the place where the village of Rybbaths had stood just that morning.

The viper was still towering in front of the cages, but its body was dark and motionless, all the flames had gone. The steaming water still splashed down its black surface but was gone too a minute later.

Will glanced at the neighbouring cage. The red eyes of

Qu Sith glowed in the darkness. He was alive.

"Now what?" the sphinx asked, still pressing his back against the rear wall of the cage. "The snake is dead, I presume. You need to cut faster."

"I don't remember where I had put the knife," Will admitted, searching his pockets with shaking hands.

"Shit!" Qu Sith cursed loudly. "We were lucky to escape those flames and those stupid savages, but now we'll die of starvation!"

"We'll find some way to get out..." Will grunted, but his voice was interrupted by the sound of breaking glass as the towering viper shattered into pieces, crashing onto the cages. Will jumped aside, barely escaping the rubble, as his whole cage twisted to the left and collapsed.

"Are you alive?" the voice of Qu Sith growled from under the rubble.

"I guess so," Will mumbled trying to get up. It took some effort to lift off the roof which was sitting on his shoulders and push aside a few broken bars before he managed to stick his head out.

The red eyes of the sphinx still glowed under the chunks and pieces of his cage. "Could you help me out, please?" the beast asked quietly.

Will struggled to free his legs without saying a word. They were bruised and painful but not broken. Then he stopped in front of the pile of rubble that was all that remained of the second cage. The eyes of Qu Sith followed him silently.

"You swore an oath," Will reminded him, looking at the

red glow. "Do you remember it?"

"Of course, I do," the sphinx grunted. "I'm not feebleminded."

"Good," Will smiled, getting a grip of a piece of roof. "I guess my back is safe then."

"You must not fear me," Qu Sith mumbled from under the rubble. "We are not enemies."

"Good to know," Will lifted the cage roof and let the sphinx out.

Just piles of flaming rubble remained of what had been the Rybbath village. Will briefly glanced at the few pieces of wood on the still rippling surface of the Lifeless Pond – all that was left of the floater. Neither the white cloth nor the body it had covered was anywhere in sight.

"Do you think there are any survivors?" Will asked the sphinx.

"I doubt it, and it's none of our business," Qu Sith hissed disdainfully. "Let's get out of here."

The night was dark, and the flickering flames of the burning village were the only light on their way across the Rybbath cemetery. Qu Sith took the lead down the narrow path between the decaying bodies hidden under the thick leaves of the blooming vines. Flowers the size of a farthing leaked a strange bittersweet aroma which, mixed with putrid stench and churned Will's stomach into knots. The dark wall of woods was no more than a couple of hundred yards away, but it seemed like miles as they passed from one grave to another. He wasn't sure if it was branches of vines or decaying limbs that brushed at his sides and he carried on without looking.

The black coat of Qu Sith was barely visible in the darkness, and Will did his best not to lose him. An owl cried somewhere in the dark woods, and he suddenly felt lonely and abandoned, stuck in this weird world. Will thought about those strange people who were taking care of his body in the hospital. They had put him into a coma, thus allowing him to stay with this dream, but would they wake him up? Those people were strange, and Will wondered why he had chosen to trust them in the first place.

He reached the forest and stopped. The sphinx was nowhere in sight, and he stood for several long minutes listening, trying to catch any sound of quiet footsteps or a breaking branch. Nothing…

The last flashes of light from the village blaze ended there, and Will was afraid to step into the complete darkness of the woods, feeling as blind as a bat. He took a few more steps away from the stench, carefully probing the way with his feet, and sat down on soft moss. He must wait until the daybreak.

That damned sphinx had left him behind. Will had never trusted the deceitful creature but hadn't expected this to happen quite so quickly. He felt the nearby trunk of a tree and lent against it, silently cursing the weather. He could be heading back to the old lava flow and searching for that orchid if that silver globe wasn't obscured by thick clouds.

A quiet swish of wings passed over him in the darkness. Seconds later, an owl cried out high above, hunting for mice. Will lifted his eyes at the sound. A pair of dark wings were barely visible in the fading light of the distant blaze. The bird circled over the Rybbath cemetery a few times then turned back. Will didn't move, and the owl landed on a branch just a few feet away from him. He smiled as two golden eyes, barely visible in the darkness, stared at him.

"What do you want?" Will asked the bird.

The owl didn't answer. They looked at each other for a few more moments, and then the bird spread its wings again, rose into the air and disappeared into the night.

Will watched the flashes of the distant blaze and wondered how those strange people would know when to wake him from the coma. Must he give them a sign? They hadn't said anything, and Will had no idea what to do. He only hoped that they wouldn't cut into his throat as they had threatened to – he was out of the cage and ready to resume his quest if that was what they wanted. Would it be sufficient to save him from that cut? *But how would they know?*

Will touched his throat, trying to imagine a knife slicing into it to fit in the tube. The thought was chilling, and he cursed. He hoped he still had a few days before that point.

"I'm on my way!" he cried out. "I just need some damned light!"

There was no response.

The blaze was almost extinguished and those rare flashes it did spit out into the night provided no light. The sky was dim grey, but the ground was as black as tar.

The moss was slightly damp beneath him, but Will didn't care. His mind was busy searching for a way to give those people a sign. He felt stupid and cursed again, closing his eyes. Outside was as dark and quiet as inside, and there was no need to keep them open.

Will listened to the silence when something began beeping to his left.

He muttered a few incoherent words before opening his eyes. The light hurt, and he frowned, trying to get his gaze to focus. His mouth was full of something, and suddenly Will felt a wave of panic rising – had they sliced into his throat? He moaned, his tongue was as stiff and dry as a piece of wood and lifted his hand – his free right hand since his left arm was attached to tubes and wires which led to that beeping machine with coloured curves running across its screen.

It began to beep more quickly and then emitted a sharp sound like a warning, with a red light flashing at the top of the screen.

Will closed his eyes, wishing he could return to that dark forest, but it was too late.

"Welcome back to the land of the living," the nurse said softly, checking the beeping machine. "I'll let the doctor know you've woken up."

She left and disappeared into the corridor. Will heard her talking to someone. He cautiously touched his throat and sighed with relief – it was still intact. An attempt to smile proved painful, as his mouth was stuffed with tubes. Another clear tube, filled with a milky substance, disappeared through his right nostril.

The nurse came back, followed by the grey-haired man, who hastily put on a friendly smile despite his concerned looks.

"How do you feel?" the grey-haired doctor asked.

Will silently pointed to his mouthful of tubes and nodded slightly.

"We'll fix that in no time," the doctor nodded to the nurse.

The next fifteen minutes were the most horrible, as she began to remove the tubes. They seemed to be everywhere! Will blushed red when his manhood uncomfortably twitched and grew stiff as she slowly removed the fixing and the tube from there.

"It may leak a little for a day or two," the nurse casually said as she replaced his sheets. "Let us know if this lasts any longer. We'll get you back to the ward a bit later."

Damn! Why did he get into it? Never before had he felt more embarrassed.

The nurse was busy collecting together all the discarded tubes and other stuff and went away, never casting a second glance at Will. Did she feel embarrassed too?

Will placed his muscular arms on top of the sheets, feeling his redness and tension subside. He must get out of this damned hospital, but he was still tied here. That damned transparent tube was still dripping some liquid into his vein, and a line of stickers still ran across his chest, connecting him to the beeping machine with its tangled wires.

The grey-haired doctor peeked in through the door. He smiled at Will and came in, bringing a file with notes in his hand.

"How do you feel?" he asked, getting closer.

"Thirsty," Will mumbled, and his tongue still felt alien in his mouth.

"Give me a minute," the doctor dropped his papers on a chair and hurried out. Moments later, he appeared with a glass of water in his hands. "Here," he extended it out to Will.

Will sniffed the glass with caution. The man grinned but refrained from any comments, and Will tasted the liquid. It was indeed, plain water. He gulped a few satisfying mouthfuls down before returning the glass.

"Do you have a headache?" the doctor asked, taking a pen out of his pocket. "Follow this, please." And he began moving it up and down in front of Will's eyes, then to both sides, while keeping his bleached eyes fixed on Will's face.

"I'm fine," Will uttered and fell into a bout of coughing. His throat was sore.

The grey-haired doctor patiently waited for him to calm down and then went through a series of examinations. He listened to Will's lungs and felt his belly, while the nurse returned and stood at the foot of his bed, waiting for the doctor's orders. Will had to stick out his tongue, and the doctor tickled the soles of his feet with a needle.

"We can take him back to the ward," was the verdict.

"I'll call the porters," the nurse said.

"Have you called his mother?"

"Yes, doctor," the nurse nodded. "She's coming in."

"Good..."

Will frowned. He wasn't ready to see his mother or listen to her rebukes. Not yet. Life had slowed down when he had been sitting in the cage. Now he was out and ready to carry on, eager to find that damned flower. His body ached from inactivity and begged for a decent workout.

"When will I be able to go home?" Will asked as the doctor collected his notes.

"I'm not sure yet, it depends what the doctors on the ward decide," the grey-haired man wore a puzzled expression on his face. "They might want to keep you in for a couple of days just to make sure you don't slip into one of those fits again."

"I won't," Will assured him. "I'm feeling fine."

"I hope so," the grey-haired man nodded. "But let the ward doctors decide, keeping in mind your best interests."

"Fine..." Will mumbled unhappily. That meant he was confined to bed for a few more days, at least. He knew, his mother wouldn't let him sneak away.

The porters came half an hour later. Two skinny blokes in their fifties valiantly dragged the bed out, leaving the beeping machines behind and pushed it down the brightly lit corridor.

Will pulled the sheets all way up to his chin, suddenly ashamed of his mighty muscular body resting in the bed, while the two skinny guys acted like a couple of determined ants and navigated him down the flow. The oncoming traffic was mainly scurrying nurses and junior doctors with only occasional wheelchairs and beds.

"Stop! Stop right now!" someone roared when the bed heading in the opposite direction lined up against Will's. He flinched and pulled the sheets up even further. The voice sounded familiar.

"I didn't know you were ill, Willy," the familiar specs peeked at him from the other bed. "I'm so sorry…"

"Leave me alone, Jill," Will mumbled feeling a growing embarrassment.

"I won't, and you know it," she was widely grinning.

"You're sick," Will mumbled and added to the porters. "Can we go now?"

"I'll email you when I get out of the hospital," Jill's hand flashed from under the sheets and firmly grabbed the edge of Will's bed. "Promise me, you'll reply!"

"I won't," Will said as firmly. "You're wasting your time and effort."

"It's my time and my effort! You don't need to worry about that," Jill attempted to sit up but fell back gasping. "I'll email you as soon as I get out of this bloody hospital."

A traffic jam had now built up on both sides of the corridor since the two beds had completely blocked the way. Will tried to avoid the angry glances flashing at him from all sides, but Jill didn't seem to care one bit.

"That won't happen too soon, lady," the porter standing at the foot of Jill's bed observed. "You seem to be quite ill."

"She is *very* ill," Will agreed.

"Could you have a chat with your grandson some other time, lady?" an angry voice from the growing crowd asked impatiently.

"I'm not her grandson," Will mumbled under his breath and pulled the slipping sheets up to his chin again.

"Lady, please…" the crowd grew increasingly impatient.

The porters swung into action, but Jill kept her grip on Will's bead with all her might, her knuckles turning white. Someone began to laugh about all the commotion, and Will felt an increasing urge to jump out of bed and run away. All that stopped him was the clear tube, still dripping fluid into his vein, and the fact that he was completely naked under his sheets.

Jill was grinning manically, and Will felt embarrassed as he attempted to free his bed from her grasp. Her skin was sweaty and cold to touch, but her hand released its grip as soon as he touched it, and Will quickly retrieved his hand when Jill's fingers had left his bed.

"Thank you," Jill whispered and added in a louder voice. "Your touch felt so good! It felt almost healing. You certainly know how to revive old blood! I'll be out of the hospital in no time!"

The statement was followed by crazy laughter and the shuffling of beds as the porters rushed to separate them while Jill still rolled her eyes in oblivion. The beds were several paces apart when she roared again at the top of her lungs. "Stop right now!"

Will sighed with relief as the porters carried on pushing his bed without paying any attention to the shouts, but Jill's bed had come to a standstill in the corridor again, blocking the traffic. Will's bed left the growing crowd and increasing mayhem behind and, before they turned around the corner, Will looked over his shoulder and gasped. Jill was screaming "I'm okay! I feel *much* better now!" and jumping on her bed in a tight hospital gown which barely contained her massive body. He couldn't make out what else she was shouting, but the voice of the old lady seemed to be full of joy.

A wave of laughter overtook them, and Will's face blushed to a deep crimson. He closed his eyes, unable to meet anyone's gaze. They were laughing at him; he was certain.

Will braved to open his eyes again only when they came to a halt in the Cheerful Sparrows ward. It seemed peaceful and quiet there, after Jill's performance in the corridor. Will's previous spot next to the window was now occupied, and the nurses directed porters to leave him at the opposite side, facing the wall.

"We've called your mother," one of the nurses said as she took the tube out of his vein. "She'll be in to see you this afternoon."

Will nodded with a stern expression as if preparing to meet his fate. His mother would be angry, he was sure – and he would have to swallow whatever she had prepared for him.

The nurses left, casually talking to each other about their

nursing things, and Will was left alone. The bed next to him was empty, and the dark green curtain hid whoever was in his former place next to the window. All he could hear was the quiet beeping of the machine.

Will closed his eyes. He was out of hands of the bloody Rybbaths, free at last. Free to go wherever he pleased. The night was dark, and his body in that dream needed a proper sleep. No harm in that. He was determined to go to the old lava flow as soon as dawn brought enough light to see the way. First thing in the morning, Will decided. Gudula's body couldn't have floated very far down the mountain.

"Hello, my name's Tim," a voice broke into Will's daydream, and he looked at the extended hand waiting to be shaken. The young guy stood next to his bed and smiled, holding out the hand. "How are you?" Tim asked politely.

"I'm fine, thanks," Will mumbled, shaking the hand. The handshake took longer than usual.

"It's a fine morning," Tim released Will's hand and said, still smiling. "The air is quite refreshing after those thunderstorms."

"Thunderstorms?" Will frowned. "I've been in a coma."

"Oh," for only a fraction of a second Tim looked puzzled. "You're doing extraordinarily well so soon after being in a coma."

"When can I go home?" Will asked.

"I've no idea," Tim admitted and shrugged.

"You're not one of the doctors or nurses, are you?" Will asked with suspicion.

"No," Tim grinned. "I'm here for the treatment of my

lymphoma. I'm hoping the doctors will be more successful this time." He paused, his grin faded. "I was just wandering around and popped in when I saw another young face on the ward."

"I won't be here for long," Will mumbled looking at the guy. There was no need to get too friendly.

"That's the only wish we all have within these walls," Tim admitted. "It's my sixth relapse."

"I'm sorry for you," Will shrugged.

"Everything will be fine this time," Tim smiled confidently. "I'm sure."

"Good luck," Will nodded. "It's not right to be ill when you're so young."

"That's true," Tim nodded. "I must go now. Good luck to you too," he extended his hand again. The handshake took even longer than the previous one, and Will glanced suspiciously at the smile that was frozen on Tim's face. The strange guy winked before turning around but didn't say another word.

When Tim had left, Will lifted the sheets to inspect his body. He had no idea what they had done to him while he was asleep.

Still, his huge muscles were in shape but badly craved some arduous training. Everything felt right, and Hel's face still smiled sadly on his chest. He touched her features with his fingertips, suddenly feeling lonely. He must find that damned flower and talk to her. She *would* forgive him, Will was sure.

He lowered the sheets and realised that he wasn't alone

anymore – shy eyes were looking at him with a spark of hope within an ocean of pain.

"Who are you? What do you want?" Will asked the woman who was meekly standing at the foot of his bed. She was in her thirties but looked much older as the disease ate its way through her body. Her bald head was hidden under a dark blue bandana, and the woman attempted to disguise her embarrassment behind a shy smile as she pressed her right hand to her shallow chest.

"I am..." she said unsurely. "Lana."

"Do I know you?"

She flinched at Will's question.

"No, you don't know me," her eyes were sad and sunken. "And I'm very sorry to disturb you. This feels like complete nonsense."

"What do you want?" Will repeated his question.

"Could you..." Lana took a few hesitant steps closer. "Could you hold my hand?"

"What?"

She flinched again but gathered her courage and took one more step closer.

"You healed that woman. I saw it with my own eyes," Lana said in a quiet voice. "I've got cancer. Breast cancer. It's everywhere inside me, and I am dying. I had no hope until I saw that woman jumping out of bed."

Will was struck by her words. That damned crazy woman Jill was still messing everything up.

"You're mistaken," he said, trying to avoid her gaze. "I healed no one. That woman is mad."

"I saw it with my own eyes," Lana whispered, tears rolling down her cheeks. "She was sick and almost died. Then you took her hand, and she was healed. Please, hold my hand for just a minute. I don't want to die. Please..."

"I'm not a doctor," Will interrupted her pleas. "I don't heal anybody. You're mistaken."

"You're the only hope I have, please," she whispered. "I'll beg you on bended knees if you want."

"Ask your doctor, not me," Will frowned. "They can do all sorts of things. They'll certainly help you."

"They won't," Lana shook her head. "The doctors have done everything they can. I went to hell and back more than once. They lost. I lost. They've told me that I only have a couple of months. I don't want to die. Please... I guess you know the real name of Death. There's a look on your face that says you know everything, I'm sure."

"Who?"

"You know Death. I'm certain of that – it's how you healed that woman," Lana's voice trembled as she nervously crumpled the side of her cardigan in her left hand. "It sounds crazy, but you know Death."

"That does indeed sound crazy," Will had to admit. "Yes, I know the woman everybody calls Death, but she has a different name. I've no idea why they call her Death – she's very sweet and lovely, and she has nothing to do with your sickness or fate. I'm certain about that. She doesn't even know you."

"You *know* the true name of Death!" Lana gasped. "I didn't expect you to be that powerful! Please, help me. I beg you. I don't have much to offer you in return. Have mercy, please. I beg you…"

The situation was ridiculous. Will stared at her with widened eyes, but his tongue refused to spit out a repudiation.

"What is it that you want me to do?" he asked reluctantly.

"Please, hold my hand," her eyes were big and wet. "Just for a minute."

"And then you'll go away and never come back?"

Lana hastily nodded.

"Here…" Will extended his right hand out. "If you need it that badly."

Her hands trembled as she touched his skin. Will patiently waited while she ran her fingers along the callouses formed from pumping iron at the gym. Lana closed her eyes and waited expectantly but, of course, nothing happened. A few minutes passed, but Will didn't dare say a word. It was utterly useless.

"Thank you," Lana opened her eyes and then lowered her head and quickly kissed Will's hand before he was able to retrieve it.

"Did it help?" he asked when his shock passed.

Lana didn't answer but turned and dashed away, hiding her face and leaving Will with a sense of guilt.

"I am not a doctor! I am not a doctor!" he repeated several times, but she was probably already too far away to hear.

Lana's footsteps trailed down the corridor. The woman

was desperate but silly, and Will saw no point in her request. He had warned her several times that she was making a mistake. She should rely on the doctors, not on him.

That touch of the dying woman was terrifying. Her skin was dry and slack, cold and repulsive, and Will frowned remembering it.

A few more minutes passed before he was finally able to calm down. Will blamed himself for why he admitted knowing Hel. Anyway, it made no difference. That disease would eventually take her life if the doctors couldn't treat her anymore. Maybe she should find another doctor?

Will was glad he was out of his own situation at last. Those doctors had said he was healthy, and he could go back to his normal previous life, go back to the gym and train. If only Jill would stop interfering. *Damn!*

Then a wheelchair squeaked in. A breathless and frightened blonde girl was sitting in it and pushing the wheels hard as she rolled in. She gasped when she caught Will's gaze, but turned her wheelchair with determination and moved closer.

Her skin was glistening and tense with countless crimson patches covered by whitish scales that broke and fell apart as she moved. Her left hand bled slightly as the skin broke as she tried to manoeuvre the wheelchair closer to Will's bed.

"You must help me," she stated firmly with a stern expression and wide eyes, still struggling to catch her breath. "You must heal me! I can't spend the rest of my life in a wheelchair!"

"I'm not a doctor, lady," Will interrupted her firmly. "I'm not healing anybody."

"You don't understand," hissed the blonde rolling her wheelchair closer. "I've suffered enough. You must help me now! I'm much more worthy than that fat blob you healed in the corridor!"

"I'm not healing anybody," Will repeated, losing his patience. "She's just a crazy old woman."

"I saw it happen," the blonde lady told him seriously. "She was almost dead until you touched her. You must do the same to me. I've no time to argue."

"Go away and leave me alone," Will was getting tired of her.

"Just do it!" the woman grabbed the edge of his bed. "And you won't see me again."

"I won't see you again anyway," Will told her.

"You don't know me yet," the blonde hissed. "I always get what I want."

"Beware, I'm sick and very contagious," Will attempted a lie.

That froze her but only for a moment.

"It can't get any worse. Look at me!" she extended her right hand leaving a few flecks of her skin on the wheelchair. "Touch me!"

Will pulled his sheets up to his chin, trying to shield himself from her. The blonde growled like a mad cow.

"You won't get away from me!" she nearly screamed, and then suddenly lifted his sheets and grabbed his right calf.

Her touch was wet and repulsive, and Will tried to jerk away, but his calf remained squeezed with surprising strength. Seconds later, she let it go with a victorious smile on her face.

"I told you," she said, backing away in her wheelchair. "Now I'll wait."

Will cursed with frustration. The situation was beginning to scare him. If Jill's madness was contagious, he must get out of this hospital. *Quickly*.

He was healthy. Will was sure about that but had no idea how to convince the doctors on the ward and, more importantly, how to convince his mother.

"I'm feeling better… I'm feeling better…" the blonde mumbled staring at the distant rooftops outside the window. "I'm feeling better!"

"Lady, are you lost?" the nurse asked, coming in. "I'll call the porters to take you back to your ward."

"I'm feeling better!" the blonde roared fiercely.

"I'm happy for you," said the nurse pushing the wheelchair out into the corridor. "But you must return to your ward."

The sounds of commotion faded down the corridor, and Will sighed with relief. The sticky touch of that diseased palm still burned his skin, and Will hastily scratched his calf, wishing he would wake up from *this* nightmare.

"Could I have my clothes back?" he asked when the nurse returned to check the other patient behind the green curtain. "I've heard the weather is nice after the thunderstorm, and I'd like a breath of fresh air if that's okay."

"Yes, sure. You don't have to stay in bed. Just don't go too far away," the nurse smiled at him, heading out. Minutes later, she returned.

"Thank you," Will gratefully accepted the bleached blue bag containing his possessions as the nurse drew the green curtain to maintain his privacy as he put on his usual T-shirt and sweatpants.

"Don't you want a snack?" the nurse asked when he emerged from behind the curtain. "It'll be here in half an hour."

"I'm not hungry, thank you," Will blatantly lied despite his loudly protesting stomach. He couldn't stay any longer in this madhouse and wait for more crazy people to come his way. He fished his rucksack out of the bag, secretly observing when the nurse had departed. His things inside were intact but not of any use in the hospital. Will found a protein bar stashed in the deep pocket behind his gym trainers. That would stave off the hunger at least for a while.

Nobody stopped him as he sneaked out. The nurses were busy at their post, and he turned right and hurried down the corridor. Will raised the hood of his tracksuit and held his rucksack in front of him, doing his best not to attract anyone's attention.

The corridor was long, and Will forced himself into a slower pace but inside felt the urge to run. A woman with wide eyes and an embarrassed look pushing a child in a wheelchair appeared at the far end of the corridor, and Will slowed down a little. The kid was terribly disfigured with saliva dripping from his mouth. Will tried to look away, having a gut feeling that the strange pair were looking for him. The madness was spreading much faster than he could ever have thought. *Damned Jill!* Was it worth all the false hope she had implanted into these sick people?

Will quietly cursed, lowered his hood and sneaked along the wall past the wheelchair. The child's eyes were unfocused and stared at the ceiling while his wrist trembled, and an acrid smell told Will that his diaper needed changing.

I can't heal him. I'm not a doctor. I won't give them even the slightest false hope. I can't! Will frowned. *Damned Jill!* His left hand had other thoughts. *Can I?*

"Poor kid," he mumbled, looming over the wheelchair. The woman jerked aside, but Will's hand simply brushed a strand of the child's hair aside, wiping away a tear that rolled down the cheek.

"Don't touch him!" the woman pushed Will's hand aside.

"Sorry..." he murmured and nearly ran down the corridor. *Damned Jill!*

Will took the stairs down. The maze of passages seemed endless, but he managed to find his way out. Nobody bothered him again. Nobody tried to stop him.

He sneaked outside through the back door, away from ambulances and sick people heading to die. There was a peaceful park with a few redwoods and larch trees grouped in the centre, and tall shady chestnuts lined at the perimeter.

It seemed like a different world after the hectic topsy-turviness of the hospital. He slowed his steps and turned left on the path that led deeper into the shade.

Jill had forced him into this crazy situation, and he could see no way out. Those people running after him were driving him mad. How could he explain to them that he wasn't a doctor? It was just a stupid show of a crazy woman, and Will regretted ever touching her. There were no miracles; he was sure. Those people had false hope, and he hated to have a part in that. But how could he hide in a hospital? It was full of sick people, and the false rumour was spreading like wildfire.

"Damned Jill!" He repeated aloud.

"Another problem with a woman, young man?" the frail voice asked behind him. "They never cease to amaze me."

Will turned around. The old gentleman was sitting on a bench set slightly away from the path under the shade of a chestnut tree. He looked familiar, and Will smiled with sudden recognition.

"Alan?" he asked. "What happen to Jim?"

"Jim is dead," the old man said sadly. "He had cancer, and the vet said there was nothing she could do for him. We had to have him put him down. I'm alone now, waiting for my turn."

"I'm sorry."

"Have a seat, young man," Alan patted the bench. "If you're not in a hurry, of course."

"I'm not," Will murmured, accepting the offer.

The air was fresh, and the gentle breeze brought a sweet

fragrance from the bright red roses, blooming nearby. Will needed a plan, and this place was as good as any, quiet and serene. Nobody would look for him here, and he didn't mind a little company.

"What brought you to the hospital?" Will asked the old gentleman.

"My blood pressure," Alan sighed. "Jim's death was too emotional for me. He was the last living creature who knew my wife, except me, of course, and his departure feels like the last thread connecting me to her has been cut off. My usual pills didn't help, so an ambulance brought me here."

"You must careful with your emotions," Will frowned. He felt uneasy advising the old man. "They can make you ill. You must be careful."

"Why?" Alan shrugged. "I know it's my turn. I've already lived for too long. I only hope I'll be able to see my Pat in the afterlife if there is any. I miss her. I don't want to live without her any longer."

Will looked at him. Alan stared at the blooming roses with not a hint of a smile. He wasn't joking. His pale blue eyes seemed empty, without pain, without hope, without emotion. Something essential had already gone. Will was surprised how much that dog had meant to the old man.

"Are you still chasing the same woman?" Alan asked after a while. "And is that other woman still chasing you?"

"Yes," Will nodded sadly. "My life is still a mess, and I've no idea how to sort it out."

"The only thing I can advise you if you chose to listen to what an old fool has to say, is to go where your heart leads you," Alan said. "Then you'll be able to face death with calmness, knowing that you've done everything you can and have no regrets."

"And what would you do about a mad woman who's chasing you?" Will asked with undisguised disgust.

"Avoid her and ignore her as much as you can," Alan shrugged. "She'll calm down eventually if you keep your distance."

"That's not easy," Will sighed. "She's crazy, and my problems have just multiplied since I met her. She finds me everywhere."

"Then you're not going far enough," Alan observed. "Keep your distance, young man, and she'll forget about you. Get closer to that other woman you're chasing, and she'll get used to you. I don't know your situation, but it would be best if you could do both things at the same time. Just listen to your heart, and you'll be fine."

"Like you did with your Pat?" Will asked.

"Yes," Alan said sincerely. "Listen to your heart even when you can't see any hope, when everybody else is holding you back and telling that you that you're out of your mind. Even then, you must sit down quietly and listen to your heart. It can't be wrong."

"Is this what you did?" Will looked at Alan, but the old man kept his eyes on the roses. "How did you find your Pat?"

"It wasn't easy," Alan shrugged. "Her blue eyes haunted me for a whole year after the war, and her French curses still rang in my ears. I knew she might have been killed during all that bloody wartime, but I still had to try, my heart was still in Normandy."

"How could you hope to find her without even knowing her name?" it sounded like a fairytale to Will.

Alan shrugged.

"That's when you must turn off your head and go wherever your heart leads you," the old man said. "Pat had been the wife of my enemy, and she loved her dead husband. I don't know; maybe it was even my bullet that killed her man. She cursed me once in French, and I knew nothing about her, not even her name. You would say it was hopeless. My brother said exactly that. But I went back to Ranville, looking."

Will shook his head.

"I wouldn't have gone," he said firmly. "I can't think of a more hopeless situation."

"Only death is more hopeless, young man," Alan objected. "I did find her."

"How?"

"I rented a flat in Ranville and began working for a fishmonger," Alan said. "The store was small but busy, and I quickly learned some French."

"She came in to buy some fish?" that seemed obvious.

"No," said Alan. "She never showed up in the shop. She hated fish, but I didn't know that. I took long walks around the town during my free time but was never able to spot her anywhere. She was like a ghost from my past without even a name. My head kept telling me that she might be dead, killed in those bloody times, but my heart wouldn't believe that so I continued my search. Sometimes I saw her in my dreams cursing me, and that gave me the strength to continue."

Alan took a moment of silence. Will didn't dare to interrupt.

"I found her in the field where my squad had killed her husband," Alan sighed. "She was standing in the same spot as her dapple-grey mare, clutching two red roses in her hand and crying. I trembled like a leaf on a high wind the moment I saw her. I was afraid to go closer. She went to that field every afternoon, and every afternoon I hid in the shrubs and watched her. It was two weeks later when I gathered enough courage to approach her."

"Did she recognise you?"

"No," Alan shook his head. "And I never dared tell her about that first time we had met when her husband had been killed. We both had our losses in that field, and this drew us closer together. She only knew a few words of English, and my French was as terrible as her English, but somehow we got along."

"What happened next?"

"We got married a year later, and she returned with me to my parents' house in Britain. She still cursed me in French when I was stupid enough to anger her," Alan smiled sadly. "Her usual was *Brûle en l'enfer, salaud*. And I would be heavenly happy to hear her say those words again."

"It seems you've had a lovely life," Will said.

"Yes, if not for that war," Alan admitted. "But I would never have met my Pat without that war. It was a divine plan, I think. I had to go through all those horrors, clear all obstacles and keep my faith. Only then did God allow me to win the prize. I can't explain it in any other way."

"I don't believe in any divine plans," Will uttered.

"I see..." Alan's voice trailed off before he added. "That's why you can't see a path around your obstacles. You must be persistent in your ways. Have faith, young man. Believe in yourself, even if you don't believe in a divine plan. Strange things can happen if you are persistent enough."

Will sighed.

"They are happening," he admitted. "But not the way I want them to."

Alan smiled a sad smile before speaking; his gaze still fixed on the roses.

"That's no wonder if your eyes choose a different path from your heart," the old man told him. "No one can help you with that but yourself."

"How do you know the difference?" Will demanded.

Alan rubbed his chin before answering.

"It is not straightforward," the old man sighed. "If your eyes take the lead, your path will be easy and pleasant but not necessarily end where you wanted. Your goal may remain buried somewhere beneath those piles of obstacles that your eyes chose to avoid. You might be quite happy living like that, but I don't know if the happiness would still be there when death stares you in the face. The path is more difficult if you allow your heart to take the lead. You may suffer a lot of pain and disappointment while you're being challenged by those obstacles, but your heart knows what the goal is even if it's hidden, and you will get there at the end. I don't know if you'd be happy with what you find there, but that goal is what you truly want."

"I see no point in this," Will murmured, disenchantment in his voice.

"Life has no point, young man," Alan said with a sigh. "It's a journey, and the only thing you can be certain of is that you will die at the end. You can't change the end of the journey, but you can choose your fellow travellers."

Will was baffled by the idea. "I'm not happy about the ending," he said firmly.

Alan shrugged. "That's the only thing you can't change." His pale eyes looked at Will. "The rest is entirely in your hands."

"I don't feel that is so," Will began to complain. "Sometimes, I feel that I don't have any free will left at all."

"Then you must stop, take a break and decide what to do with your life," Alan said. "No one can make your decisions for you."

"That's easier to say than do."

"You're a big young man," Alan frowned, looking at him. "Why are you complaining like a small child hiding behind his mother's skirts?"

Will shrugged. That struck him with a sense of guilt. He wasn't hiding, in fact. His mother had kept him tied. Nevertheless, the result was still the same.

"It's been a pleasure talking with you, young man," Alan said, watching a nurse escaping from the hospital with a concerned look and searching around. "It seems that my period of tranquillity is over."

"Mr Lengthorn!" the nurse waved, spotting them on the bench. "It's time for your procedures!"

"Your life doesn't belong to you at the end," Alan observed and stood up, leaning heavily on his walking stick.

"Then my end is very near too…" Will mumbled and kept his eyes on the old man who carefully walked down the path away from him.

The nurse waved her hands impatiently and took Alan by his elbow. Will couldn't hear what she was telling him, but Alan kept shaking his head until the door swallowed them back into the hospital.

Will kept on staring at the distant door, but nobody else emerged. Alan was gone.

The day was serene with beautiful sunshine and a light breeze. Will was alone in the park as far as he could see. The gravel paths were empty. Nobody enjoyed the shade of the giant chestnuts.

Will opened his rucksack and inspected the contents – the trainers, T-shirt, jeans, and the towel were in place. He dug a little deeper to find another protein bar and his phone. His stomach jumped at the sight of food, so Will had to feed it first. The phone was off, and Will frowned wondering if there was anything left in the battery. The screen came on, and he grinned – someone had prudently switched it off when he had been put into the coma, saving most of the charge.

He cleared the long rows of Jill's emails with an evil

grin. That felt good, but not entirely liberating. Will was certain she would keep sending them.

It was the slightest of touches on his wrist that made him stop and freeze that silly smile. Will's eyes almost popped out of his head, but still, he could see nothing, yet he could swear that a strand of hair had lightly brushed his skin. A moment later, the ghostly sensation had gone. *What was that?*

He looked around but, as before, not a soul was out enjoying the serene weather in the park. The wind had calmed down to a standstill, leaving behind the scent of roses it had brought.

It must be my nerves after that coma, Will thought and returned his gaze to his phone.

It rang unexpectedly.

"Where are you, Willy?" the voice was impatient and demanding.

"I'm in the park, mum," Will sighed. "Getting some fresh air."

"Are you crazy?" the mother gasped. "You've just woken up from a coma!"

"It was artificial, remember?" Will did his best to sound encouraging. "The doctor's have told me I'm fine and in no need of any treatment."

"Good news," his mother said in a flat voice. "But why are they searching for you on the ward, Willy?"

"I've no idea," Will assured her. "There's nothing they can do for me, and the doctor told me that I'm past having all those fits. I just need a little observation."

"Come back to the ward at once, Willy. I'm waiting for you here!" his mother left no room for an argument.

Will's throat went dry at the mention of the ward. He couldn't go back to face all that madness that had been richly seeded by Jill. He clutched his rucksack and took a deep breath.

"No, mum," he said at last. "I can't."

"*What?*"

"I can't explain it to you," Will's tongue grew numb. "I just can't. They've said I'm healthy, and the observation is only a precaution only. You can observe me as much as you like at home. There'll be no more fits."

The phone was silent for too long.

"Don't you dare to argue with your mother!" she gasped at last. "You're still sleeping under my roof and eating my bread! Do as I tell you, Willy! Get back to the ward at once! The doctors are chasing you!"

Will looked at the empty space on the bench where Alan had been sitting just minutes ago. The old man had gone back to the hospital without too much complaint. His life was nearing its end, and he had merely obeyed, losing his grip. Will shook his head silently – his own life wasn't ending; not now, not like this. He must be firm. He must resist the poison Jill was spreading around him. That insane crowd would tear him into pieces. He couldn't go back and surrender.

"No," he whispered into the phone – quietly but firmly.

"Willy!"

"No, mum," he repeated a little louder, still firmly.

"They've told me I'm healthy. I don't need a hospital."

"Don't you dare…"

"I'm not going back to the ward, mum…" Will's voice trailed off.

"How dare you? You're still living under my roof!" his mother gasped. "Don't you dare come home if you are flouting me! Come back to the ward at once!"

"No," Will repeated, and then he did the unthinkable – he hung up. The silence was deafening.

Will looked around him. The leaves on the trees and roses were swaying lazily in the faint wind. A few squirrels had decided that he posed no threat to them and jumped around on the ground searching for food in the neatly trimmed grass. Nothing else disturbed the serenity.

The phone rang again. Will frowned looking at the number of his mother flashing up but didn't answer and silenced the ringer instead. He couldn't go back, not with that army of madmen waiting for him.

Will picked up his rucksack and ran his gaze across the park for one more time. Then he turned left and went down the alley leaving the hospital behind. His phone frantically vibrated as he followed the path under the shade of the mighty chestnut trees, but he kept it deep in his pocket without bothering to have a look. His mother was mad at him, and Will had to wait until her anger had calmed down. He knew he was fine, and the doctors had said that he was fine – there was no need to spend one more minute in the hospital despite what his mother might think. Will was a big boy and could take care of himself. He only had to get away from the madness Jill was spreading, and life would get back to normal.

Will went down the winding path, scaring away the squirrels.

He stopped just for a second at the rusty gates of the park and hesitantly looked back at the distant light grey building of the hospital. Will was glad it was now far away, barely visible behind the chestnut trees, and he just managed to stop himself from sticking his tongue out at Jill who was probably wandering around the hospital corridors. *No more madness*, Will thought with a grin. Then he felt his hair begin to rise with that unmistakable feeling of being watched.

Endless streams of cars rushed in both directions on the busy street beyond the gate. He looked around. It seemed he was the only pedestrian, and nobody had followed him out of the park. This puzzled Will, and he looked around again, this time more slowly and carefully.

The cars sped by both ways without slowing down. Will poked his head through the gate and looked up and down the pavement. *Empty!* But the feeling didn't go away. Will watched a flock of pigeons circling above the distant rooftops before he spotted her. A young girl in jogging gear was standing on the other side of the street behind the heavy traffic. Her left hand was raised at the chest level as if preparing to check a smartwatch, but her body remained frozen still with her eyes fixed upon Will. He didn't know her, and it was a strange way to attract attention. Will attempted a shy smile and even waved at her, but the girl's face remained expressionless.

Was she one of those giggling magpies from the row of treadmills? Will frowned trying to get a better look, but the girl seemed unfamiliar. He couldn't be sure anyway since he never paid any serious attention to those gigglers. Still, the situation was weird.

Will waved again, trying to ease the strange tension, but the girl didn't even blink. Her feet remained firmly fixed on the pavement, and her left hand remained raised.

"Shit!" Will cursed loudly and turned left, hurrying down the street.

He still felt the gaze of that weird girl following him like a searchlight until he turned around the corner. Will slipped into the first side street trying to escape that feeling and ran down the pavement, followed by the barking of dogs. The weird girl didn't follow.

"What's happening?" Will mumbled rushing down the street and taking a few more turns into other side streets. For some reason, he felt afraid. That girl with her vacant gaze had looked like a zombie. Was she going to run after him? Bite him? The thought was ridiculous, but he couldn't get rid of it.

A few streets later Will slowed down, then cursed and stopped. He was a big boy and shouldn't be afraid of some girl who had stared at his muscles with bulging eyes and a gaping mouth. *Yes, it must have been my muscles she was staring at,* Will decided. *Nothing to worry about.*

The street was empty, and he strolled down the sunny side, still casting glances over his shoulder. Nobody followed him, and the image of the girl slowly faded.

Nothing to worry about...

His phone vibrated several more times, but Will didn't bother to take it out of his pocket. He wasn't going back to the hospital, no matter what his mother told him to do. He owed nothing to those doctors. All he wanted was to get back to his former life, away from Jill and away from the madness she was spreading.

Will was sure his mother was furious, and it was better to stay away for a while until she had calmed down. He decided to call her later, in the evening, hoping that the pressure would have eased by then. *There was nothing to worry about.*

The thought of home sent his stomach into spasms. That protein bar had been digested and forgotten long ago, and he needed some stuffing, some real food to get him through the day.

Will frowned at the thought of crowds in the town centre but turned right at the next crossroad, heading closer to the High Street. The girl in jogging gear never showed up again. He looked back several times.

The day was heading into the afternoon, and his hungry stomach urged Will to move faster. He raised his hood before turning left onto the High Street. The crowds were less than he expected. Still, some crazy people from the hospital could be running around here, searching for him. He glanced around cautiously before going to the nearest ATM to check his savings.

The machine displayed those few hundreds of pounds that were left after the last raid on the account. Feeling rich,

Will withdrew a twenty-pound note and went down the street grinning. His stomach growled approval when he turned into a kebab shop a few paces later.

"Afternoon, Ali," Will nodded to the man on the other side of the counter.

"It's so nice to see you, my friend," Ali grinned widely. "What would you like today?"

"My usual stuff, please," Will told him without thinking too much.

"Oh," Ali nodded with a knowing smile. "The Manly Meal?"

"Yes," Will extended the note out to him.

"Ten quid, my friend," Ali took the note and began shuffling food around. "Take a seat wherever you like. I'll bring it to you."

The place was small, and the generous sounding offer to take a seat was limited to the three scratched chairs at similarly scratched tables. Will headed to the one in the far corner and sat down facing the wide open entrance. He gulped down a mouthful of saliva when the pleasantly spiced aroma of frying meat reached his nostrils. People were hurrying along the street, minding their own business, not paying too much attention to the inviting smells. Ali's kebab shop was just one of many along the road and, although far from luxurious, the food was cheap here but well made. Will rarely dined outside his mother's kitchen, but when he did, he always went to Ali's on those rare occasions.

Will patiently waited until Ali placed a huge plate in

front of him, piled high with meat and a handful of fried vegetables, a big glass of strawberry milkshake and a piece of a carrot cake.

"My cousin just texted me such a funny thing, I can't stop laughing," Ali said, placing plastic cutlery in front of Will.

"What is it?" Will asked, picking up the fork and digging into the meat.

Ali winked and took the phone out of his pocket.

"Here it is," he frowned scrolling through the messages. "Some lunatic woman has claimed she was healed by someone's touch in hospital and now half of the hospital is running around back and forth, trying to find that healer! Can you believe it?"

Will stopped chewing.

"That's silly," he uttered in a flat voice.

"I can't believe how crazy some people can get," Ali grinned replacing his phone in his pocket. "Healed by a touch! That guy could make millions!"

"Did your cousin tell you who the healer was?" Will coughed before asking.

"No," Ali shook his head. "It seems nobody knows for sure. They're just running around and touching everybody on their way. Isn't that funny?"

"No, it's silly," Will shrugged before putting another piece of meat in his mouth.

"All right," Ali winked with a grin. *"Bon appétit,* my friend!"

Will watched as he retreated to his counter. How far

would people go with this madness? He only hoped that it wouldn't spill out of the hospital. The doctors must deal with it the proper way. It wasn't his problem anymore.

He kept on destroying the pile of meat as disturbing thoughts sneaked back into his mind. What if Jill began preaching about her so-called healing in the town? She might find followers. The world was full of crazy people, after all. They might launch a hunt for him. *Should he hide?* Or would it be better to confront her? But then that dirty little secret about the circumstances of their acquaintance would surface with its shitty side facing up. Will couldn't let that happen. His mother would get really mad with him, hearing that news. But she was mad already...

This was all too complicated.

Will gulped down the vegetables followed by the remaining meat. His stomach felt warm and full, and he grinned before pushing the empty plate away and digging into the carrot cake. It was too sweet for his liking but went down nicely anyway.

Ali suddenly burst into laughter, staring at his phone.

"You must have a look at this, man," he shook his head, wiping tears of laughter away. "It's so funny! They've put it on the internet!"

Will stopped drinking his milkshake and put the half-full glass on the table, feeling his heart sinking slowly.

"I need to have a look," he stood up.

"Here," Ali turned his phone to Will, still laughing.

Will frowned. It was the giant blob named Jill happily jumping on her bed in a bursting-tight hospital gown. His face turned red, but then he sighed with relief – only a small corner of his bed was visible, and it had departed before Jill had begun jumping. Will forced a weird grin just to keep Ali's suspicions away.

"Funny, isn't it?" Ali replaced his phone in his pocket. "Would you like anything else?"

"No, I'm full. Thank you," Will returned to his table and downed the remaining milkshake in a single gulp. Then he handed the empty dishes to Ali.

"Thank you, my friend," Ali put a broad smile on his face. "Hope to see you soon!"

Will just nodded silently and slipped back onto the High Street. Nobody looked at him, but he lowered the hood as far as it would go, trying to hide his face. *Damn Jill and the day he had put that advert on the internet!* He might find himself to be the laughing stock of the whole town. He only hoped nobody had been able to film "the healing touch" when he was trying to get rid of that crazy woman.

Will turned left at the next crossroad wandering back into nearly empty side streets. Nobody bothered him, and his phone had gone suspiciously quiet. He even took it out to check the battery – still, more than half left, but there were no missed calls or texts, not counting the steady, endless stream of emails from Jill.

Will wandered aimlessly through the streets and sat in the parks staring at young mothers pushing their prams around, watching over their children. The weather was calm and gentle, with full sunshine and the lightest of breezes. He sat in the shade, hugging his rucksack and waited patiently.

It was early evening when he finally dared to move. By his estimation, several long hours would be sufficient time for his mother to have calmed down and be ready to hear his side of the story.

Will couldn't tell it all. He decided to keep quiet about his dream, about Hel and her blue orchid, about the lava fields and that damned geyser which had brought those fits at the same time each evening. He was free again, away from the cages, and those fits that had concerned his mother so much were now a thing of the past.

The only problem was how to explain his relationship with Jill if his mother had found out about them. Will bit his lip and scratched his head, but nothing useful came to mind. He'd just have to make something up as he went along.

The streetlights came on, as grey evening dusk descended on the town. Will stopped in front of his home. The window of his own room was dark, but his sister's window was brightly lit, and he could see his mother busy in the kitchen. A pleasant aroma of roasting chicken and frying potatoes leaked through the open window.

Will took his key out of his pocket and hesitantly went closer. It was always was a piece of cake to plug it in, but then the key became stuck before it was fully inside the lock. Someone had left a key in on the other side. There was no way now he could sneak inside unnoticed.

Damn! Will quietly cursed, suddenly afraid to ring the bell. He glanced through the kitchen window – his mother was putting plates and cutlery on the table where a big bowl of fried potatoes and a fresh salad already flanked a beautifully browned chicken. There were only two plates and two sets of cutlery on the table.

Will took his key out of the lock and pressed the doorbell.

He saw his mother leave the kitchen and heard her footsteps in the hallway.

"Who is it?" she asked behind the locked door.

"It's me, mum," Will mumbled.

"Who?" the question was repeated on a higher note.

"It's me, mum, your son Willy," he said loudly. "Let me in."

The next few seconds of silence seemed painfully long.

"I don't know anybody called Willy," she said at last. "And I don't have a son. Go away."

"Mum?" he rapped the door. "Mum…"

"Go away," she said firmly. "Or I'll call the police."

"Mum! Please…"

She was silent again.

"Open the door, please," he whispered, trying to hide the desperation in his voice.

"Go away," she shuffled through her pockets. "That was your last warning. I'm calling the police!"

Will couldn't believe what was happening. He backed away a few paces staring at the door which didn't open. *How could this be possible?* Why was she doing this to him?

"Hello," he heard his mother speaking on the phone. "I need help, officer. Someone's breaking into my house… No, I don't know him… Yes, I've warned him several times… Thank you, officer. I'll wait."

Will backed a few more paces away, shaking his head – this couldn't be true! It was just another bad dream, and he would soon wake up in that damned hospital bed. *Did he take a nap?*

A police siren wailed in the distance, getting nearer. Will waited for a few more seconds – the door didn't open, and he sprinted away, as blue flashes appeared at the far end of the street.

He couldn't remember clearly how fast or how far he ran. When he stopped, at last, breathing heavily, and looked around, he found himself in the dark alley of the old park with a full moon glistening in the dusk above the slowly moving river. He was alone.

Why had she done that?

Will sat down on the nearest bench holding back tears – he was too big to cry, even if nobody was looking. The question still rang in his head, unanswered – *why?*

The next thought that sneaked into his mind was even scarier – what should he do next? Where could he go? The night was falling, and he needed a roof over his head.

Will felt scared, hungry and lonely clutching his rucksack on the park bench with only a skyful of bats and owls above his head. The town quietly hummed around the park with families gathering at tables, having their dinner, talking, laughing… Why had his mother done that to him? *She had asked too much!* He couldn't go back to the ward with all that madness about "healing". It was all Jill's fault. That crazy woman had made his life miserable. *What could he do now?*

Would his mother ever forgive him? She might need some more time to calm down and allow her anger to fade. Will would then be able to return home and eat his dinner before going to bed. He just needed a few days to let her think it over and change her mind. *Would she change her mind?*

He cursed. The world as he knew it was crumbling in front of him, revealing a dark, frightening unknown. *Was he now homeless?* Probably…

"You're sitting on my bench, mate," a harsh voice snarled behind him.

Will flinched and turned around. There was a dark shape behind him dressed in rags carrying the strong odour of a cheap beer and urine and god-knows-what- else.

"There's plenty of benches in the park," Will observed.

"But this bench is mine, mate," the shape insisted, coming closer. Something narrow and metallic flashed in the silver moonlight. "I can make a few holes in you, mate, so that you can have a comfortable bed in hospital, but the bench is mine!"

Will jumped to his feet. The threat was real, as the knife flashed a few inches away from him.

"There's plenty of benches in the park as you said, mate," the knife flashed a few more times. "Go away!"

Will was much larger than the man with the knife, but what could he do barehanded? He might end up back in the hospital where the insanity instigated by Jill was already flourishing. *Damn!* Why must life be so complicated?

The vagrant growled as he shuffled through his bags,

but Will went away without looking back. He must find a shelter, a safe place where he could spend the night. *Perhaps the gym?* It was open around the clock, and maybe with a little luck, he could find a quiet corner? The thought was soothing, and Will grinned as he hurried away from the park.

He still had time for a quick workout, and then he could persuade the guy at the counter to direct him into some quiet corner where he could stay until morning. He was sure there would be some place available. Maybe some storage space next to the changing rooms?

Will bought a few protein bars on his way and chewed one immediately. He'd find a solution. He was sure. He just had to speak to the guy at the gym.

Then his hopes crashed. Will could only gasp, staring at the dark windows. He couldn't believe his bad luck. The gym had been closed for renovation while he was in the hospital and now stood locked and silent. It felt like the ground was slowly slipping from under his feet.

Will turned right and walked away. The High Street was still crowded, and he strolled aimlessly downhill with his rucksack over his shoulder. He pulled his hood low over his face, feeling like an outcast or a criminal, sneaking about in the midst of the rushing crowd with no real place to go. Nobody looked at him twice, nobody cared.

Still, he probably had two places where he would be more than welcome – the hospital and Jill's boudoir, but even the thought of that was repulsive. *Should he try his luck back in the park?*

Reluctantly he went downhill looking at the brightly lit windows of the shops and cafés, at the cars rushing up and down the street and at both smiling and serious faces. He felt like a ghost with gazes brushing over him but never stopping. Will passed a stupidly dressed hen party but didn't get any attention from them either, not even a wolf whistle at his muscles. This was a complete disaster. *Should he go back home and beg his mother for forgiveness on his knees?*

The High Street went left at the roundabout, and Will followed the flow, slightly uphill this time. A few blocks later, he had to stop, as a crowd suddenly burst out of a brightly lit building, temporarily barring his way. A train had arrived, and people were rushing home.

The train station was painted yellow. The large windows showed the dispersing crowds and a coffee shop on the right-hand side of the waiting room. The Manly Meal was now long gone and forgotten, and Will's stomach began to stake its claim, sensing the pleasant aromas leaking outside. *Only a sandwich*, a thought flashed through Will's mind as he licked his lips. *Or maybe a baguette.*

He went inside. The waiting room was almost empty already, as the train had now left and most of the passengers who had arrived with it had already rushed off home to their families. A girl behind the counter in the coffee shop was reading a book and only briefly glanced at Will. He went along the display staring at cakes, sandwiches and baguettes as if seeing them for the first time. Never before had the contents of his wallet felt so lightweight, and he wanted the best value for his money.

"Can't make your mind up?" the girl asked, glancing at him over the book.

Will shrugged. Then he grabbed the biggest baguette of turkey trimmings and brie cheese and showed it to the girl.

"Anything to drink?" she put her book aside.

"A cup of tea, perhaps," Will mumbled.

"With milk and sugar?" the girl demanded.

"Yes, both please," Will nodded.

He patiently waited while the girl took his money and prepared him a cup of tea. Then he took a seat in front of the window and began to chew the baguette. The girl went back to her book, and Will realised that he was alone in the waiting room except for that girl and the man who was selling train tickets.

The baguette was too small for his liking, and he chewed each bite carefully in a silly attempt to extend the moment. It was dark outside when he had finished dealing with the turkey trimmings and pressed the cup of tea to his lips. Will looked at the passing cars with empty eyes and an absentminded smile.

"Are you travelling somewhere?" the question woke him up from his daydream.

The man from the ticket office was standing in front of him, and Will caught some bad determination flashing in his eyes.

"Yes," he nodded. "Why do you ask?"

"This waiting room is for passengers," the man told him. "We're not happy about someone who's not travelling and has no place to go, just sitting here and spending the night."

"I am travelling," Will assured him.

"Then you need a ticket," the man said.

"I'll buy one as soon as I've finished my tea," Will attempted a smile, but it wasn't convincing.

The man shrugged and returned to the ticket office. Will looked around as if seeking help, but the girl was immersed in her book, and no one else was waiting for a train.

The tea grew cold, as he unhurriedly sipped the brew. He turned the empty cup in his hands when he finished. The death stare he received from the ticket office clearly indicated that his time was up. Will stood up, gathered and disposed of his garbage and then went to the ticket office.

"One-way ticket, please," Will said to the man on the other side of the counter.

"Where to?" the man demanded with a yawn.

"London."

Afterword

You have just read a story from the Sleeper Chronicles series and may wonder which book will take you deeper into the world of Sleepers. It's a difficult question, and the advice is not as straightforward as it may seem. The Sleeper Chronicles is a non-linear series, where the story in book B doesn't necessarily follow book A, and book C doesn't precede the story in book D. Each main character tells his own story as a piece of a jigsaw puzzle. That piece may be as short as a short story or grow into several books. Still, not a single piece can reveal the picture of the whole universe, but more details emerge when those pieces are added together.

The stories are listed on the webpage www.sleeperchronicles.com – in no particular order. Of course, the books are available in Kindle format if you prefer electronic devices. They are also beautifully narrated by a Downton Abbey actor on Audible. It's up to you to decide which piece of the puzzle to pick next.

Ray Zdan

Printed in Great Britain
by Amazon

75119663R00194